SUPERB
and SEXY

SUPERB
and SEXY

JILL SHALVIS

BRAVA

KENSINGTON PUBLISHING CORP.
http://www.kensingtonbooks.com

BRAVA BOOKS are published by

Kensington Publishing Corp.
850 Third Avenue
New York, NY 10022

All Kensington titles, imprints and distributed lines are available at special quantity discounts for bulk purchases for sales promotions, premiums, fund-raising, educational or institutional use.

Special book excerpts or customized printings can also be created to fit specific needs. For details, write or phone the office of the Kensington Special Sales Manager: Kensington Publishing Corp., 850 Third Avenue, New York, NY 10022. Attn. Special Sales Department. Phone: 1-800-221-2647.

Brava and the B logo Reg. U.S. Pat. & TM Off.

ISBN-13: 978-0-7582-2184-1
ISBN-10: 0-7582-2184-3

First Kensington Trade Paperback Printing: June 2008
10 9 8 7 6 5 4 3 2 1

Printed in the United States of America

SUPERB
and SEXY

Chapter 1

The man pulled up in a rumbling, bad boy Camaro like he owned his world, and Maddie had good reason to know he did.

Brody West owned his world all right, and completely rocked hers.

What the hell was he doing here?

It'd been a long time since she'd seen him. Six weeks, two and a half days, and waaaaay too many minutes. Not that she was counting.

But to be honest, that she hadn't seen him was all her own doing. She'd left town to recover.

To think.

To make a Plan with a capital P.

Hence staying in the mountains where no one could bother her—including Brody.

Especially Brody.

With him, no contact was good contact since they clashed at every turn, bickered when they weren't clashing, and in general, brought out the worst in each other. She hadn't even thought about him while she'd been gone, sitting here on the porch of the log-style cabin that she'd rented for its rustic, isolated beauty, emphasis on isolated.

Okay, so she'd thought about him. She just hadn't *wanted* to think about him. Probably, she was just overreacting. Honestly, maybe it wasn't even him in the car.

And yet, she knew better. Her body knew better. The simple act of hearing the engine rev had made the hair on the nape of her neck rise in sudden, unexpected awareness.

Yeah, it was him because she felt . . .

God, she felt so much, but thunderstruck led the pack, though an undeniable excitement came in close second.

He was here, forty-five miles off the beaten path from his home in the Burbank Hills to the Angeles Crest Forest.

But *why?* Why wasn't he holed up in his office, or on one of his planes he loved more than anything, working himself into an early grave as he liked to do?

She knew that he, along with his partners Shayne and Noah, wanted her back at work, seemed desperate for her to be back. Shayne had told her yesterday on the phone that Sky High had gone through four temp concierges in the time she'd been gone on leave, all of whom Brody had chased off with his sunny nature.

Translation: he'd been brooding and edgy and terrifying.

Yeah. Sounded like him.

But the brooding and edgy thing had never bothered her much. Maybe because she'd always been drawn to the bad boys. The reason for that was simple. Bad boys wanted the same things she did—no strings attached.

She didn't do strings.

Outside, Brody turned off the Camaro, and silence filled the air.

A heavy, weighted, questioning silence.

And suddenly, Maddie's chest felt too tight. Damn it. She let out a long, calming breath, which of course, didn't work. It never worked. Neither did just sitting at the window staring down at him, but God, she was tired, and still recovering.

Yeah, that's what this asinine weakness in her knees was—recovery. Because it sure as hell wasn't for him.

No way.

They didn't even like each other . . .

And yet she leaned over so she could see out the window again, past the tall twin pines trying to block her view of the nearly six feet, four inches of rough and tumble, sexy as hell male as he unfolded his long legs from the muscle car.

Her pulse took another unfortunate leap. The last time she'd seen him, he'd been in his pilot's uniform, and even though it was ridiculous and juvenile and wrong, it had turned her on. The thought of seeing him *out* of it? Even more so.

Yeah, she had a problem. She'd been shamelessly, secretly crushing on him all damn year. But that was her own humiliating secret, and one she'd take to the grave. And here was another—that fateful last day at work six weeks ago now, when she'd been just a little ticked off that she couldn't get him to notice her as a woman, she'd dressed solely to gain his attention—miniskirt, snug cami, teetering heels, the whole shebang. She'd been gratified when it'd worked, when he'd executed a comical double take at her and then spilled coffee down the front of his shirt.

Mission accomplished. He'd most definitely noticed her as a woman.

The excitement level had been so high she couldn't stand it. And then she'd smart-mouthed a psychopath and gotten herself shot, and her life had been put on pause.

Fast-forward to now.

Shutting the driver's door of the Camaro, he stared at the cabin. He wore a T-shirt, cargoes, and scuffed boots, all in black, emphasizing that world-class bod she'd spent many, many days drooling over while pretending to work.

Unlike her, the man was genetically incapable of pretending anything. Nope, he rarely bothered to hide his thoughts, especially as they pertained to her, thoughts that had at one

time or another run the gamut from baffled to that one time
she'd done the unthinkable and pressed him back against a
wall and kissed him.

And for that one blissful moment, he hadn't been vexed or
grumpy. He'd been stunned and aroused and all sleepy-eyed
and sexy with it.

Not now, though.

Now he stood there, tall and sure, a frown on his face, his
dark hair falling carelessly across his brow, and at just past his
collar, longer than one would expect a pilot's hair to be. She
knew that it wasn't that way because he cared about being in
style, but because he simply forgot to get it cut. Sometimes
she thought he'd forget his own head if it wasn't attached.

The only things he never forgot were his damn planes or his
business. Sky High Air was an exclusive, luxurious, sophisticated airline service. Pretty damned hilarious considering that
the three guys who ran it had been troubled youths, to say it
kindly. They'd started Sky High last year by the seat of their
pants and their collective wits. They'd put their heads and
bank accounts together, managing, barely, to eke enough money
to get it going, then keep it going.

But a miracle had occurred. The LA rich and spoiled had
discovered them, *loved* them and the services they provided,
and all the buckets and buckets of antacids they'd consumed
over the cost of the start-up were finally paying off.

Below, Brody stopped on the walk and looked up.

She held her breath. Hard to believe they made geeks in
such outrageously magnificent male packages, but there it
stood, looking for her.

His eyes were hidden behind mirrored aviator sunglasses,
but she knew them to be a mesmerizing pewter gray that
could turn to ice or flame given his mood, and they were filled
with secrets she'd never managed to plumb.

They drove her crazy, those secrets. She'd always wanted to
know their depths, wanted to know what made him tick, his

likes, his dislikes . . . and the yearning had driven her even more crazy.

Had.

Because she no longer had the luxury of dreaming about him. She had other things to dream about—things like life and death.

But he didn't know that as he headed for the door. Around his neck were the earphones for his iPod, which probably had Linkin Park blasting out at decibel levels uncharted. How the man hadn't gone deaf was beyond her, but that wasn't what she wondered as her gaze ran all over him like he was cotton candy. No, she wondered how she was going to keep her hands to herself if she had to talk to him one-on-one . . .

Get a grip.

After all, his partners had stolen her heart from day one, too, and she didn't want to jump them. Shayne and Noah were bad boys as well, and when she'd gotten the job working for them, the rebel inside her had rejoiced to find a place where she belonged. She loved them both, loved them like the older brothers she never had.

But nothing about her feelings for the edgy, brooding Brody was brotherly.

Nowhere even close.

Very annoying, and hard to hide as well, though she'd managed. She always managed, no matter the task. Cool as a cucumber, that was Maddie, always.

She needed to find that cool now. Oh boy, how she needed to find that cool.

Not easy when that dark, silky hair of his called to her fingers, and then there was that lean, angular face she wanted to touch, or that tough, muscular body she wanted to lick from top to bottom.

Damn it, she'd told herself she was over her little schoolgirl crush, over whatever it was about him that melted her brain cells, not to mention her bones, leaving her a ridiculously vulnerable puddle of longing every time he so much as looked at her.

She was tougher than this.

But not with him.

That thought came out of nowhere, and she beat it back, along with the knowledge that he, unlike any other man she'd ever met, had somehow sneaked past her defenses, past her carefully erected brick walls, and saw the woman beneath.

He stopped walking. Stopped and tilted his dark head up to the second story window, and then seemed to look right into her eyes.

Oh, God.

Unprepared for the reaction that barreled through her, she actually sat there, still, rooted to the spot for one long heartbeat.

"Who is that?"

Maddie jumped as her sister came into the room. Tiptoed, as if someone was still on her trail, in the jerky, self-conscious movement of someone used to being pushed around.

Goddamnit. "No one, Leena. It's okay."

Leena leaned over Maddie's shoulder, gnawing her lower lip between her teeth as she took in the man on the walk below. "My God," she murmured and shivered.

Yes, Maddie thought. My God. Brody induced that reaction from her, too.

"That's not no one."

True enough. She took another quick peek and felt a shiver herself, not of fear of that impressive size and height, but because she knew what that impressive size and height felt like full frontal and plastered up against her. "It's okay. He's my boss."

Leena let out a low breath as she stared at Brody. "You work for *him*?"

"And two others. Three pilots."

"You work for three men like *that*?"

No use telling her that not all men were manipulative jerks who ruled with their superior size or fist. That was something she'd have to learn on her own.

After all, Maddie had.

"You can't let him in," Leena said, a growing panic in her voice, a panic Maddie felt as her own.

Because Leena was right. She couldn't let him in. Couldn't because there was far too much at stake here.

No matter that she and Brody had unresolved issues, mostly hers. There were other more pressing issues, issues that had nothing to do with him.

Serious issues.

Like those life and death issues . . .

If she let him in, he'd take one look at her and know something was wrong because brooding and edgy as he might be, he had the intuition and instincts of a panther—sharp and unwavering.

In Brody's world, things were black and white. Right and wrong. When something was broken, he fixed it. If someone needed him, he moved heaven and earth to do whatever needed to be done, and he would do so for a perfect stranger.

Maddie was no stranger, perfect or otherwise.

Yeah, he'd want to help.

Only he couldn't.

No one could.

Staring down at Brody, her pulse raced with a horrible mixture of yearning and wariness. Him showing up was the worst thing that could have happened, for the both of them.

Not that he could know that or the fact that she was in over her head in a way she hadn't been since he'd hired her and unknowingly given her a much needed security that she valued above all else.

But apparently unable to read her mind, he headed straight for the front door, his long-limbed stride filled with a casual ease that said even if he'd known about any potential danger, it wouldn't have stopped him.

God, she loved that about him.

Beside her, Leena made a sound of distress and wrung her hands together.

Maddie's reaction wasn't much different. Her heart took another hard knock against her ribs. She had no idea what it was about Brody's attitude that went straight to her gut—and several other good spots as well—but with that scowl on his face, he looked every inch the wild, bad boy rebel pilot that she knew him to be.

And from deep within her came a new emotion, one she hadn't thought still existed inside her.

Hope.

It made absolutely no sense, no sense at all, and she quickly squashed it flat because that particular emotion, or anything close to it, had no place here, and she'd do well to remember it.

That was the hard part. Remembering it.

"Maddie," Leena whispered.

"I know."

For all of their sakes, she had to get rid of him.

Fast.

Chapter 2

Brody knocked on the door of the cabin as if he was Avon calling, but in truth, he felt much more like the big, bad wolf standing outside Maddie's house of straw.

Or at least a big oaf.

He had no idea why, but around her, he felt clumsy and off kilter. Oh, wait. He knew exactly why. She was smart and amazing and hot and funny and *hot*, and so far out of his league he couldn't even see the league.

He knocked again, glancing at Maddie's Jeep in the driveway and the car next to it, wondering if she was alone, wondering why she was here, in the mountains, miles from the nearest high-end clothing store. Maddie was a sophisticated, elegant, big city lover who considered anything less than a four-star hotel roughing it.

She wasn't exactly roughing it, not in this big, beautiful rustic cabin, built with a rather staggering view of majestic mountains and valleys as far as the eye could see. The front yard was a homage to The Ponderosa era, with a wagon wheel on either side of the walkway and railroad ties lining the path, all of it rather beautiful really, in a very Wild West sort of way.

But this was definitely a distant world for Maddie. So what

the hell was she doing out here, far from the work she loved, apparently unconcerned about earning money?

The thought was alien to him.

Give him the stability of work, and the money earned for that work, and he was good. Not worrying about the roof over his head or his next meal was pretty much all he required from life.

And flying.

Flying was a close second to eating. Flying made him whole, flying made him happy. Flying was everything.

Maddie was an enigma because she didn't seem to need any one thing, or anyone, for that matter. Maybe that's what made her so good at her job. She was a freak of nature who could work a keyboard, a cell phone, and a scheduling board and run Sky High Air at the same time, all without seeming to care what anyone thought.

She was his employee. His responsibility, and she drove him batshit crazy. He'd told himself it was her persona. She looked like a punk rocker superhero. Her hair could be spiky platinum one day, straight jet black with magenta streaks the next. She had several visible body piercings, and wondering about the ones not visible had kept him up on more than one long night. She wore leather and silk with equal élan, and her exotic footwear alone had given him more fantasies than he cared to admit.

He wanted her more than he'd ever wanted a woman. Hell, more than he'd ever wanted a plane, and that was saying something.

She walked as if she'd been born the Queen of the Free World, which only further confused him because usually, he was drawn to sweet and easy. And, okay, maybe just a little bit naughty.

There was nothing sweet or easy about Maddie, and he doubted that she was only a little bit naughty. Everything about her, from her baby blues to the tip of her manicured toes, everything screamed look-but-don't-touch, and in her presence, he was always swamped with conflicting emotions—the urge to rumple her up and the need to put his hands in his pockets to keep them off her.

Yeah. She really got to him. It was the equal mix of quick wit and trouble in her eyes. It was the sharp humor she revealed in her smile, which was so damn contagious he often found himself smiling back with or without being in on the joke. It was how she cared so deeply about the people around her, people like Noah and Shayne, and also him.

Especially when it was him.

Once he'd fallen off a ladder and landed on his ass, and she'd been the first one to get to him. She'd thrown herself at him, fear in her voice, and for that moment before she'd figured out he wasn't hurt, before she'd smacked him and yelled at him never to scare her like that again, he'd really enjoyed the feel of her curves hugging up all over him. Another time, he'd heard her on the phone telling a client about his piloting skills, bragging about how he was the best of the best, and he'd actually felt his chest puff up.

Yeah, he really liked it when she revealed how much she cared.

But this wasn't about him or how she seriously screwed with his head on a daily basis. This was about work. About Sky High Air.

He handled the majority of the flights himself. Noah specialized in personalized adventures, finding and fine-tuning them for their clients. Shayne, the people person of the group, brought in their rich clients. Together, they made the whole package, whether that meant flying a turbo prop or a jet on a moment's notice, taking a charter flight to Santa Barbara or a business group to Alaska, it got handled efficiently, discreetly, and luxuriously.

And it was all managed by Maddie, the best concierge on the planet. Sky High couldn't have achieved half their success without her, and none of them ever doubted it for a minute. Glorious, hotheaded, temperamental, beautiful Maddie Stone.

They needed her back.

Like yesterday.

No one could replace her, and he'd learned that the hard way. He was here to deliver that exact message. He planned to beg her, if necessary, and then get the hell back to where he belonged.

In the air.

He wanted her to show up for work, nose thrust higher than any of his planes, telling him to go to hell in that soft, come-fuck-me voice while stopping his world with one look from those sharp light blue eyes. And when she smiled? Jesus. He had a rep for being damned near indomitable, and yet her smile absolutely broke him every single time.

Untouchable . . .

It shocked him, really. The effect she had on him. She was tough and resilient and by turns, hard as nails or soft as butter melting on hot bread, and she never, ever compromised.

And yet there was no doubt in his mind that when she looked at him, she held back. She held back a lot, never quite letting him see the real her, except for that one time when for just a moment, he'd caught a glimpse of her entire heart and soul.

It'd shaken him. It'd opened his eyes to her. It'd told him his gut was right—that beneath that tough ass exterior beat the heart of a woman he could fall for. Terrifying, really. So he did his best to keep a certain distance, or at least, that had been his plan.

Until she'd gotten shot while working in *his* lobby, on *his* goddamn watch, and then vanished from the face of the earth for six hellishly long weeks during which he'd just about lost his mind until she'd called.

She didn't answer the door. Of course she didn't answer her door because that would have been easy. Stepping back, he glanced back up at the window above, but if he'd seen a flash of her a moment ago, she was gone now.

Avoidance. He recognized the technique, just not the need for it. Maybe she'd expected them to ignore her disappearance, or if not, then she'd have thought either Shayne or Noah would have come, both of whom had a much softer, easier relationship with her.

Well, too bad, they'd sent him. The hard ass.

He knocked again and waited with barely concealed impatience. He needed to get back to LA. He had flights scheduled, and the Piper needed a full work over . . .

That's when he heard it, a soft whisper.

A rustling.

Someone stood just behind the front door, possibly looking through the peephole decorated with a horseshoe. Someone, no doubt, just waiting for him to leave. "Maddie?"

A hushed silence greeted him. A very fully loaded hushed silence.

"Maddie, come on. Open up."

More of that loaded nothing, and he tried a different technique. "I have a stack of mail that came for you at Sky High. All your magazines . . ." He figured that would get her. She loved her magazines: *US Weekly*, *People*, anything pop culture, she inhaled.

But she didn't open the door.

Okay, next tactic. "You should know, Shayne crashed your scheduling program all to hell. We've got planes coming and going, and maybe some are even getting off the tarmac without getting billed."

More of the nothing, but a new, even tighter tension filled it. Nothing Maddie hated more than money being wasted. In that way, they were kindred souls.

In all other ways, they were classic opposites—oil and water, day and night—and like the *Sesame Street* song went, they were two things that did *not* go together. "Come on, Mad. Shayne and Noah are worried sick about you. Open up for me, show me you're good to go, that you can slay me with just one of your classic glacial stares, and I'll leave you the hell alone, I swear."

When she didn't, he had to admit to the smallest flash of relief that she was at least okay enough to be pissy, that she obviously didn't need anything from him. He could walk away. But doing so would make him a coward.

He'd been a lot of things in his life, but never that.

Except, apparently, where Maddie Stone was concerned.

Hell. "Maddie?" He had one last ace in the hole. "I also brought your paycheck . . ." He pulled it out of his pocket and waved it in front of the peephole. "I *know* you want this. I'm not just leaving it out here, so you're going to have to open up."

Utter silence.

Well, hell. He wasn't a bad guy or a bad boss. Sure, he had his faults, but nothing that warranted leaving him standing on the steps while she did God knew what in there. "Goddamnit, Maddie."

After an interminably long moment, someone fumbled with the door, and he felt his gut clench. The last time he'd seen her had been in the hospital after her surgery, when the doctor had told them all that she might never regain full use of her left shoulder and arm. She'd been stoic, gamefully nodding her understanding, but Brody had had to leave the room and pound the shit out of something. He'd settled for flying hard and fast, where only he and the sky knew how he'd grieved for her.

She pulled the door open and stood there in her doorway while his heart rolled over in his chest and exposed its soft underbelly. Her hair was blonde today, with electric blue tips flowing past her shoulders and brushing the tops of her breasts, which were covered in a skintight, long-sleeved top of some kind that nipped in and pushed up and out, making his eyes instantly cross with lust. But the top was nothing compared to the jeans that had to have been spray painted on. Oddly enough, she wasn't wearing her usual myriad of earrings, or an ounce of makeup for that matter, and he immediately looked into her baby blues to see misery, pain, and anguish.

And every self-righteous bone in his body melted away, leaving him weak as a goddamn kitten. "Maddie."

She blinked once, slow as an owl. Only Maddie had never been anything close to slow. As he'd noted on more than one occasion, she was the smartest, fastest, sharpest, most amazing woman he'd ever met, but his gaze had snagged on hers and held. He couldn't look away to save his life. He'd never seen her without full makeup. Without it, she might have been sixteen, but it was the way she was looking at him, right through him, as if she'd never seen him before that drew him up short.

Before he could say a word, she snatched the paycheck out of his fingers.

Then she slammed the door in his face.

And then it was *his* turn to blink. *What in the hell had just happened?* And why had she acted like she'd never seen him before? Whipping out his cell phone, he punched in Noah's number.

"Yo," his partner answered softly, as if he was in the middle of something. And he probably was. In the middle of doing his new wife Bailey because the two of them had become like a pair of rabbits. Normally, Brody would have at least had Shayne to commiserate the loss of bachelorhood with, but unbelievably, Shayne had also done the unthinkable and gotten himself involved, too, and now he had a fiancée.

Brody was the lone single man holdout. "There's something wrong with Maddie," he said.

That got Noah's attention. "What do you mean? Her shoulder or—"

"She slammed the door in my face."

"What did you do?"

"Nothing."

"Seriously."

"*Nothing!*"

A pause. Then Noah said, "You had to have done something."

"Fuck you."

"Sorry, you're not my type."

Brody pinched the bridge of his nose. "Are you going to help me out here?"

"Yeah. Knock on the door. When she opens it, you smile, then cute talk her into smiling, too, so you can then haul her sweet ass back here."

Brody shook his head. "Let me repeat. She slammed her door in my face."

"Did you smile?"

"I was getting to that."

"Did you bring her flowers?"

"Come on, flowers?"

"Yes, flowers!"

"No way. She wouldn't have fallen for that."

"Hook, line, and sinker, she would have," Noah promised with utter conviction. "Women love that shit."

"I had something better."

"What's that?"

"I told her I had her magazines and paycheck."

Noah sighed.

"What?"

"And here I thought you knew women."

"She loves her paychecks."

"Go get the freakin' flowers and try again."

"I'm in the mountains. There's no florist."

"Pick some wildflowers."

He could. Except in his gut, Brody knew that Maddie hadn't turned him away because he'd showed up without flowers.

The truth had been there to see in her eyes, an emptiness he'd never seen in her before.

And a fear.

He hung up on Noah and turned back to the door. Even knowing his chances of her answering were slim to none, he knocked again because if he didn't go back to Sky High Air with some answers, Noah would continue to peck at him like a hen.

He figured his knocking had to be annoying. Hell, it was annoying him. Two months ago, Maddie would have whipped the door open and given him a piece of her mind. Two months ago, she'd have stood in front of him in that tough girl stance of hers, the air shimmering with a sexual tension that had nearly exploded the two of them into flames every time they were in the same room.

What had happened?

"Maddie?" he said to the door.

Nothing.

Not promising.

He added a word he probably didn't use nearly often enough. "Please?"

To his utter shock, it worked. She opened the door, looking even more pale than before, if that was possible.

Without thinking, he reached for her, only she did the oddest thing.

She jumped back, away from him, as if afraid.

What the hell?

Everything within him went still because Maddie, his in-charge-of-the-entire-world Maddie, would never jump at his touch. She'd give him hell if she wanted, yeah, but she'd never jump.

And just like that, a real fear hit him, a deep gut-wrenching fear. "Maddie, are you alone here?"

"I can't deal with you right now."

"Are you alone?"

"Y-yes."

But her words were hitched with emotion. And so were her next ones.

"I just can't, okay? I can't do this. Not on top of everything else."

Yeah, a gut-wrenching, devastating emotion that hurt him just to hear her, but that wasn't the worse of it.

Because before he could stop her, or even wedge a foot in the door, she'd once again slammed it in his face.

Chapter 3

L eena ran back up the stairs and skidded to a shaky stop in the doorway of the master bedroom where Maddie still sat at the window.

"I think he's going," Leena whispered.

"No." Maddie watched Brody move down the walk, his broad-as-a-mountain-range shoulders deceptively loose, his gait easy. No matter what it looked like, she knew he wasn't going anywhere. She'd heard his voice at the door, low and tense, and knew that Leena had inadvertently awoken the curiosity within the beast.

Damn it.

It'd been a grave tactical error on Maddie's part to let Leena go to the door to get rid of him simply because she hadn't wanted to face him.

Because Leena hadn't quite pulled it off.

To be fair, no one could have. She and Brody might bicker like a pair of Siamese twins, but the bottom line was that they shared an unnamable, unbreakable, and certainly unfathomable bond that even she didn't get.

He could have no idea of the truth or even halfway guessed it. After all, the truth was so insane no one would believe it. But he knew something was wrong, and that was enough for him.

Unfortunately for her, an inquisitive and nosy Brody could be more tenacious than a bulldog.

She'd seen it happen.

Exhausted, she set her forehead to the window casing and just breathed. She didn't know if she could handle all this—her sister needing help "disappearing" and all the memories that went with that, memories she'd shoved back but now threatened to roll through her like a tidal wave, and her uncle either already looking for the both of their heads on a platter, literally, or getting ready to.

And now Brody here, nose twitching.

All too much, just too damn much.

But then the sound of an engine starting up drifted through her window. The badass Camaro roaring to life like a well-tuned lion.

Whoa. Leena *had* done it?

Surprised to the core, she stared at the car as it pulled away from the cabin.

He was actually leaving. The only man she could have, *should* have asked for help, had actually done what she'd asked—for once—and walked away.

Which was for the best.

Really.

Really, truly.

Yeah. Now all she had to do was believe it.

"You can't go all the way there and then leave without talking to her," Shayne said in Brody's ear via cell phone.

Yeah, Brody already knew that, thanks, but he hated to be told what to do. Hated to be in this situation in the first place. His fingers tightened on the wheel as he slowed down. *Really* hated this. Not a new feeling for him as he tended to look at the negative side of things. It served him well as a pilot because it meant he was always prepared for the worst.

In life, however, it hadn't been quite as helpful.

"Dani will kill me," Shayne told him. "You have to go back in."

"You afraid of your fiancée now?"

"I promised her, all right? And Noah promised Bailey. Which means you need to get to the bottom of this. You don't know what it's like."

"To have my dick in a sling? No, you're right. I don't, something I'm grateful for." Now that Shayne and Noah were both head over heels in love, they thought everyone should be.

But Brody did not agree.

So did not agree.

Now head over heels in lust? That he could get behind. He was halfway there with Maddie, in fact, and had been ever since she'd shoved him against a wall in the lobby at work and kissed him—a slow, wet, deep kiss like maybe her next breath depended on them to keep kissing for a good long time.

He'd been game for that. So game just remembering flooded his circuits with all that pleasure and need again.

"It'll happen to you," Shayne said confidently. "Some day you'll want to get married."

"Okay, I'm hanging up on you now."

"Go back in there, and get some answers from her."

"I don't think so."

"You have to."

"Yeah? Why?"

"Because if you don't, I'll . . . take you down."

Brody snorted. Out of the three of them, Shayne was the pacifist, always had been. "Seriously? *You?*"

"Okay, fine. I'll have Noah do it."

Shayne couldn't kick Brody's ass on his best day, but Noah? Noah could give Brody a run for his money if he put his mind to it. As best friends, the three of them had brawled just as many times as not, and it was always good for a tension reliever. And he was pretty filled with tension at the moment. But then he thought of the look on Maddie's face and knew he wasn't going anywhere to fight or otherwise. Not because he was afraid of Noah. Hell, he wasn't afraid of Noah. He wasn't afraid of much.

But he was afraid for Maddie.

So he tucked his cell phone between his ear and his shoulder and parked in the damn bush where the car wouldn't be seen by anyone happening by, not that *that* seemed likely. Maddie had chosen a place waaaay out of the way, and come to think of it, he'd like to know why. "I'm not leaving. I'm going undercover."

"Undercover."

"I'm going to break in."

There was a silent beat. "Okay, hold up. You've gone to the bad place. Come back here. I'll go and—"

"I'm already here."

"In body, yes. In mind, I'm not so sure."

"I haven't lost it."

"Clearly you have."

"Look, you made me do this, and I'm going to see this through."

To prove it, he got out of the Camaro, and walked through the woods to the back of Maddie's place, and eyed the back deck and, bingo, the sliding glass door. Probably, it was locked. Not a problem for a former juvenile delinquent with talented fingers. "I'm going in."

"Brody, you're crazy. What if she calls the cops? I'm not going to bail you out again."

"Once. You bailed me out of jail once."

"You still owe me five hundred bucks for that, by the way."

"Jesus. We were eighteen years old and in Mexico, and it was your fault I got caught with that open alcohol in the backseat since you were the one drinking it."

"Just saying."

"We're miles from the nearest cop." Brody was well aware of his past sins, many public knowledge, some not so much.

After all, he'd been born in a gutter, had lived in one, and would no doubt still be there, or in jail or worse, if at age twelve he hadn't tried to pickpocket an off-duty cop who'd decided to feed and house him instead of jailing him.

Later had come Shayne and Brody, and though they'd been codelinquents together for a while, meeting weekly, sometimes daily in school detention, neither of his two new partners in crime had really ever toed the line of the law like he had.

Somehow, their friendship had kept him mostly free of temptation and on the straight and narrow.

Except for the occasional fuckup.

Now that he had the dubious advantage of maturity, he rarely felt the need to create mayhem by doing anything illegal. But he felt it now.

He eyed the deck. Yeah, undoubtedly, he had a big fuckup coming his way. But come hell or high water, he was getting inside to talk to Maddie face to face, without a closed door between them.

With a stealth that came from a whole lot of years getting himself in and out of situations he shouldn't have been in in the first place, he got to the deck.

Tested the door.

The sliding glass door was, indeed, locked.

Not a problem. Old habits died hard, and sticky fingers never forgot how to be sticky.

Chapter 4

Maddie leaned out her bedroom window so far that Leena let out a terrified squeak and raced forward, grabbing her legs. "Don't jump! Ohmigod, don't jump!"

"I'm not!" Maddie pushed Leena's hands away. "Are you kidding? I'm not crazy."

"Okay." Her sister gulped in air with a hand to her chest. "Okay, that's good. You scared me."

"I just wanted to see if he was really gone."

"Is he?"

"Yes," Maddie lied. She'd lied more today than she thought she'd ever have to lie again. She sure hoped Karma wasn't paying attention because she could be a vindictive bitch.

Leena took a peek out the window as well, still breathing unevenly. "Sorry. I might have overreacted."

Maddie shot her a look. "Really?"

"I'm nervous, okay? The Plan and all."

Yes, The Plan.

They'd first hatched it when they were young, getting serious on their sixteenth birthday—run away and start a new life.

Only on the fateful day of execution, Leena hadn't gone with Maddie.

Nope, it'd taken her ten years to decide to catch up, ten

years during which Maddie had made a new life for herself. Now here Leena was, petrified, finally ready for The Plan, and Maddie was going to have to do it, have to start all over because she'd promised.

"It's just that he's so . . ." Still staring at Brody, Leena shrugged helplessly.

Big? Bad? Gorgeous? Pick one.

"Intimidating."

"Not when you know him," Maddie murmured.

"He was scowling at me. Like he wanted to eat me for breakfast, lunch, and dinner."

Maddie had seen that look from him before. Only, she hadn't found it scary, but unbearably erotic. "He wouldn't hurt you."

"You don't know that."

"Yes, I do."

"How?" Leena took a deeper look at her twin. "How do you know that for sure? Are you into him or something?"

Or something. "Don't be ridiculous."

"You are," Leena breathed, shaking her head in disbelief. "You're totally into him."

"Trust me," Maddie said with a laugh. "The two of us can't even be in a room together without riling each other up. I drive him crazy. He drives me crazy. We both drive—"

"Each other crazy. I get it." Leena continued to study her thoughtfully. They hadn't spent much, if any, time together in years. Maddie lived in LA, Leena in Florida and the Bahamas. Maddie supported herself and kept her distance from her past. Leena clung to their past . . .

Or had.

Until now, when she'd come to Maddie for help.

"I thought you gave up men." Leena was looking at her in surprise. "Back when—"

"I did," Maddie said quickly, not wanting to go on a trip down memory lane. "Mostly."

"Good. Because he's . . ." She gave a helpless shrug.

Yeah. When it came to describing Brody, words failed Maddie, too. "He's actually very nice."

"Seriously?"

"Okay, not necessarily *nice*, but he's a good man."

"I thought good and man were oxymorons."

"Not all men are assholes, Leena."

Unable, or unwilling, to believe, her sister shrugged. "It doesn't matter anyway, right? We're leaving?"

"Yeah." Maddie rubbed the ache in the center of her chest. She understood her sister's fears about needing to vanish, but Maddie hadn't lived in that world in a long, long time.

She intended to never live there again and hoped to make sure Leena didn't either. "Listen, why don't you go take your shower and that nap you wanted? Everything's going to be okay."

"Everything's never okay."

"A little positive thinking here, Leen. It goes a long way."

"Okay." Leena managed a smile and feigned a toast. "To positive thinking. To our plan."

Maddie returned the smile, pretending for both of their sakes that it was real. She realized nothing about The Plan was the smartest thing, at least not for her, but she didn't have a choice. A promise was a promise, with her sister's life on the line. "To The Plan."

Looking relieved, Leena nodded and grabbed her cell phone off the nightstand, sticking it in her pocket as she headed to the door.

Maddie waited until she was gone before turning back to the window and letting out a long breath. Lying . . . making promises she couldn't keep. . . . Yeah, she was on a roll today.

Because everything was not going to be okay, not by a long shot. Not unless she personally made it so. And it looked as if maybe she'd have no choice but to do just that or live in constant fear again.

Not going to happen.

Still, she had another, more immediate problem. Brody had left, yes, but she hadn't been born yesterday, and neither had he, damn him. And suddenly, she knew. She left the bedroom at a run, skidding to a stop at the top of the stairs, craning her neck to peek out the high, rounded beveled glass window that allowed extra light to beam down the steps and into the living room.

Yes, there. The glint of something not natural parked in the woods.

A Camaro.

Driven by an avenging angel in tough guy clothes with tousled hair and a badass attitude.

Her heart skipped a beat, and she got goose bumps. He was coming for her.

Damn it. *Damn him.*

She went running down the hardwood stairs, racing through the living room to the sliding glass door she'd kept locked since she'd gotten here, the door she'd been double-checking ever since the moment her sister appeared out of the blue after several years of no contact. Locked, but the shades hadn't been pulled. She needed to get to them before—

Too late.

Breathless, she gripped the shades as if they were a lifeline, staring at Brody standing on the other side of the glass.

He slowly arched a daring brow at her. *Really?* his expression and stance said. *You really think a locked door can keep me out if I want in?*

"I'll call the police," she said through the glass.

He let out a half smile and shook his head. She wouldn't. She knew it, and so did he. And as he stepped closer to the glass, there was a deceptive and unnerving quietness to his movements, to the way he looked at her, which told her that she wasn't getting out of talking to him until he'd gotten whatever answers he sought.

Damn it! She should have just dealt with him, answered the

front door herself and taken her paychecks, told him whatever he needed to hear, and he'd have been long gone by now.

Instead, he was on to her—not knowing exactly what he was on to, but on to her nevertheless. His smile might be laid-back and easygoing, but his body shimmered with tension, and also a strength and a solidity she knew she could count on.

He eyed the locked door, then lifted his head so that their gazes met. "Let me in."

Oh, God. A part of her wanted to. Wanted to more than anything. But she shook her head.

"Then tell me what's wrong."

She found her voice, even managed to inject a tone of irritation in it. Not too difficult when she *was* irritated, not to mention frustrated, exhausted, and the doozy . . . terrified. Hell of a combination. "Nothing's wrong, except you're bugging the hell out of me."

His eyes narrowed as they took her in from head to toe, which once upon a time, would have positively stolen her breath because he had a way of looking at her, really looking. She actually did experience some of that usual breathlessness, but it was because she realized she'd really screwed up. She and Leena weren't wearing the same thing.

Appearances were important to her. Very important. Her life could be in the toilet along with her self-esteem, but with the right makeup, the right clothes, and the right expression, no one would know it.

She'd spent the past year wearing such façades at Sky High Air, looking completely on top of her world, when in reality, it could all crumble at a moment's notice.

As it had with Leena's appearance.

She should have known. Karma *was* a bitch, and inescapable. Especially since unlike Leena, she wore only a pair of loose sweats low on her hips and a sports bra, and nothing else. No makeup, no armor of any kind.

Brody eyed her limbs, specifically her left shoulder, which

had three scars—one a six inch surgery incision, a second where they'd slid in a camera probe, and a third where the bullet had gone in and shattered her collarbone.

At the sight, Brody's jaw tightened visibly, and his mouth went grim.

She already knew he blamed himself, which was ridiculous, and she fought the urge to run for cover.

"You changed quickly," he said through the glass.

She lifted her good shoulder.

"And your hair . . ."

Shit. "I was wearing a wig before." Or Leena was. She'd had fun going through Maddie's wigs. As for herself, she was her own natural auburn for a change.

He nodded, though she couldn't tell if he bought the lie or not. Couldn't tell a damn thing behind those mirrored sunglasses. Then he slid his hands into his pockets and rocked back on his heels. "I'd really like to talk to you."

Yes, but she didn't want to talk to him. Not now, not until she solved all her other problems, the biggest one being her identical twin in the other room. "How did you find me?"

"It wasn't easy. You ever hear of returning a phone call?"

"How, Brody?"

He sighed. "You called Sky High from the landline once."

"Two days ago, when my cell phone battery had died."

"Yeah. We got Shayne's brother to track you."

"Wow." She shook her head. "What an unbelievable invasion of privacy."

"I'd say sorry—"

"But you're not." It was all over his face how not sorry he was. "Look, Brody, now's not good, okay? Maybe another time . . ."

Like, unfortunately, never.

He shoved his sunglasses to the top of his head, and his steely gaze narrowed in on her, full of frustration and heat.

She didn't know what to make of the heat, other than the answering flicker of flame that occurred in all her good parts.

The hell of it was even though she'd been fantasizing about him for way too long, she actually didn't have time to go with that right now.

What with The Plan and all.

"You were afraid before," he said, revealing a new emotion from him, a deep concern, which did something funny to a spot low in her belly.

"No," she denied. "Not afraid." Look at that, another lie. Man, she was getting good.

"Yes, you were at the front door. You were terrified. And now . . ." Cocking his head, he looked her over slowly, so damn slowly she felt those helpless reactions begin again at the base of her spine, working outward.

"It's not just the clothes," he said, frowning. "You look different."

Okay, he was *way* too close to the truth, and with a sound of distress she told herself he couldn't hear, she began to pull the shades shut, blocking him out.

"Maddie, goddamnit." He put his hand on the glass. "Don't."

"Sorry."

And she actually was sorry. So damned sorry that she felt her throat tighten and her eyes burn. And actually, if she wasn't careful, she was going to lose it right here, just completely lose it in a way she hadn't in years. Because she didn't want to go. Didn't want to never see him again . . .

"Maddie."

She closed her eyes, needing that little shield, no matter how telling.

"Hey, how about this," he said. "I'll give you a raise if you let me in. A big, fat, pretty raise. Come on, you know how you want one."

Oh, God. He already overpaid her, but that was only because Shayne and Noah made him. If he had his way, they'd all be working for free, squirreling away every penny for a rainy day.

It wasn't because he was cheap.

Okay, it was because he was cheap. He was so cheap he squeaked when he walked, but he'd grown up poor, had had to literally beg, borrow, and steal his way through childhood. Now, for the first time in his entire life, he had money, thanks to his own hard work and brains, and she knew he wasn't quite used to it yet. "You said the word raise without getting hives," she murmured, telling herself it shouldn't be endearing because he was trying to manipulate her.

"Let me in, and I'll say it again."

She meant something to him. She meant a lot. Even more shocking, he meant something to her, too. He meant so damn much it hurt to look at him. At the knowledge, she swallowed hard. Not going to cry . . .

"Maddie." He touched the glass as if he wanted, needed, to touch her. "Don't do this."

She closed her eyes again.

"I'll double your salary."

"Stop," she whispered.

"Let me in, and I'll stop. I'll do whatever you want."

Oh, God, now *there* was a promise. Close to doing just that, a noise from the other room stopped her cold.

Her sister's shocked gasp.

What now?

Maddie locked eyes with Brody. All these past weeks, seeing him had been a secret wish, an unconscious desire like breathing air. Having him come after her, having him want to be with her . . .

Except now, right this minute, when her sister's life was on the line and therefore, hers as well. If Brody stayed, then he, too, would be in danger. But she knew him, knew that he wasn't going anywhere unless she managed to distract him. "Okay, you're right. Something's wrong."

"Finally."

"I'm waiting on my physical therapist to come out for a session, but we had five inches of rain a few days ago and the road in here is still a little tricky. He's got a little Honda and won't come. Maybe you could go get him." She grabbed a notepad from a small desk near the door and scribbled down an address, then opened the door and slapped it to his chest. "Thanks."

Praying to God he left to track down the PT who didn't exist at the address that also didn't exist, giving her enough time to speed up The Plan, she locked the door again and yanked the shades over the window.

"Maddie!"

Tuning him out, she ran for her sister.

Chapter 5

Maddie raced into the kitchen to find Leena holding her cell phone to her ear, shaking from head to toe. "Leena? What are you—"

Leena shut her phone and stared at it like it was a poisonous spider. "He left a message."

No need to ask who the *he* was. Only one person could put that look on Leena's face.

Or Maddie's, for that matter.

Good old Uncle Rick.

"He already knew I'm not on that cruise like I told him. He thinks I might be on the run."

Maddie stared at her, absorbing all that Leena wasn't saying. Uncle Rick and his merry men weren't stupid. They knew Leena wouldn't run on her own.

Nope, of course she'd have gone straight to Maddie.

Damn.

Chances were, they'd never *not* known where Maddie was, but up until now, they hadn't needed her. Not when they had Leena.

"He's playing it cool," Leena said. "Pretending I'm not gone. He said if I just come back and do a job for him, I can get back to my vacation."

"You don't have to do what he says. You've left Stone Cay behind."

"Maybe no one ever really leaves."

"I did. You know I did."

"Yeah, you left. You had to sneak out in the middle of the night without a forwarding address, and you couldn't look back. You had to run hard and fast, thousands of miles away. You were young and all on your own, and you were nothing but a child."

"But I did it."

"But you had to hide. You had to start a new life." Leena said this in wonder. "No money, no friends or family or anything. Back then, I couldn't imagine the courage it took, and now . . . now that I'm here, I don't know if I'm strong enough to do the same."

"Well, I know. Besides, you're older than I was, and you're not alone. You have me. You can do this. You can, Leena. I promise."

They stared at each other, Leena's fear and Maddie's strength battling it out. Unfortunately, fear was a formidable opponent, and contagious, as well. Hers and Leena's differences had always been very obvious, but suddenly, the gap seemed to shrink to nothing until they were both young and scared stupid all over again.

"I want to do this," Leena whispered.

"And you will."

"But it's asking so much of you."

"Look, you're out of there. That's all that matters. The rest will be fine." Maddie only hoped that was true, but God, she didn't really want to vanish again. She loved the life she'd made for herself.

Loved.

It.

But she loved Leena more, even if it meant saying good-bye to everyone else. All they'd needed was a few more days, and she'd have had The Plan in motion. They'd have been gone. But now, Rick already knew Leena wasn't where she'd said she was, and the man Maddie didn't want to have to say good-bye to had shown up.

God.

"If Rick finds us—"

"If he tries to push us around, we'll push back," Maddie said firmly. "We'll get the authorities involved."

Leena was already shaking her head before Maddie finished. "Manny," she said, and the name stopped Maddie cold.

Manny had been one of Rick's grunt men, young and built, and Leena had gone out with him once. After their date, he'd come on to her strong, wanting sex. Leena hadn't been ready. She'd refused him anything but a quick kiss, but Manny hadn't been happy with that and tried for more. Leena'd shoved free of him, and he'd fallen down the stairs.

And died.

That was Leena's story.

Unfortunately, Rick had another one because Manny had been found with a knife wound in his gut. Back then, Rick had cleaned up that mess, but it wouldn't stay clean.

"If I stay gone," Leena said, "Rick's going to bring me up on murder charges."

Which would affect them both. "Okay, well, we'll cross that bridge when we get to it."

"Ohmigod." Leena shook her head. "I'm really doing this."

"Yes." Maddie thought of Brody, hopefully on his wild-goose chase after her PT. "But we need to move up the timetable to, like, now."

"We can't. I have someone I want to say good-bye to first. In New Orleans."

"Now?" Leena shook her head. "New Orleans? Who's in New Orleans—"

"Ben."

Now it was Maddie's turn to shake her head. "Leena, no. We can't do good-byes. We have to leave. Now."

"No." Leena's chin was set. Never a good thing. "I'm sorry, Mad, but I'm not like you, all tough and impenetrable, letting nothing get to me. I have to say good-bye."

Is that how Leena saw her? Really? Tough? Impenetrable? Cold? Is that how Brody would see her when she was gone? "I let plenty get to me. I just don't let any of it rule me. You have to be strong."

"No one's as strong as you."

"You are, and I'll prove it to you. Wait right here." With a calm she didn't feel, Maddie raced up the stairs. In the master bedroom, she went to the dresser that she'd commandeered as her own for her stay. Specifically, the underwear drawer. Beneath all the silk and lace that was her own vanity-vice, past the gun she kept there, sat a small jewelry box.

The only thing she had of their mother's.

It was wooden, intricately carved, and Russian, and she carried it with her because it gave her comfort. Supposedly, her mother's mother's mother had brought it over when she'd first come to the States. Inside was a string of pearls and a three-by-five picture of twin four-year-olds—Maddie and Leena, dressed for Halloween, wearing Batman and Robin costumes.

Superheroes.

They were grinning for the camera, arms slung around each other, their world as wide open in front of them as the gap in their mouths where their front teeth had been.

Maddie ran her thumb over the photo, her wistful smile fading. It'd been shortly after this picture had been taken that their mother had left them, just walked away to go after her dream of riches and fame in Hollywood rather than see her own children grow up. Rumor had it she'd made it only as far as one of the strip clubs in Miami.

Maddie and Leena had been raised on Stone Cay, a private Bahama island, in a huge, luxurious compound that made up their father's family heritage. Family being a loose term, of course. Their father had been with them until Maddie's and

Leena's eighth birthday, when he'd died of a heart attack after a fight with his brother over how to run a portion of their import-export gem business, the illegal portion.

Maddie and Leena had grown up in the lap of decadence and luxury, but they'd also grown up quickly. Classic poor little rich girls, one twin with an aptitude for survival skills and one gifted with a genius for jewelry design.

Leena.

After that little talent had been discovered by Uncle Rick, they'd pulled Leena into the business almost nonchalantly—oh, here, Leena, an important client wants to buy this million dollar gem from us, please design a piece for it. Then Uncle Rick would swap the gem out for a replica, sell the designed piece to their customer and the gem to someone else, and pocket the cash from both deals with their customer never the wiser.

When Maddie had learned of it, she'd freaked, knowing that when Rick got caught, Leena would go down in flames right alongside him. Maddie also knew that the only way to save Leena was to get her off the island, but every time she planned an escape, Leena would back out. Maddie might have stayed on Stone Cay all these years just to keep watching after Leena if it hadn't been for that one last fateful night, which had forced her to run hard and fast and never look back.

Staring down at the picture now, Maddie felt the regret nearly choke her. She'd walked away from Leena, left her alone and defenseless.

Seemed she wasn't so unlike her mother after all.

But the mistakes of her past were just that. She didn't have to repeat them. She wouldn't repeat them. Leena had come to her. She was ready. They could do this.

Together.

Slipping the picture in her pocket, she left the room to prove it to her sister.

* * *

Physical therapist, Brody's ass. PTs didn't make house calls, not even to gorgeous liars.

And Maddie *was* desperate. There'd been many, many times when he'd daydreamed about her being desperate . . . desperate for his body was his favorite.

But that's not what she was desperate for now. Nope, she was killing herself trying to get rid of him, and that wasn't going to happen.

It took him about four minutes to jimmy the lock on the sliding glass door. It would have taken less, but halfway through, Shayne buzzed him on his cell to ask if he'd handled things yet.

"Working on it."

"What's taking you so long? You losing your touch with women?"

Brody snarled, and with a laugh, Shayne disconnected.

Anger was a good motivator, but angst was a better one, and Brody slid the door open. Helping himself, he stepped inside. Someone had gone a little overboard with the wild, wild West theme in the place, but even without the cowboy paraphernalia, the interior screamed expensive taste, much like the woman who lived here.

There was no one in the living room, but he followed a low murmur of voices into a hallway, where there was a line of skis and snowshoes that he absolutely could not see Maddie using. She liked cars and planes, things with engines, nothing that required her own steam.

Why was she here, so out of her element?

Then he heard a cell phone ring, and Maddie's voice answer, low and unhappy. He moved into the kitchen where he found her talking to her cell phone, opened on the counter.

"I've been out of range," she said.

"That's a problem." The man spoke in a harsh warning tone. "You need to get back in range."

"You don't understand." Maddie wrung her hands. "I just

want to live my life. I want to . . . travel. I won't tell anyone
what we've done, I promise. Just let me go."

This made Brody even more tense, as did the fact that she
was back to being a platinum blonde and wearing the sprayed
on jeans.

What the hell? She looked like the kick-ass Maddie he
knew, but she did not sound like her, not with the uncertain
tone and stance that suggested she could be bullied and intimidated.

The Maddie he knew would never give anything away, certainly not a single vulnerability, and she sure as hell never let
anyone bully or intimidate her.

Never.

He was missing something, and the niggling of it rumbled
through him.

"I know you won't tell a soul," said the man through the
speaker. "Just as I know you'll get back here. You have a job."

"I'm . . . no longer interested."

"Get reinterested. Fast."

"But—"

"Okay, let me make things clearer. Get back here, or I'll
send someone for you. And you won't like that, believe me.
You know you won't."

At Sky High, Maddie would have cut the guy off at the
knees, if not the balls, and Brody waited for her to do just that.
Instead, she shuddered in fear. "No, please. Don't."

Okay, fuck this, he thought and strode across the room toward her.

She whirled and at the sight of him, let out a terrified little
squeak that stopped him short.

"Brody?" she whispered, hand fluttering up to her throat
like a damsel in distress, which confused him all the more.

"Who's Brody?" the man on the phone demanded.

Brody slowed his steps, not liking the way she was retreat-
ing from him, backing up against the counter. He'd figured

she'd slug him or do anything in her usual take no prisoners way. Instead she was cowering to the tile, eyes huge on his. "Brody's my . . ."

"What?" the cell phone commanded. "He's your what?"

"I forgot to tell you. I'm . . . married."

Dead silence all around.

Well, except for Brody's heart, which skidded to a stunned stop, then began a heavy, hard beat that threatened to give him heart failure.

Married?

"Yeah," Maddie said, eyes still locked on Brody. "And he makes enough money for the both of us, so I don't ever have to work for you again, Rick. And if you're smart, you'll just let me go."

Brody was still on the married portion of that sentence. What the hell was she talking about? She dated occasionally, he knew. He hated it. But he'd always taken some comfort in the fact that when she did date, she rarely repeated a guy.

But married? That required a lot of repeating, and he would have definitely noticed that.

"You're married," the man on the phone said in clear disbelief.

"Yes." Maddie's eyes were still locked on Brody. "And Brody doesn't like the islands, so we can't come back. Sorry."

Jesus. Why would she say she was married to *him?*

"You're the one who's going to be sorry if you don't get back here to Stone Cay," the man said, and the following click, along with the aggression and fury in the sound, echoed through the kitchen, distinctive and succinct.

Brody stared at the woman who his eyes were telling him was Maddie while his brain screamed otherwise, but then she did something even more extremely un-Maddielike.

She put the cell phone in her pocket and burst into tears.

Absolutely struck stupid by all of it, he moved as if underwater, reaching for her, pulling her into his arms.

"Maddie's going to kill me," she cried against his chest.

He went still as stone as her tears soaked into his shirt, then stared down at her. Maddie was going to kill Maddie?

What the hell?

But she just leaned on him and sobbed. Only Maddie had never leaned on him, not once. As far as he knew, she'd never leaned on another soul. What she also did was stand her ground, always.

Then something even more shocking happened, if that was possible. Another woman stepped into the room, the mirror image of the Maddie in his arms.

She wasn't sobbing, nothing close, and he divided a glance between them, suddenly feeling better, a whole lot better, in fact, because he wasn't crazy, he was simply stupid.

The other Maddie, the *real* Maddie, walked right up to him, and not quite certain what she intended, he drew in a breath because she had a reputation for leading with her right hook, or a hard smack upside the head.

But she ignored her "husband" entirely and simply pulled her twin out of his arms and hugged her close.

"Identical," he murmured and shook his head. Damn, he'd been schooled, hard.

Looking over her sister's head, Maddie met Brody's gaze. She was *au natural* in a way he'd never seen her before, her auburn hair down and loose, no makeup, somehow more beautiful than he'd ever seen her. She was also completely together, extremely so, and he wondered how the hell he'd ever mistaken her sister for her.

"Thanks for getting the physical therapist," she said dryly.

"There is no physical therapist. You were trying to get rid of me."

Her mouth tightened.

"Admit it."

"Leena," she murmured, still looking at Brody. "Wait for me upstairs?"

With a nod, Leena pulled free and left the room.

Maddie kept looking at Brody.

He looked back. Her eyes were cool, her head high. Her hair fell in an intriguing curtain of glossy, perfect silk behind her shoulders, except for one strand that brushed her creamy skin at her collarbone, and as mesmerizing as that was, it had nothing on where the ends landed—at her breasts, covered only in that sports bra. When she tossed the strands back, he saw that her nipples had hardened.

He took a careful breath. And then another. Because he had no business noticing her breasts with her nipples poking at the material, or otherwise, and to remind him of that, he looked at her bullet and surgery scar, the one that ripped at his heart. Yeah, that was a good way to put things in perspective.

"Brody."

He lifted his gaze.

"Okay, there's no PT waiting for a ride. But there is a package at the post office. I—*we* need that package. Clearly, I'm not going to get rid of you, so—"

"Damn right."

"So maybe you could go get the package for us."

"Sure. If you come with me."

She sighed. "Brody—"

"You come with me. That's the deal."

She frowned. "I'd have thought at the word *husband*, you'd be running for the hills."

That was just true enough that he really couldn't take offense. "How about we put aside all my many faults and concentrate on you for a minute?"

"Are you sure?" she said. "Because there are so many faults to pick from that we could discuss."

He dragged a hand over his face in frustration and decided she was still trying to distract him. Only she didn't get it. It wasn't going to work. "What's going on?"

"Nothing that concerns you."

"Really? Because I'm pretty sure being the husband concerns me."

She simply turned away from him, ignoring him completely but giving him a nice view of her nearly bare back. Her spine was ramrod straight, her shoulders proud.

Yeah, there was the Maddie he knew, the take charge, capable woman. At Sky High, she'd intimidated the hell out of him with all her elegance, sophistication, all that easy class that screamed Don't-Touch.

Nothing much had changed.

But he still wasn't leaving.

Chapter 6

Could this day have gotten any worse? Maddie wondered as Brody followed her through the house. She passed through the laundry room where Leena had some of her bras hanging up to dry. She ducked beneath them, but even when he ducked, Brody managed to hit a hanger. A black, lacy panty fell to the floor.

He bent and picked it up, the thing looking incredibly small and feminine in his hands.

With a sound that she meant to be annoyance but might have been something else entirely, she snatched it from him, stretching to hang it back up. As she moved, she felt him at her back. She always felt him, but more today than she ever had before.

She'd missed him.

Hell of an admission.

He was eyeing the rest of the drying lingerie, not saying a word but clearly thinking plenty. "My sister's," she said and walked on.

He followed. Of course, he followed.

She couldn't shake him, and she sure as hell hadn't managed to distract him either. She was definitely losing her touch. Stopping in the front hall, she looked pointedly at the door. He set a big, warm hand on the small of her back until she turned and looked at him.

She got that she'd inadvertently triggered all of his alpha male, drag-his-knuckles-on-the-ground tendencies. It was all over his face, in the hard angles of his jaw, in the set lines of his mouth, in the way his eyes were so intense and stormy and utterly focused on her.

He knew her far better than she'd imagined. Though how that was possible, what with him always doing his damnedest to keep his distance from her at work . . .

But she'd obsess about that later.

Much later.

She had bigger issues at the moment. Life and death issues. Leena's. Hers.

And now his.

Because yes, she'd heard Rick's message loud and clear. Her Uncle Rick expected Leena back on Stone Cay, and if she didn't go, there'd be trouble.

There'd be problems.

There'd be blood. "Brody."

"Maddie," he said with shocking calm. A furious calm, if she wasn't mistaken, but still.

"I'm on leave of absence," she reminded him, not telling him that it looked like it might be permanent. Hell, she could hardly think it, much less say it out loud. "As in, I'm not currently working for you. So what's happening in my life is none of your business."

"That might have been true a few minutes ago. But now we're related."

"Stop it."

"No, you stop it." Yes, definitely fury. "What the hell is this all about, Maddie? Who was that asshole on the phone?"

She wasn't moved by much, but him standing there in that tall, muscled package, wrapped by all that raw and dangerous male beauty made her swallow hard. "You wouldn't believe me if I told you."

"Try me."

Try him? That had been her greatest fantasy up until Leena had shown up and Maddie's entire world of glass had shattered. Before that, she'd wanted to try him every which way possible, but that was going to be just a fantasy now, a remote one. She reached for the front door, but before she could open it, he placed his hand on the wood, effortlessly holding it closed above her head.

Facing the door, she eyeballed his arm, taut with strength. The fingers of his hand were spread wide. He had long fingers, scarred from all the planes he'd rebuilt. They were capable fingers, always warm, and the clincher . . . they knew how to touch. He'd held her face that time she'd kissed him, and if she closed her eyes, she could still feel them on her jaw. She'd spent a lifetime schooling herself against feeling too much, against giving away too much of herself, especially to men. But the men she'd been with didn't make her nerves sing and her pulse jump by just looking at them.

Brody did.

"Maddie."

"It was nice of you to visit. But as you can see, now's not a good time."

He lifted his hand and traced a finger over the exit wound on the back of her shoulder. "Are you feeling okay?"

She loved his touch. Way too much. "Yes." Unfortunately, the man was a virtual mule when he wanted to be, unmovable, staunch in his opinions. On her best day, she might have gone toe to toe with him, no problem, using that voice of honey she'd perfected, her smile of ice, and the argumentative skills she'd honed well over the years. She was every bit as stubborn as he, and she would have won—she'd have seen to it.

But this wasn't her best day, not by far. In fact, it was

quickly gearing up to be one of her top three worst ever. "Don't make me kick your ass out of here."

"I think I can take you."

With a sigh, she dropped her forehead to the door and just breathed. Not easy with well over six feet of solid, warm muscle encroaching into the personal space behind her.

And he *was* encroaching.

Not that her body minded. Nope, it had apparently disengaged from her brain and was making a break for freedom.

But then he did something that made it all the more difficult. He stepped even closer so that she actually felt his thighs brush the backs of hers. His chest did the same to her back, and then, oh God, and then she felt his breath on her temple.

She had to close her eyes. *Don't turn around because then you'll be in his arms, and you just might be stupid enough to kiss him again, get lost in him . . .*

He slipped an arm around her waist, hard and corded with strength. Adrenaline and something else, something much more dangerous to her well-being, washed through her veins, followed by a high tide of stark desperation.

If she pushed back against that body, she could rub all her good spots to his. No.

Yes.

Her mind continued to war with her hormones, but then he leaned in, just a little, and put his mouth to her ear. "Tell me one thing, at least."

She swallowed hard because he even smelled good. Sort of woodsy and so very, *very* male. She could feel her heart racing, which was at complete odds with his, beating slow and sure and smooth. Damn it. She was supposed to be slow and sure and smooth! "What?"

"Where's Stone Cay?"

Oh, God.

"I can look it up, but I'm going to guess . . . The Keys?"

"Bahamas. It's a small private island in the Bahamas."

"Okay." He sounded relieved to be getting somewhere, but that relief would be short-lived because he wasn't going to get any further.

Nope.

"Do you think I can't see your fear?" he murmured, his mouth still so close to her ear that his lips brushed against her lobe when he spoke. "That I don't know how unlike you this is?"

His lips brushed her skin again, and her entire body began to hum. "That was Leena's fear," she managed. God. He was too close. And he was too raw, too masculine, and far too big for the small hallway.

"But it's you now. Right here, right now with me. Afraid." As he spoke, his mouth moved against her, his warmth seeping into her chilled bones and with all that hard strength up against her, and it was too much, making her squirm to free herself.

He merely pressed up against her, fully now, so that he couldn't take a breath without her knowing it, and vice versa.

"Talk to me, Maddie."

Impossible. With all that testosterone wrapped in sinew pressing against her, his face so close she could feel the stubble from his jaw brush hers, and that intoxicating scent of frustrated man, she could hardly think. Talking? Forget about it.

"Are you in trouble?"

Truth? Trouble was her new middle name. She bit back her short bark of laughter because it would have come out sounding far too hysterical. Plus, she might not have been able to stop. "No." And there went another lie. Hope Santa wasn't listening, but it was for Brody's own good . . .

"Jesus, Maddie, come on. It's all over your face."

She imagined it was. At some point between Leena showing up and realizing Rick was on her tail looking for blood and then the guy of her secret fantasies arriving in his Camaro-chariot, Maddie had lost her ability to hold it together, much less hide her emotions.

She really needed to get a grip on that pronto. Showing emotion was dangerous, both to her physical well-being and to her heart and soul.

Not that she was worried about her heart and soul. Nope, at the moment, it was mostly her physical being she had concerns about.

And Leena's.

And if she didn't shake Brody, his as well. God. Was she in trouble? Hell, yeah. The worst sort of trouble. But she could handle it.

She always did.

Except this time . . . this time, there was a small part of her that had doubts, a small part of her that said her luck had finally run out and the past she'd been one step ahead of for ten years just might have caught up to her. "There's some trouble," she admitted.

"Your sister?"

Okay, maybe she could admit that part, too. "It's a misunderstanding. Nothing we can't handle."

Look at that, another lie right off her tongue. They were really racking up today.

"Let me help."

No. Definitely not. Not with Rick involved, not with her past hanging out, leaving her feeling way too exposed. So was the way Brody was holding her with extreme care, making sure not to put too much pressure on her shoulder, but she couldn't get free—a bit demoralizing given all those years of self-defense classes she'd taken.

Squirming did nothing but make her extremely aware of their position, of her butt snugged to his crotch, for example, and how she wished they were in this position for another reason entirely.

He turned just his head so that once again his jaw brushed hers. The feeling shouldn't have stopped her heart and made her belly quiver, but it did, and that just pissed her off. "I think this qualifies as you butting your nose in where it doesn't belong. You don't let me do that to you."

"Are you kidding?" he asked with a low laugh. "When you're at work, you butt into my life every damn day of the week."

"Oh, you mean when you're in your office, all pouting and edgy and barking at the rest of us?"

"Excuse me. *Pouting?*"

"That's right. Pouting like a woman over your deep, dark secrets."

He choked on that, then went silent a moment. "I have no secrets."

"Uh-huh, and you're an open book."

Now he let out a low huff of frustrated air, which disturbed the hair on her temple and a whole bunch of things inside her.

Too many things.

Damn it. She couldn't keep it together with him here. "You're hurting me."

At that, he pulled back so fast her head spun. Her relief was short-lived, however, because then his hands were on her waist, gently but inexorably turning her to face him.

So she played chicken and closed her eyes.

"Maddie. Look at me."

No, thanks. Because she could stand here, just like this, close to him without being too close, being able to smell him but not see him, for a good long time.

Forever, maybe, except then her body gave her away by swaying toward him.

Traitorous body.

"Maddie, goddamnit."

She sighed and opened her eyes.

His held hers and wouldn't let go. "I know you want me gone so you can take care of this 'misunderstanding.'"

"It *is* a misunderstanding."

He rolled his eyes. "Whatever. But as your husband, I'm equipped to help."

"Why? Because you have a penis?" She struggled for patience and decided she needed a moment to cool off. Giving him a little push to clear her path, she walked away.

Walked away and rubbed at the spot in the center of her chest that ached like a son of a bitch because she needed one last lie. The king of lies, she thought as she climbed the stairs. Something that would make him think he was helping and get him the hell out of here.

Leena hadn't wanted to leave her sister alone with the tall, dark, and absolutely attitude-ridden Brody, nor did she want to step up and say so.

She wasn't good at stepping up, especially to men. One look at her life would tell anyone that. She hadn't stepped up to Rick, and he'd single-handedly ruined her life. She hadn't stepped up when Manny had wanted her and she hadn't wanted him. She hadn't stepped up when she'd become attracted to one of the men she'd helped Rick rip off, leaving that man, Ben Kingman, in possession of one gorgeous and very fake diamond ring, which was all her fault . . .

God. Sometimes, she really hated herself.

She paused to listen to how her sister was faring with her boss and heard Maddie say "Don't make me kick your ass out of here."

See? Maddie didn't let anyone push her around; she took care of herself.

How Leena envied that because she wasn't any better at taking care of herself than she was at standing up for herself. Actually, she wasn't good at much, really, except for creating truly original, one of a kind, beautiful jewelry on spec for whoever happened to have money in their pocket to pay Rick for such things.

Yeah, she was good all right. Real good.

Not that she was proud . . .

Of course, the swindles had all occurred against her will and with the threat of all sorts of Sopranolike violence if she didn't keep her trap shut, but she doubted the law would see things her way. If Rick was ever even caught.

Rick had promised her he wouldn't be. And that going to jail was nothing compared to what he'd do to her if she ever turned him in. For herself, she didn't care.

Okay, she cared.

But for Maddie . . . tough, resilient, brave Maddie who'd gotten away on her own, who'd done so before she'd had anything to be ashamed of, who'd managed to make a life for herself, which she deserved . . .

Leena couldn't, wouldn't do anything to jeopardize that.

But you already have, just by coming here . . .

Ashamed, she closed her eyes. She'd screwed up again. Always . . .

Giving her sister some privacy, she moved out the back door and stood on the deck, then reached into her pocket for a cigarette before remembering she'd given up all the things that were bad for her. Wishing she'd left herself that one vice, she wandered into the woods, eyeing the towering pines, the wildflowers swaying in the breeze, everything so beautiful and in its place.

She'd never found her place. She'd never belonged.

And hell, if that wasn't an overly dramatic, self-pitying thought, when she'd given up both dramatic and self-pitying thoughts along with the cigarettes.

Damn it.

Out here in no-man's-land, she didn't hear any voices, raised or otherwise, which meant Maddie had either kicked some Brody ass or she'd gotten rid of him. She still couldn't believe that Maddie would actually work for someone like him, someone so . . . nerve-wrackingly big and bad and . . . undeniably sexy.

If one was into nerve-wrackingly big and bad and undeniably sexy.

Personally, she was not. Nor had she expected Maddie to
be. But it'd been a long time since Maddie and Leena had
been together. Things had changed.

A lot of things. With a sigh, she went back inside, where it
was quiet, very, very quiet. "Maddie?"

"Up here."

Leena found her in the master bedroom, looking through
the small, intricately carved wooden box that had belonged to
their mother.

That surprised her. Maddie wasn't sentimental; neither of
them were.

They'd never really been given a chance to be.

Maybe Leena wasn't the only one feeling a little pes-
simistic about their future. "Where's Brody?"

"Hopefully thinking about leaving soon."

"Hopefully?"

"Don't worry. He's not a problem. I'll figure it out."

"You could just tell him the truth."

"No, I can't," Maddie said. "That would leave a loose string,
someone who knows."

"You said you trust him."

Maddie stared at her. "Well. That's a new word for you. Trust."

Leena lifted a shoulder. "I just think that it seems like
maybe . . . maybe there's something more between you two
than just work."

"If there is, it no longer matters."

Because of The Plan.

Guilt stabbed at her, hard. "Maddie—"

"Forget him a minute." Maddie pressed a photo into her
hand. "This is what I wanted to show you."

Leena looked down at the old picture of the two of them in
the Halloween costumes, missing their front teeth and pretending to be superheroes, and along with the guilt came a
new and completely unexpected surge of emotion.

Love.

"We were both strong then," Maddie reminded her. "We can both be strong again."

Leena lifted her gaze from the picture and looked at Maddie. In her sister's eyes was more of that love, and that swamped her, too. Her heart couldn't take any more, but she could admit this. "Yes. You're right."

A smile crossed Maddie's mouth. "I like the sound of that."

"But Maddie? I'm still going to go say good-bye to Ben—"

"Leena—"

"No, listen. Please. You have to understand. For years, I've gone about my life with my eyes closed, letting Rick rule my whole world. But I can't keep pretending not to see what's going on around me anymore. I have to change. And to do that, I have to face what I've done." She took Maddie's hand. "I have to try to make it right."

"By admitting your part in criminal activity to Ben, a man who can use that admission to press charges against you?"

"By not being shallow. By growing a backbone."

"Okay, give me a minute." Maddie pressed her fingers to her mouth. "I admire the thought, but Jesus, Leena—"

"I know, but I have to right that wrong if I'm going to go on. I have to, or I *can't* go on."

Maddie stared at her, both deeply impressed and deeply terrified. "I want to pull the older twin card here and say fine, but you're not going alone. No way in hell."

Leena's eyes were filled with an admirable steely determination. "I know I'm doing the right thing. And you're only four minutes older."

"Five minutes."

Leena smiled. "Older sister or not, I'm doing this. And then we can put The Plan into motion. The Vanishing Off The Face Of The Earth Plan."

In that moment, Maddie realized something a little shocking—all this time she'd thought of herself as the stronger of the two of them, but that wasn't actually true.

Leena was the stronger.

Because unlike herself, Leena was going to actually have her good-bye.

Don't worry so much," Leena said softly. "It's time for me to take care of myself."

"Fine. But I've got your back."

Ten years of karate classes and other various self-defense classes would have both of their backs, as well as the gun in her underwear drawer and the knife she always had strapped to her thigh because it never hurt to be prepared.

"You're always going to try to take care of me, aren't you?" Leena asked.

Maddie hesitated. "I guess I am." She waited for Leena to object, but her sister surprised her.

"I'm glad," Leena said and hugged her hard. "To The Plan then."

"To The Plan."

Chapter 7

Brody heard the soft murmur of the sisters talking upstairs. He'd watched Maddie walk away from him, moving with sheer, dazzling attitude and grace, like a dancer in motion, even with the one shoulder that she couldn't quite square and the one arm that didn't quite flow like the other.

A fact that just about ripped out his fucking heart, but that was another issue. As was the fact that he'd caught her looking at him with such a sense of loss that she was scaring the crap out of him.

Why did she feel like she was losing him when he was right here?

He didn't know, but he was on a mission to figure it out. To further that, he opened the front door, paused for effect, and then without stepping outside, flicked his wrist and let the door slam shut, practically hearing Maddie's sigh of relief from upstairs.

And then he walked through the living room, heading straight for the desk he'd eyed when he'd first entered the place. Maddie wasn't forthcoming with answers. No problem. He'd find them for himself.

It was the husbandly thing to do.

Maddie would be furious, but he didn't care. Having a

woman be furious at him wasn't anything new, nor was having
one ask him to leave her presence. His own mother hadn't
known what to do with him and had washed her hands of him
at a young age, not that he blamed her—he'd been more than
a handful.

Later, when he'd discovered women, they'd always been
drawn to him until they realized his priorities, which were
planes, flying, more planes, food, roof over his head, planes . . .
and lastly, any possible relationship.

Yeah, he'd been asked to go away a lot. But he wasn't going
this time. No way, no how. The threat from the man on the
phone had been real, and directed at Maddie.

The top of the desk was neat as a pin, without so much as a
stapler or paper clip or spare piece of paper. The drawers were
locked. He did feel a brief stab of conscience as he broke into
the thing, but it was very brief. When he opened the top two
drawers, he wasn't surprised to find nothing but office sup-
plies, all neat and unused.

The third drawer held the jackpot. A laptop. He booted it
up and was momentarily stymied at the required password
when he heard her footsteps behind him.

"*Are you kidding me?*"

Swiveling in the desk chair, he took in the woman standing
in the doorway. She had auburn hair, but she no longer wore a
sports bra and sweats. They'd been replaced with a white
miniskirt, and he did mean mini, with a lacy baby blue number on top that showed off the class A curves she was packing.
There was a narrow strip of smooth, sleek abs showing at her
belly button, and the sexy twinkling jeweled piercing there,
which made him want to fall to his knees and worship the spot
with his mouth.

Oh, and the boots didn't hurt. His first thought was to strip
her out of the lace and mini and leave just the boots.

Yeah, *there* was an image. But which twin? He wanted to say
Maddie . . . "You're not triplets, right?"

She put one hand on her hip in a stance that was self-explanatory. Pissed off female alert. Whether she didn't use both hands because she'd been shot on the job, *his* job, or because she didn't want to expend any more energy than necessary, he had no idea.

"So you're still here," she said.

Okay, she looked like Maddie and sounded like Maddie . . . but did she *taste* like Maddie? He squelched that inappropriate thought the best he could, which wasn't very well. "I can't leave."

"Can't? Or won't?"

"Yeah. That one."

Looking sizzling hot, she blew out another breath. "You're more stubborn than my sister."

Yes. Yes, he sure as hell was. She was speaking quietly, so quietly he practically had to cup his ear to hear her.

Very un-Maddielike.

Maddie wanted him gone. Enough to have her sister to pretend—again—to be her while she escaped?

Probably.

Standing, he went to the window and looked out, seeing nothing but forest. "You could have avoided me coming here." He turned back to her. "You know that, right?"

She arched a questioning brow. "Are you fishing for a hint to which twin you've got?"

He decided to plead the Fifth on that one.

"We're completely identical, you know. Except for only one of us having a small birthmark on the back of the right thigh."

A most interesting image, one he tried to forget as he eyed her body, trying to tell if she was favoring her arm. "I know another difference."

And Maddie did, too. At least the real Maddie did.

"What's that?"

"The tattoo." And if she'd just turn around and bend over, her skirt was low enough on her hips that it might reveal enough of her heart-stopping ass to show at least some of the highly stylized inked Chinese symbol she had there, the one that translated to Dream Big.

She'd never said, but he had a feeling that once upon a time, dreaming big had been all she'd had, something he most definitely empathized with.

They were definitely kindred survivors, but with the way she practically screamed high class and him hardly even knowing what class was, that's where their similarities ended.

"Right," she said. "The tattoo. But that's not for public viewing."

Now see, Maddie would have just flashed him the ink; he was sure of it. She'd done it before, to him and Shayne both, and he'd nearly had to kill Shayne for drooling over the sight.

Maybe he could grab her hand, pull her over his knee, and tug down her skirt to see for himself, but as much fun as that would be, he valued his life very much. "I've seen the tattoo. You showed it to me yourself." He waited for a reaction. Yeah, there, that flash of heat and temper. *Maddie.* It was all in the eyes, the undeniable awareness of him, even though she was trying to fight it. *Join my club, babe.*

"I'm going to ask you nicely this one last time," she said. "And then you're going to be sorry."

"Actually, you're not asking all that nicely."

"Oh, forget it." She shoved up her sleeves. "I'll kick you out myself."

Ah, a threat. Definitely Maddie. "I can help you. I can help you both."

"How? You don't even know which twin you have."

And that made her mad. It was in the tight lines of her gorgeous, kissable mouth. And damn, she was holding her arm close to her side as if her shoulder hurt. Rising out of his chair, he moved toward her.

She gave one startled squeak and took a step back, right up against the wall now.

Good one, he thought. She might have been Leena right down to that unhappy glint in her eye, except for the I'll-kick-your-ass tilt of the chin. He definitely knew which twin he had, and wondering how he'd ever doubted it, he stepped up close and personal, toe to toe, flattening his hands on the wall on either side of her head.

"What do you think you're doing?" she demanded.

"I don't know. *Leena.*"

Steam came out of her pretty ears at that. Oh, yeah, his gorgeous, strong, stubborn as hell Maddie was good and ticked off now.

Which made two of them. Why the hell wouldn't she trust him enough to let him in on what was happening? Did she think he couldn't sense that this was serious, deadly serious, and that she was in danger? It scared him. She scared him.

Frustrated and hot under the collar, he leaned in, wishing she didn't smell so damn good . . .

"Maddie'll—"

"What?" he murmured, watching the pulse at the base of her neck race. "Maddie'll what?"

Her eyes narrowed as she clearly fought between admitting that she wasn't Leena and her own damn pride, which wouldn't allow her to admit anything. Neither could she fully squash the flash of hurt that he hadn't known her.

Ah, Maddie. I know you. I know you inside and out. Watch me prove it . . .

Their noses were nearly brushing, and that wasn't the only thing. Her breathing had changed, quickened, and with each shallow little pant, the tips of her breasts slid against his chest. He tried not to notice that or the way her nipples had hardened into two tight points, but was a complete failure at both.

She was softening, melting for him, and God, he loved that. Loved when she let him see the real her . . .

Failing at keeping his damned distance, he lifted his palms from the wall and slid his fingers into her hair.

Another sound escaped her, this one different from the first, low and uneven, which shot straight to his groin.

"What are you doing?" she asked, so breathy he nearly moaned.

What was he doing? He hadn't a clue. All he knew was that he'd planned on getting her to agree to come back to work and then hightailing it out of here. But now, that was the furthest thing from his mind.

Which he'd apparently lost.

Yeah, his mind was gone, and he was crazy because he was going to kiss her. "I already know how Maddie kisses," he murmured and slid the tip of his nose along her jaw, slowly exhaling in her ear, absorbing her shiver. "I thought I'd find out how you kiss."

She gasped, but he shifted infinitely closer, letting his gaze drop to her sweet as sin lips, letting her know that he was thinking about much more than kissing.

And then she was thinking more, too, he could tell. Heat swirled in those baby blues as certain as it swirled in his gut.

And lower.

Christ, this was stupid. Spectacularly stupid. They'd kissed once before, and he'd barely recovered. He'd dreamed about, thought about, obsessed about that single kiss.

Now he wanted to do it again. *Was* going to do it again, stupid or not, mostly because his head wasn't in charge. At least not the one of top of his shoulders. If it had been, he'd be still sitting at her desk, making her tell him what the hell was going on from a distance.

A healthy distance.

Instead, here he was, pressing her to the wall, practically inhaling her. And then his mouth was on hers.

She could have stopped him if she wanted to, and for a breath, he waited for her to do just that.

Instead, she let out a surprised, pleasure-filled sigh. She slid an arm up and around his neck, her other hand going to the small of his back as if to hold him in place.

And just like that, he was lost, lost in the feel and taste of her, lost in the sensation of being with her like this after fantasizing about it night and day.

No one could destroy him with a single kiss like she could, no one . . .

And then she said the word he'd hoped not to hear.

"Stop."

Damn. With shocking reluctance, he lifted his head.

Mouth wet, she stared up at him, desire and yearning pouring off of her in waves.

He glided his thumb over her full lower lip. "What?"

Her lips parted, but no words came out, just a soft sound, one filled with desire and confusion and frustration.

Leaning forward, he swallowed the next one with his mouth, kissing her again, and then again, his breath catching in an almost painful knot in his throat as he absorbed the gratifying, alluring warmth of her mouth, her hands tightening on him, running over his chest as if she had to touch him or die.

A goner.

He was a complete goner, and he pulled her closer, deepening the kiss, falling headfirst into his own seduction. God, it was sweet, sinking into her, feeling her tongue slide alongside his, the scent of her hair teasing him, the feel of her hands gripping him so tight.

Tight was good, tight was fan-fucking-tastic, and going with that, he spread his fingers wide to touch as much of her as he could, knowing that this was a dream, one that he could be deprived of any time, and he wanted to be able to remember this. Wanted to remember every second.

She was tight, toned, but had curves in all the right places, lush, soft curves he wanted to bury himself in, and given the way she arched into him, those whispery pants in his ear, she felt the same. He slid his hand down over her sweet ass and the backs of her thighs, his other skimming beneath her top to the warm, sleek skin of her back, coming around to touch her belly, which was rising and falling with her quick breath.

"Brody."

He heard it in her voice—she was going to stop him again, and he didn't want her to. He could tell himself it was because it had been so long since he'd held a woman, but that would be an excuse. It was her.

He couldn't stop touching *her*.

He slid his fingers over her ribs and was working his way north as his other hand continued the march on the southern territory, his fingers catching on . . .

Ah, Christ, yeah, a thong. "God, you feel good, so damn good." His hands were busy, very busy, and so were hers, under his shirt, too, digging into the muscles of his back . . . "I want you naked," he murmured. "Naked and all over me."

She made a little sound that he decided was agreement, and he actually craned his neck to see where they could do this whole naked and all over him thing. "The desk."

She followed his line of vision and choked out a laugh, sliding her hands around to his chest. "Oh, no."

"It'll hold—"

"No way. Seriously. Don't even think about it." But he was thinking and thinking hard. "Brody, listen to me."

He turned to her. "Oh, I'm all ears. Maddie."

She gaped at him. "You knew all along?"

"Did you really think I would kiss Leena like that?"

"This isn't about the kiss."

"No. It's about me knowing you. And I do know you. Which is why *you* need to listen. I'm sticking, okay? Until the bitter end. So you might as well start talking."

Chapter 8

Leena stood by herself upstairs, staring down at the picture of her and Maddie as little kids. Back then, they'd been equal in strength.

Then, slowly, she'd somehow let her faults run her life—that's what had happened. And there'd been many. She'd been weak. Selfish. So damned selfish. Yes, she'd stayed with Rick and done his bidding out of habit, and certainly fear.

Lots of fear.

But if she was being honest, then she had to admit all of it. The lifestyle hadn't hurt—island fun, the gorgeous house, traveling on Rick's credit card whenever the fancy struck her . . . all luxuries she'd never have known otherwise.

But there'd been a price for those luxuries, and not just her self-esteem. She'd somehow managed to compartmentalize the bad, but that particular compartment had broken down. She could no longer ignore the facts. She'd screwed up. Made mistakes.

Bad ones.

She'd let herself be bullied into living a life that she never should have lived, and what made it worse was that she had come here to Maddie, expecting her to be willing to pick up and go with a ten-year-old plan, without thinking about what she'd be asking of her twin.

But she was thinking now.

She'd seen how Maddie looked at Brody. Seen, too, the brief hesitation on Maddie's face when they'd talked about going away together and starting over. It'd been so brief Leena might have imagined it, but she hadn't.

Maddie would never say so, but she liked the life she'd made for herself, and she deserved that life. She shouldn't have to give it up.

And suddenly, she recognized and understood the new emotion inside her. Strength. Because maybe Maddie was right. Maybe she was stronger than she'd thought. And maybe . . . maybe she could do this all on her own so that Maddie didn't have to give up her life.

Leena could follow The Plan on her own. It could work. Rick couldn't do anything to Maddie because one, her sister wasn't a jewelry designer, and two, if he even thought about getting the authorities involved, he'd be implicating himself.

Yeah, Leena really could vanish on her own. She could vanish and let Maddie live her life.

Maddie would never let her do it, of course. Never. Knowing it, knowing there was no better time than now, she grabbed her bag and then at the last moment, took the photo, too, slipping it into her bag next to her cell phone before quietly heading outside.

Maddie's lips were still tingling. She didn't take her eyes off Brody as confusion and heat flowed through her veins instead of blood. So much damn heat . . .

He'd kissed her.

Holy smokes, he'd nearly kissed her right into a spontaneous orgasm. Her pulse couldn't seem to recover, nor could the rest of her. Her skin felt too tight, her breathing still labored.

Brody hadn't taken his eyes off her, either. His own breathing didn't seem any too steady, and when he spoke, his voice was low and rough, his expression as baffled as she imagined hers was.

"I can't believe you could kiss me like that," he said. "With all that tongue and heat, and still not tell me what the hell is going on."

"I thought that you thought that you were kissing Leena."

"Yeah, well, you thought wrong."

Okay, so he wasn't slow. She knew that. He was a pilot, a man with sharp reflexes and a sharp mind.

But she was sharper.

She'd had to be.

All her life, she'd had to be.

Not Brody. Brody flew planes for a living and hung out with friends for a pastime. On weekends, he played basketball like a pro and gravitated toward big, stupid muscle cars. He was kind to old ladies and dogs. He liked pizza and loud music. When he dated, the women were usually warm and sweet, and vanished as fast as they appeared.

He did not, as a rule, worry or stress or angst about his existence, and if his past ever bothered him, he never let on. It certainly did not come back to bite him on his ass. Even thinking about him being a little boy was absurd because he was a man, a big, tall, rough and tumble man who made her hormones stand straight up and tap dance, damn it.

But she could set that aside. She *would* set that aside. He had no idea what she was going through, and he never would.

And yet . . .

And yet he'd known it was her . . .

That thought niggled at her, just a bit, because it was a warning, a little flare in her brain cautioning her not to underestimate him again, but at the moment, she had no choice but to believe herself stronger than him.

"If nothing else," he told her quietly, still a little sleepy-eyed from that kiss, "we're friends. Friends talk. Friends share."

Oh, God, he could have no idea how she wished she could share with him. "Friends? No. We either snipe at each other or kiss. Not talk or share."

"At the very least, we're also boss and employee, and that's a fact. I'm responsible for you."

"That's a stretch, considering how far from Sky High we are."

"I want an answer to at least one of my questions, Mad."

"Fine. Ask one."

"Let's start with why you have a knife strapped to your thigh." With lightning speed, he slid his hand up her leg, beneath her skirt and commandeered said knife.

Holy shit, she'd never seen him move so fast. Apparently, when they'd been making out, her mind had shut off.

But his hadn't. She stared at the knife now in his fingers. "It's for emergencies."

"Okay. And since you're the smartest woman I've ever met, you can probably figure out my next question."

He thought her the smartest woman he'd ever met? Interesting, considering she thought him the most amazing man she'd ever met.

Amazing, frustrating, completely pig-headed, world-class kisser . . .

He had the knife between his two fingers like it was distasteful, his arm loose at his side, and with her own lightning speed, she grabbed it back, not holding it loosely, but up as if she meant business.

He merely stepped forward so that the blade was only an inch from his chest.

Then, while she debated her next move, he put his mouth to her ear, irritation personified. "Are you mad because you thought I didn't know you, Mad? Or because I do? Because let's clear up one thing right now, knife or not, attitude or not, I'll *always* know."

God. She actually let her eyes drift closed at that, but caught herself and flashed her eyes open again to find him watching her intently.

Then he took another step forward, and now the tip of the blade touched his chest, not that he seemed to care. "What's it going to be, Maddie?"

The fight draining out of her, she turned away, letting the knife fall to her side, both shocked and uncomfortably aroused. He wanted answers, and unfortunately, she had them. "I told you Leena's in trouble."

"Yes."

"I'm going to help her out of it." She didn't even realize she was rubbing her shoulder until she felt him gently nudging her fingers away, touching her scars, touching her heart.

And other places, too, places that wanted to get back to that whole kissing thing, which would be an even bigger mistake than all her other mistakes combined, and that was saying something.

"How?" he murmured, his mouth brushing her shoulder and then the side of her throat . . .

Oh, God.

She was going to melt into a boneless puddle of longing right here on the floor. "Don't." She said this in a pathetically low, whispery voice, not knowing exactly what she was saying don't to.

Don't stop touching me . . .

Don't stop any of it . . .

His fingers continued to work on her, slipping beneath her shirt to touch bare skin now as his jaw slowly rubbed alongside of hers. "Are you going to pretend to be her?"

"No. Brody, stop—"

But he didn't. Somehow, he knew exactly what muscles were sore, and what to touch, and how to leave her a bowl of jelly. It had to stop. "I mean it."

But he kept doing.

All of it.

"But you're going to somehow risk yourself to save her, is that it?"

Close. Too close, and frustrated, hot, God, so hot, she simply reacted. Whipping around, she hooked her leg behind his knee and dropped him to the floor, which he hit with a heavy thud.

Sprawled on his back, he stared up at her. "What was *that?*"

Not proud of the move, she backed up a step. "I said don't."

Wincing, he sat up and rubbed a spot low on his back. *"Ouch."*

Okay, so now she'd used her unfair advantage of martial arts against a man who'd done nothing but drive her crazy.

And turn her on. Let's not forget that part. Guilt-ridden, she bent over him and offered her hand. "I'm sorry—*hey*—"

That's all she got out before he grabbed her hand and tugged hard so that she fell right over the top of him. Or would have, but he caught her and rolled.

The next thing she knew, her knife had flown across the room, and she was flat on her back on the floor where he'd just been, held there by well over six feet of frustrated, temperamental, leanly muscled male.

She struggled, oh, how she struggled, but it was all in vain. He deflected every move she made as if he knew martial arts as well as she.

That only infuriated her all the more, and she fought with everything she had, but he held her down effortlessly, subduing her without hurting her, a consideration she hadn't given him.

"Damn it!" Furious, she tried to knee him, tried anything, everything, but nothing worked.

Finally, he looked at her, expression unreadable. "Give up?" His voice suggested he was bored.

Bored while she'd used every bit of energy she had, and then some. His every move had been precise, calculated, and efficient.

Controlled.

She was good, she'd made sure of it, but he was better. In fact, he'd wiped the floor with her. And now he wanted her to give up.

Never. She blew a strand of hair out of her face and glared at him. "You know how to fight."

"Yeah. So?"

"So . . ." She didn't know really, except that he definitely had his own secrets.

Which didn't matter because she was going to kick his ass and be done with this. She rolled, but before she could twist free, he flipped her over so that she was face to the carpet.

Then, in further insult, he gathered both her hands in his. Her good arm he yanked up over her head, the other arm he kept at her side, her wrist manacled by his long, work-roughened fingers.

Because apparently, even while being a pissed-off, nosy bastard, he was still caring and thoughtful.

Craning her head to the side, she managed to glare up at him. "Damn it!"

He simply made himself comfortable on top of her. "You've already said that," he noted. "Now . . ." He shot her a grim smile. "How about we finish our chat?"

Chapter 9

Maddie decided not to answer on the grounds that after she killed Brody dead as a doornail, she didn't want to have to admit in a court of law that the murder had been premeditated.

He was still holding her so that she couldn't get free, his big, warm body to hers. He was good. How the hell had he gotten so good?

And why?

At work, he and Shayne and Noah joked around a lot, wrestling occasionally, tackling each other over a candy bar or a CD or something equally stupidly male, but on the whole, they were a fairly laid-back, easygoing group.

And yet he'd fought her like a consummate pro. Even more startling, he'd subdued her without hurting her. "You're crazy."

"Probably."

"Seriously." She was still struggling to get the upper hand and still failing miserably. "Certifiable."

"No arguments here, babe."

She opened her mouth to blast him again, but he merely shifted. His thigh, the one holding hers open, glided against the core of her, and just like that, a switch flicked on in her brain, and she went from violent to something just as devastating.

No. *More* devastating.

Lust.

The sensations bombarded her body, wave after wave of them—the feel of his heated, strong arms on the outside of hers, the way he held her hands in a grip that was presumptuous, bordering on dominating and aggressive, and yet . . . and yet she couldn't hold on to her anger to go with those things.

Just lust.

And then there was the humdinger—either he had something in his pocket, or he'd enjoyed that little tussle.

A lot.

Oh, God.

He was hard. And big. And the knowledge created even more embarrassing reactions . . .

Not good.

In fact, this was the opposite of good. Her mind raced, and it came to her, the one and only way to get Brody to back off. It was cruel and low, even for her, but difficult times called for difficult measures.

"Ow," she murmured very softly, wincing, grimacing. "You're hurting me."

Before her heart hit its next beat, anguish crossed his face, and his body lifted off hers so fast her head spun.

"I'm sorry," he said quietly. "I—"

"Just give me a minute." She let out a long, slow breath. "I need to just lie here a minute."

His eyes were tortured. "I'm sorry, so sorry. You were moving like you were fine, and—"

"I'm okay," she said weakly. "Really. I'll be fine in a minute—" But she broke off with a gasp when he scooped her up in his arms. "*What are you doing?*"

"Putting you to bed." His jaw was tight, the muscles jumping with tension as he headed to the stairs. "Where you are going to be a good little girl and stay."

"Put me down."

Instead, he strode up the stairs like she weighed less than a gnat, which she definitely did not. "Seriously, I am *not* going to bed with you."

"You know, you're the second person today to turn me down for sex when I didn't even offer it."

Odd, that quick stab of hot emotion that she refused to acknowledge might be jealousy. "Who was the first?"

Only his eyes cut to hers. "Why?"

"Because if it was that bimbo you were dating before I got shot . . . Bambi? Barbie? You could do better."

A corner of his mouth quirked. "It was Shayne, actually."

"Oh."

"Bambi?" he repeated, definitely sounding amused. "Barbie?"

"Whatever." It wasn't easy to maintain her dignity, but she managed. "You can see whoever you want."

"Yeah. I can. Funny how I don't want to."

Though he'd spoken lightly enough, she swallowed hard because nothing in his eyes said light. No, those eyes were all flinty steel, and not cool steel either, but smoking hot.

"Where did you learn to fight like that?" she asked.

"Where did you?"

She closed her mouth.

So did he.

Fine. A crossroads. The story of their lives.

He strode down the hallway with her in his arms as if she weighed nothing. After the surgery, she'd definitely lost some weight. She wasn't fully back on her game, and yeah, she might never be, but she could handle herself. "This is really going over and above the call of duty."

"Which you would think would bring me some gratitude," he said.

"I don't do gratitude. You must really have hated those temps."

"Actually, they were all quite polite. Not one of them argued with me on a daily basis."

"And yet you scared them all away."

He didn't say anything to that, and she didn't know what she'd expected. A confession that he'd done so because he'd missed her? She might as well wait for an invitation to fly to the moon. "I can walk."

He shot her a quick glare, then stopped on the landing, still not winded.

She really hated him.

"I assume your bedroom is up here. That's where you were watching me from when I first got here, right? Probably having a helluva laugh over sending your sister to the door instead of coming yourself."

"I wasn't laughing."

He slanted her another look, also unreadable. "Where's your shoulder brace?"

"My physical therapist said I could go without it now, unless I'm hurting."

"You are hurting."

"Yes, because some idiot decided to wrestle with me."

"Who's the idiot with the knife?"

Before she could object to his calling her the idiot, he went on in a scathing tone. "A *knife*. You held a fucking knife on me like I was the fucking bad guy."

"I'm out of the airport for a month, and your language goes all to hell."

"Six weeks."

"What?"

"You've been out of the airport for six weeks, and you're still in pain." At that, he stopped talking. Just stopped and put his forehead to hers. He didn't move a muscle, but she could feel the tension in his big, tough body. They stood just like that, utterly still, for that one beat in time united in their frustration.

"You're killing me," he whispered. "You know that?"

His misery stopped her cold and drained her temper. Somehow, her hand came up and touched his jaw. "It wasn't your fault."

"You should have been safe there."

"It wasn't your fault, Brody."

He shouldered open her bedroom door and then stopped short in the doorway at the sight of Cowgirl Central, complete with leather and pink lace everywhere. "Your bed."

Oh, God. She'd forgotten. "It's not mine."

"It's pink," he said, sounding as stunned as he looked, which pissed her off. "Lace."

"I didn't pick it."

He stared at the huge, high four-poster bed barely visible through the heaping piles of pillows and soft, luxurious bedding done up in, indeed, pink lace. "It's . . ."

"Girly. I know. It's my arm and shoulder, Brody. Not my legs."

As if mesmerized, he moved to the bed. The headboard was an old brown barn door, lacquered to a high shine. Above it, a lasso hung on the wall in the shape of a halo. "Wow."

She wriggled, and he slowly, carefully set her down in the center of the froufrou setup.

She had to remind herself that she was playing weak and hurt in order to get him out of her hair. But damn, the hardest thing she'd ever done was allow herself to sag back as if she didn't have the energy to even get beneath the covers.

"You're surrounded by mountains of pink." He looked confused. "And miles of lace. *You.*"

She shouldn't have been insulted, but she was. "It's ridiculous, I realize that."

"No, it's—"

"I didn't pick it out, okay?" If he smiled, she was going to kill him.

"Okay." His mouth twitched, but he didn't smile. Smart man. "Your sister's staying here with you?"

"Sort of."

"Why didn't you ever tell us you had a sister?"

Us. As in him, Noah, and Shayne. She wondered if the word choice was a subtle way of distancing himself, of being just someone from work.

Distance worked for her. "Why should I have? She doesn't affect my ability to do my job."

"Maddie."

The low, soft chiding tone to his voice cut right through her righteousness and unexpectedly left her feeling stripped bare. Closing her eyes, she lay back, suddenly not having to fake being weak.

And stupid.

Let's not forget very, very stupid. "I'm sorry. I'm not used to someone . . ."

"Caring?"

"Yes."

"Well, at least you know I do care. I'll take that as a good sign. Now if I could just get you to stop kicking at me."

God, she knew it. "I'm sorry for that, too. And I'm sorry I said we weren't friends."

The light that came into his eyes would have warmed her soul if not for the knowledge that soon, she was leaving. For good. "I'm tired," she whispered, throat tight. "I'm going to rest." Lifting her arm, she settled it over her eyes to keep her from being tempted to keep looking at him, needing her fill.

But then she felt his hands on her foot, and then came the rasp of a zipper before he tugged her boot off.

And her other.

Which left her bare feet in his big, work-roughened palms. He took in her toenails, painted purple today, which didn't mean anything except she'd been bored the other night. She had a silver ring on her second toe, which didn't mean anything either. Nothing around her meant much, especially lately, and honestly, she was getting a little worried about that.

She needed something to mean something. And she wished

it could be him. God, she wished that she could stop pushing and just let him in, really in.

Then his thumb skimmed over her instep, and she felt the touch in all the places she shouldn't. She did her best not to melt under his touch, once again asking him the burning question of the day. "Where did you learn to fight?"

His eyes met hers, stubborn to the depths. "Where did you?"

"Do you always answer a question with another question?"

He sighed. "I grew up in Compton. Skinny little white boys didn't fare so well unless they knew how to protect themselves."

Staring up into his inscrutable face, she tried to see any of that vulnerability that must have been a part of him then. "You don't talk about your family."

"No."

"Why?"

"Because." When she just looked at him, he gave in. "My parents were barely able to score their next fix, much less worry about their street brat."

"I see." She knew it'd been bad, she just didn't know how bad. She'd been lusting after the tall, enigmatic, gorgeous pilot for what, nearly a year now, and yet in all that time, she'd never seen him as anything less than a sure, steady, sharp, sophisticated man, a man who could, by turns, make her laugh, want to tear her hair out in both lust and temper, and in general, drive her mad.

She'd never pictured him doing as she had, overcoming mountains of shit to be where he was, and that was her selfish shame. "So you learned how to fight out of necessity."

"Survival of the fittest."

And he was fit. Incredibly so. Mouthwateringly so. But to find out it wasn't just lucky genetics or a love of a good gym seemed to give him a whole new dimension for her to chew on.

"Now you," he said.

"Classes," she admitted. No need to hide that. "I learned to fight in classes. Lots and lots of classes."

"Why?"

"A girl needs to be able to protect herself."

He took that in, his gaze never leaving hers. "A girl shouldn't have to. Especially a young girl. How old were you?"

"When I what?"

"Needed to know how to defend yourself."

Okay, too close. She crossed her arms, or tried to, belatedly remembering it was a bad idea. When she winced this time, it was for real, and his mouth went grim. "Lift up," he told her, and when she did, he pulled the blanket from beneath her to cover her up.

Which had been her plan. Let him put her to bed.

Except he didn't look like he was planning on going anywhere. She needed to get him to leave for long enough that she and Leena could get out without him following. The only idea that came to her seemed fairly evil, even for herself, but she had no choice. "I can't sleep in my clothes."

He went still, then lifted only his gaze. "No?"

"I need help undressing."

A dizzying mix of reluctant arousal and discomfort crossed his face. "Oh."

"Yeah. Why don't you go to the post office for me, and I'll get Leena to do this."

At his expression, she knew she'd done it. Finally. He was about to run like a little girl and choose the post office.

Chapter 10

Brody stared at Maddie lying in the bed, looking wan and helpless, and very unlike herself. If he hadn't kissed her, he might really wonder if he, indeed, had the right twin. Slowly, he repeated the important part of her statement because it bore repeating. "You need help undressing."

"Yes." She tossed back the blanket, reminding him of how little she was wearing. "But don't worry. Leena'll help me undress and make me hot tea for the pain meds while you go to the post office."

Uh-huh. Except . . . yeah. She sounded just a little too eager for him to go.

Big surprise.

He took in her teeny tiny little miniskirt, something he'd been doing his damnedest not to. It had crept up so high on her silky smooth, creamy thighs that he could just see a barely there hint of silk between. Her top, that lacy number, fit her like a glove and had risen too, revealing a strip of belly and that sparkly piercing twinkling at him like a beacon.

Jesus.

Sliding her fingers up her body until they rested low on her abs, her thumb playing with the hem of the shirt. "I'm not sure I can get this off by myself."

As if to prove it, she tried, using her good hand, pulling the material up to just beneath her breasts, squirming as she strained to get her arm out. With some work, she did get the one arm out, and then she was caught halfway in, halfway out, her head beneath the stretchy material.

Beneath the lace, she had silk. Tiger-striped silk in the form of a demi bra cut so low that all her wriggling and squirming threatened her coverage.

Not to mention, shot his distance theory all to hell.

"Uh-oh." She bounced up and down. Yeah, like that was going to do anything except maybe give him a heart attack because her breasts were bouncing too, shimmying and shaking, and he actually felt a coronary coming on—

And then it happened.

A nipple popped right out of her bra, a sweet rose-colored nipple.

Riveted to the spot, he stood there, heart pounding, blood roaring like a white water rapid as it rushed through his body to pool between his legs.

"Damn it, I'm stuck. Can you get Leena?" Her voice was muffled through the shirt. She had her bad arm pinned to her side, her good arm straight up over her head, her top still half on and half off.

And a nipplegate situation going on.

He had to clear his throat to talk and even then managed only a barely audible "I said I'd do it."

Because he was stupid. Very, very stupid.

For her part, she kept valiantly trying to free herself, which involved more bouncing. He tried to move, but in reality, he could do nothing but stare at her breast, the tip puckering up tight right before his eyes, making his mouth water.

"Brody? You out there?"

He nodded, then realized she couldn't see him. "Yeah," he managed hoarsely.

She tugged again and then let out a low cry of pain, which

pretty much galvanized him into reluctant action. Setting a knee on the bed, he leaned over her. Christ, where to put his hands? "Be still," he demanded, but the woman never listened. She kept moving, moving, moving, and her bared breast kept bouncing, bouncing, bouncing. "Seriously. Sit still."

He held her raised arm with one hand and ordering himself not to look, grabbed the hem of her shirt to try to get the thing off her, all the while taking care of her bad arm.

And not looking.

He succeeded at the first and failed miserably at the second. The shirt snagged on her elbow, and once he fixed that, he was nearly home free until he caught the material on her earring.

"Ouch."

"Don't move!"

"I'm not!"

Not earring. Earrings. She had four silver hoops in her ear, and he had no idea why, other than the tiny hoops made a sweet little tinkling sound when she moved, and for some reason, the sight of them made him want to nibble there.

But there were lots of places he wanted to nibble at the moment. With Herculean effort, he finally dragged her free of the shirt and tossed it aside.

In unison, they looked down at her exposed breast. "Whoops," she said and tucked her nipple back into the cup of her bra.

He'd carried her through the house and up the stairs without breaking a sweat, but he was sweating now. "Okay, then. I'll just . . ." Dream about your body, and that nipple, for the rest of my life. ". . . get you that tea."

"But I'm not all the way undressed."

He eyed her skirt. The smallest skirt in the history of skirts. "Right. I guess that has to come off."

"The zipper's in the back," she said helpfully.

And then she all but stopped his heart by rolling to her belly, exposing the smooth, sweet skin of her slim back, broken only by the strap of her bra and that scrap of material mas-

querading as a skirt, which revealed her tattoo and empha-
sized the sweetest ass he'd ever seen, not to mention the two
tightly toned legs that could take him weeks and weeks to explore.

"Do you see the zipper?" she asked, her face pressed into
the bed.

The one that ran a whole whopping two inches from the
small of her back just below her small tattoo to halfway down
the already aforementioned sweet ass? Yeah, he saw it.

"Brody?"

"On it." His palms itched. His fingers twitched. Everything
twitched. He should have gone to the damn post office. With a
knee still on the bed, he leaned over her and grabbed the zipper tab.

Then pulled.

She wriggled, widening the gap, and if he'd thought her
skirt tiny, it had nothing on her thong panties, a matching
tiger-striped, narrow strip bisecting the most amazing, mouth-
watering ass he'd ever seen.

Reaching down with her good hand, she shoved the skirt off
one hip and then wriggled—*Jesus H. Christ*—wriggled to try to
lower the other side as well. She did have a small birthmark on
the back of her right thigh, and at the thought, a strangled
sound of lust tumbled from his lips.

Craning her neck, she blinked at him. "You okay?"

No. No, he wasn't. All of the blood in his body, every single
drop, had left his brain for parts south.

"I can't—" She struggled some more, those sweet cheeks
lifting off the bed, and he found himself actually leaning in as
if to kiss them.

Or take a bite out of them.

"A hand?"

Yeah, a hand. How about both hands? He could cup and
squeeze—

"Brody?"

"Yeah."

You are so fucked, he told himself and slipped his fingers into the waistband of her skirt to tug. Shrink-wrapped to her skin, the skirt only gave an inch. But that inch . . . more sweet flesh, more of the thong . . . holy mother of God, he wasn't going to recover from this. He really wasn't.

Another tug, and the skirt slid to her upper thighs, exposing her in full, including the line of the thong as it narrowed and vanished between her legs. And then she scissor kicked the skirt off her legs, giving him an all too quick, tantalizing view of the barely covered treasure in between.

"Brody?"

He blinked and realized she'd turned back over and was waiting for him in nothing but tiger stripes. "Huh?"

"Blanket?"

"Right." He yanked it over her and swiped his forehead. "It's hot in here. Is it hot in here?"

Her eyes were already drifting shut. "It's just perfect. Thanks for your help . . ."

Okay, then. He strode to the door as fast as he could, needing out, needing air, needing . . . well, what he needed didn't bear thinking about.

The minute Brody left the room, Maddie slapped her forehead. Asinine. Her great plan had totally and completely backfired on her because now she was shaking. Shaking and quivery and so turned on she could hardly stand it. She shoved the covers back off and took a deep breath.

He'd wanted her.

By the look in his eyes, he'd wanted all of her, fast and wild and maybe a little dirty. *Whew*. Fanning her face, she got out of the bed, then went looking for Leena.

They had to go. Like yesterday.

Only Leena was already gone. Her bag, her suitcase . . . gone.

Oh, God. Maddie stood in the center of the spare bedroom,

the spare *empty* bedroom, and then ran to the window. Leena's car was gone.

Damn it! She'd decided to execute The Plan on her own.

But Maddie couldn't let her do it. Stupid plan or not, they were stronger together than apart, and she was going after her to prove it.

Leena bought the last ticket on a plane bound for New Orleans and hoped to be at Ben's art gallery by dawn.

Assuming her courage caught up with her.

She let out a long breath and walked past the airport bar. The kind of drink she could use about now would only cost her four bucks, but she'd given up alcohol along with the cigarettes and everything else that she missed.

She thought of Maddie and wondered how much her sister would mind that Leena had accidentally grabbed Maddie's cell phone instead of her own, since apparently they still thought alike and had bought identical phone covers.

Or that Leena had abused the mini credit card she'd found in the back of Maddie's leather cell phone cover to buy her airline ticket.

Oh, boy. She distracted herself by thinking of Ben. She'd designed a series of exquisite original pieces for his gallery, and by the time she'd finished his job, she'd left a part of her heart and soul there. Because of her art, certainly, but it went deeper than that.

Ben had been in on the design. Not in corroboration so much, but just watching and experiencing her process. It'd been part of the deal, his deal, because he loved to be involved in the artistry of the pieces he collected and sold.

Leena had flown to his gallery several times with the designs, and once she'd begun work on the pieces, Ben had flown to Stone Cay to watch her work.

She'd expected him to be old, stuffy, maybe fat, and definitely snooty. Rick's people were always snooty. Men with too much money and too much power were spoiled and used to getting their own way. Knowing it, she'd been braced to hate him.

And then she'd entered his gallery.

It was a wide open space with splashes of color that had caused the oddest reaction. Leena had immediately felt invigorated, vibrant . . . happy. That first day he'd come out from the back in well-worn jeans faded white in the stress points, a white T-shirt, work boots, all splattered in paint. He'd held out his hand for her to shake but had then caught a glimpse of the paint on his skin and laughed, pulling it back before he could get anything on her. "Sorry," he'd said in a rugged voice tinged with Irish. "I'm in the middle."

She'd blinked, a little surprised by the fact that he hadn't been old, stuffy, or anywhere close to fat. In fact, he was maybe thirty, and tall and lanky lean. He was an artist, too, from his paint-splattered boots to the deep soul shining out of his warm chocolate eyes . . .

He'd liked her. He'd liked her a lot and had wanted to explore that between them, but she'd been there for business only.

Rick's business.

And yet she'd found a way to wrangle several trips to New Orleans, citing design problems, which had only been an excuse to look at Ben some more.

She was certain he'd seen right through her, but he'd never been anything but sweet and kind, melting her every which way but Sunday with that low, Irish-tinted voice of his . . .

In spite of dragging it out as long as possible, eventually, she'd finished the jewelry for his gallery, and the job had come to an end. Rick himself had delivered the jewelry, with the priceless precious gems switched out for fakes, of course.

As for Leena, she'd been paid for a job well done and hadn't seen Ben since.

He'd called several times, and she was so ashamed and terrified of the part she'd played in his being ripped off, she'd not returned a single one.

Just one more thing to hate Rick for.

And herself.

But she was on her way to fixing her wrong in the only way she knew how.

Brody stood in the kitchen waiting for the damn water to boil. He'd never understood the appeal of hot tea. It smelled like old ladies and tasted like flowers.

But whatever. It kept his hands busy. And they needed to be busy. He'd bring the tea to Maddie, who was hopefully still covered with her quilt up to her chin. Because chins weren't sexy. Chins didn't make him ache.

In the meantime, hopefully, his body would calm down, but he had a feeling he could brew all the tea in China and his body wouldn't calm down, not after that little episode upstairs.

His fingers were trembling. He was trembling. And still hard.

He found a mug in the cabinet and checked the water for the hundredth time.

Still not boiling.

He looked at the boxes of tea lined up on the counter. Seven. Earl Grey, Black Cherry, Lemon Mint, Chamomile, green tea, black tea, white tea. . . . Who needed seven different kinds of tea? A dull ache throbbed between his eyes, so he closed them and snatched a box blind.

Lemon mint. Whatever. The water still wasn't boiling. "Work with me here," he told the pot, which finally began to bubble, and he decided he should probably bring her something to eat, too, since she'd lost a little weight. So he shoved a few pieces of bread into the toaster.

Look at him, all domestic.

When he finally had the tea and toast ready, he made his way back up the stairs, eyeing the rooms as he went because the silence suddenly got to him. It was a big silence. A you're-screwed sort of silence, and his spidey sense quivered.

Then he stepped into Maddie's bedroom. Maddie's *empty* bedroom, and the doubt became something bigger. One quick look out the window told him the truth. Maddie's Jeep was gone, and so was the rental car.

She'd ditched him; they both had.

And didn't that just top off his damn day. Suddenly he hoped that they were triplets, or quadruplets, or better yet, quints. Because being had by only two women seemed just too ridiculous.

Maddie's purse was gone. It'd been sitting on her dresser, a black and silver number with lots of buckles and pockets. Next to it had been her cell phone, also gone. For shits and giggles, he pulled out his own cell and called hers, not surprised in the least when it went straight to voice mail.

Goddamnit.

With no compunction at all, he opened a dresser drawer, looking for clues to where she might have gone, but he ended up staring down at the pile of silky stuff. Hooking a satiny black number on his finger, he lifted it up. Panties barely the size of his palm.

He tossed the thing back into the drawer, then frowned at something else there, a box, and he nudged aside some more silk to expose . . . bullets.

And this time when his heart kicked, it kicked hard enough to nearly crack a rib.

She'd had a gun in here as well, a gun that was now gone. He was chewing on that when Shayne called him.

"Lost her, huh?"

"How do you know?"

"Because she's on her way here."

"*What?*" Brody took off running for the door. "What's she doing there?"

"Sneaking away from you apparently."

"Fuck. Tell me she's going there to work and not to get on a plane."

"Sorry, no can do."

"Let me guess." He stopped outside his car, slapping his pockets for his keys. "She wants a plane?"

"Give the man a prize. She called ahead. How did you know?"

His keys weren't in his pockets. He was not a man who lost his damn keys ever. "Just stop her."

"Yeah, I'm on that. What's going on, Brody?"

"Hell if I know, except that she has a sister. A twin sister. And she's in trouble."

"She's never mentioned a twin sister."

Where the hell were his keys? "Trust me, Leena is alive and well. At least at the moment. But she's involved in something, and they're both in way over their head. They had a threatening phone call from someone they knew."

"Maddie went to Dani for help." Shayne sounded as unhappy as Brody felt that Maddie hadn't trusted them. "She asked her for a flight under an assumed name. She wanted to keep it secret. Why the hell would she need to keep anything secret from us?"

Brody had a couple of ideas, but none that appealed. "Is Dani planning on stalling her?"

"Yes, and if she finds out I'm a narc, I'm never going to get to have sex again."

This from the man who only a year ago, would have gotten hives at the thought of having sex with the same woman for the rest of his life. "Just stall her when she gets there." Brody shoved his phone back in his pocket and stared at the car he was locked out of.

He had no idea what was going on, but it was more than that. Maddie hadn't trusted him. It was unbelievable to him that she hadn't. She'd kissed him like he'd been better than air. She'd let him strip her, let him make her goddamn tea, but she hadn't trusted him with this, and on top of that, she'd stolen his keys, and that sucked.

Chapter 11

Maddie walked through the lobby at Sky High. She needed a direct flight to New Orleans, pronto, because if Leena got too far ahead of her, if she said her good-bye to Ben and vanished, Maddie might never catch up with her.

There was no better way to get a direct flight than through her world.

It was a risk coming here, definitely, but as she'd personally made sure, the place specialized in making customers happy. As a customer, she needed a flight out like yesterday, and only speed would make her happy.

But she had to get out of here before Brody showed up. She wondered if he'd tried calling her. It was likely.

More than likely.

But as she'd discovered on the drive down the mountain, Leena had grabbed Maddie's cell phone.

Which meant Maddie had Leena's. She'd used it to call her own cell, trying to get Leena to no avail. Leena had turned it off.

So Maddie had called ahead to Sky High, specifically to Dani, and now she walked through the lobby, soaking up the place that had been her home away from home, knowing that it very well might be the last time she set her eyes on the place.

The building was new, all steel and glass, with a wall of windows looking out on to the tarmac lined with millions of dollars worth of planes. Beyond that lay an incredible view of the LA skyline.

Hard to remember that only a year ago, all of Sky High had been housed in a single leased hangar with borrowed planes and boatloads of debt.

But the three guys, her three guys, had built this place from sweat and guts and sheer determination. Now they ran a luxury jet service to the stinking rich, and she was a part of it.

Or she had been.

That was the thing about burning bridges. And she'd burned a big one when she'd left Brody in the mountains with his keys in her pocket.

Even having lifted his keys, she knew she had a limited amount of time before he figured out a way to get here and went all Neanderthal on her. So she left the lobby for the tarmac, waiting for her plane. She was financially stable, thanks to a great paycheck, but even with that paycheck, she wasn't in a position to afford a charter flight. With Dani's help, she'd shamelessly used her employee status to deeply discount the flight.

Once the plane was rolled out, she could board, and since she would do so under an assumed name, Brody would never know. She wondered how many times he'd called. Was he worried or just plain pissed off? God, she wished it didn't have to be this way, that things had turned out differently, but she didn't have time for regrets.

Too bad her heart didn't seem to get the message.

When her sister's phone vibrated, she jumped on it, expecting it to be Leena, but she was about as wrong as she could get.

It was Rick.

Good to know you came to your senses about protecting Maddie. We'll expect you on the island at 9:00 a.m. tomorrow morning to do the job.

Oh, God. Did that mean . . . no. Leena hadn't gone to New Orleans. Somehow, some way, she'd spoken to Rick and was headed to the island.

To protect Maddie.

"No. No, no, no, no . . ." As quickly as she could make her fingers move, she hit send, entered her own number, and typed in, DON'T DO IT!

But Leena wasn't exactly on a roll of listening to Maddie, was she? Which meant she needed to stop Leena from getting to Stone Cay.

Where was her plane? Just as she thought it, two linemen finally came out of hangar two, towing the Learjet she'd ordered, but before she could board, Shayne exited the lobby.

Crap.

He strode down the tarmac toward her in his easygoing, long-limbed gait, looking for all the world like any one of the wealthy, sophisticated clients they served on a daily basis.

But she knew that was just the veneer he pulled on like those designer duds he favored. His family might be wealthy and sophisticated, but on the inside, Shayne was a guy's guy, a regular blue-collar type, holding his own with the streetwise Noah and Brody.

Shayne didn't say a word, just pulled her into his arms. He was tall and lean but strong as hell, and for a moment, she absorbed his strength and affection while fighting a stupid urge to cry.

"You scared the hell out of us," he murmured, pressing his cheek to her hair, holding her tight. "All of us."

She knew. And she hated it because they were her family here. They were her life, but she'd done what she had to.

"Why didn't you return any of my calls? Are you okay?"

Throat tight, she nodded.

"So what's going on, Mad?"

At that, she went from nodding to shaking her head in the negative.

Still gently holding on to her, he pulled back enough to search her gaze. "Tell me this much. Are you quitting? Because I need to schedule in hanging myself if you are."

That tugged a laugh out of her, and he smiled. "Okay, so you're not quitting. Do you need help?"

"Obviously, you know I ordered a flight."

"Yes."

"Am I going to get out of here without a problem?"

"This is Sky High. The customer never has problems."

She laughed, but it was bittersweet.

"Jason's flying you," he said, referring to their new pilot. "And he's good. Better than good. But I'm working on switching my flight so I can fly you—"

"No." Her heart all but stopped. Just what she did not need, Shayne flying her. "Don't do that. It's no big deal. Brody completely exaggerated anything he said."

"I don't think I told you what Brody said."

"He is who he is. He said something." She smiled and did her best to make it real. "Look, I'm fine, everything's fine. I just need that flight. Though I need a destination change."

"Oh?"

"I'll work it out with Jason. Where is he?"

"He'll be here any minute, I'm sure. Where are you going then?"

She looked into his eyes and wondered if he was stalling her. "The Bahamas."

"Interested in telling me why?"

"No."

He sighed. "Women never tell me anything."

She laughed. "Dani apparently tells you everything. Is that an engaged thing?"

"It's a respect thing."

She sighed.

"You saw Brody."

Her smile faded, and so did Shayne's. "Ah, hell," he said. "What did the big lug do now?"

"Nothing."

He just looked at her.

"Nothing," she repeated.

"Really? Then why is my bullshit meter ringing?"

Maddie rolled her eyes. "Stop."

Shayne let out a breath and hesitated, which was very unlike him, so much so that she braced herself. "What?"

"Okay." He offered a smile meant to charm. "I'm the one who sent Brody to see you because to be honest . . ."

Oh, God. No. Don't be honest . . .

"I sensed there was something going on between you two." He watched her very carefully for a reaction, and she did her best not to give him one.

"Why would you think that?" she eventually was able to say.

"Because when you were in the hospital, I've never seen him so absolutely devastated. Never."

"That was guilt."

"Maybe. Partially. But there was more."

"I doubt it."

Shayne wasn't buying it. "Look, we both know our boy has had it rough from the get-go."

Yes. She did know. Just as she knew that Shayne had been born with a silver spoon in his mouth. Not Brody. Anything he'd ever had, he'd had to fight for, physically and mentally, and it'd molded him.

She knew it now more than ever.

And secretly, she admired that about him. Brody didn't take any shit from anyone, and she admired that, too.

"Really rough," Shayne said again quietly. "And for the most part, he's let it all go, lets it all bounce right off him. He does that because he's tough as nails—"

"You mean he has the hide of an elephant."

A smile fought for a place on his mouth. "Yes, exactly. Nothing penetrates. It's how he functions. But you . . ."

Don't say it . . .

"You penetrated."

"I drive him crazy," she corrected.

"Crazy hot, maybe."

Maddie's composure took a hit at that because back at her house, Brody had made her pretty damn crazy hot, too. "I don't know what you're talking about."

"No? I would have thought the kiss would explain things pretty good."

And the direct hit . . . "What kiss?"

"Yeah, now see . . . " Shayne looked amused as he rubbed his jaw. "Brody gave me that same look. I'm thinking you two aren't so different after all."

"I do *not* have the hide of an elephant."

"No, you most certainly do not," he agreed with great appreciation. "At least not on the outside. And see that's what I'm getting at . . ." Reaching out, he squeezed her hand. "It's the inside I'm worried about. He doesn't show it, Mad, but he's vulnerable, especially to you."

"He's not vulnerable to anyone. Or anything." But even as she said it, she knew that wasn't true. She'd seen a flash of that vulnerability at her place when she'd brought up his past. The man had far more layers to him than she'd ever guessed.

"He'll never admit it," Shayne told her. "But you get inside. You get past that thick skin like no one else ever has." Leaning in, he brushed a kiss over her cheek. "So be gentle with him."

That anyone could suggest she be gentle with the six foot, four inches of solid testosterone that made up Brody West was ridiculous, and she laughed. "Come on."

"Don't worry. I'll make sure he's gentle with you, too."

"I don't need gentle."

"Yeah, yeah. The two of you can kick ass from here to the

moon and back and never admit to any vulnerabilities, I get it." He shook his head, his eyes still amused. "Yeah, Dani was right. It's going to be really fun watching the two of you fall."

Okay, whoa. "I'm not—"

"Yeah, you are." To soften the blow, he drew her in for another hug, then held her arm and looked into her eyes. "Remember, you can call me. Any of us, anytime, night or day."

"I know. I'm not falling."

He smiled. "Love you, Mad. Come back to us soon." And with that, he strode off.

"I'm not falling!" She just watched him go and sighed.

Come back to us soon.

What she would give to be able to do just that, go back to the way it'd been two months ago, without any worries except whatever the hell Shayne had done to the books.

She boarded the Lear, then paced the luxurious cabin, her gaze going to the window every time she pivoted. There were other planes on the tarmac: a King Air, a Westwind, a Cessna Citation, and the Moody she knew Brody had purchased a few months back and considered his brand new baby.

He loved this place with all his heart and soul.

And so did she: the elegant, sophisticated lobby she'd helped decorate herself, the three huge hangars that smelled like oil and gas and hopes and dreams, everything about it. She'd come to work here with her own hopes and dreams—to find a niche, to belong.

And she had found both. Here, she was home. Here, she belonged and was cared for, which had her heart catching because that would all be over. She was going to the Bahamas to somehow stop her sister from getting to Stone Cay, and then they'd execute The Plan.

Frustrated, antsy, she went to the private master suite in the back of the Lear so that she wouldn't have to converse with her pilot. She didn't feel talkative.

She heard him board a few minutes later, and relief filled

her. *Finally*. But when she turned to face the door, everything inside her went still because yeah, she had a pilot all right.

The biggest bad boy pilot of them all.

Brody stood there in the doorway in all his furious glory, of which there was lots.

Oh, God. *Lots*.

Eyes positively crackling with withering temper, he pointed at her.

You.

He stepped inside like he didn't give a shit what anyone thought of him, and she happened to know that was most definitely true. He really didn't.

His stride was long-legged, easy, and confident as hell as he came toward her.

She'd have paid every penny she would ever earn in her entire life to have a fraction of that confidence. Oh, she had no doubt that she walked a good game, talked a good game, and could fake it with the best of them.

But she wanted the real thing.

Brody was the real thing. Tall, dark, and completely one-hundred percent attitude-ridden, he stopped in front of her, legs spread, arms crossed over his chest.

Maybe he was here to wish her a good trip. Ha. And maybe Santa Claus would actually come this year.

Chapter 12

Maddie stared up at the one man she'd thought she'd never get to see again. How had he gotten his car started so quickly without keys? He was only thirty minutes behind her—

"Hot-wired it," he said. "In case you're wondering."

Damn, he was good, but that didn't explain how he knew she'd be here.

Shutting the door behind him to give them privacy, privacy she most definitely did not want, he leaned back against it, arms still crossed.

Casual pose.

Not a casual man.

"Dani ratted me out," she guessed.

He merely arched a brow, clearly inviting her to give this more thought.

"She called Shayne," she decided. "Shayne called you, then stalled me. Damn almost-married people, they're all too loyal and trusting."

"Speaking as a relatively new husband myself," he said with a boatload of dry sarcasm, "all the trust in the room really boggles. Where's your gun?"

She blinked. "My what?"

"I saw the bullets in your underwear drawer, Maddie. Where's the gun to go with them?"

"You went through my panties?"

"The gun, Maddie."

She shrugged, then winced at the movement in her shoulder, and he went utterly still, reminding her that he was a helluva lot easier to handle when he thought she was hurting. Whether that was lingering guilt because she'd been shot here at Sky High or just simply the weight of his penis bogging him down, she had no idea, but she was going to shamelessly use it to her advantage.

She had no choice.

"You didn't take your painkillers," he said tightly. "Since you left before I brought them to you."

"I'm weaning myself off them."

"Noah said that Bailey said that your doctor said you still need them."

"Noah and Bailey need to worry about themselves. Everyone needs to worry about themselves."

"Shit." Looking stymied by her very existence, he let out a long, careful breath.

Not the only one frustrated here, she understood the sentiment perfectly.

With another long exhale, he paced the length of the suite as she'd done only a moment before, then moved toward the bed where she sat, his body and all the muscles in it—of which there were tantalizingly many—moving like poetry in motion. "You're in no shape to be flying anywhere."

"I'm fine." But she lay back and closed her eyes. Playing it up, even just a little, wasn't all that hard, she discovered, since she was weak with fear for her sister. "Where's my pilot?"

"You're looking at him."

Her eyes flew open. He could fly like nobody's business; she'd seen him in action hundreds of times. He flew with concentrated proficiency, his eyes sharp, his body deceptively relaxed. But it couldn't be him, not for this trip. "I didn't hire you."

"No, I hired you."

"I'm not talking about my job, Brody, and you know it. Today, I'm a paying customer. And I paid for Jason."

"If you're flying anywhere today, I'm taking you."

"Bad idea."

"I'm your husband, remember?"

She winced. "Would you stop flinging that word around like it's real?"

"Sure. Soon as you stop walking away from anyone and everyone who cares about you. What happened to the kick-ass Maddie Stone? Because the one I knew would never run away like a little girl."

"I'm not running. And for the record, it's Leena who pretended to be married to you."

"Ah. And where is Leena?"

"She's . . . " She debated for a beat, then gave in. Sort of. "She's in bigger trouble than I thought."

"Shock."

"I'm going to go help her."

"Again with the I."

Frustration had her tossing up her hands. "Brody, don't you get it? It's not that I don't want you to understand what's going on here, or that I wouldn't rather have you with me, but that I can't ask it of you."

That took him back. "Why not?"

"Why not?" She sputtered for a moment, trying to figure out a good reason why not. She ended up trying something new— the whole, unadulterated truth. He deserved it. "Because I'm afraid for you. Okay? I can't do what I have to do while I'm worried about you."

His eyes softened, but his tough guy stance did not. "I'm a big boy, Mad. I can take care of myself."

Actually, she'd noticed that. In fact, with his walking-talking attitude and all that sinew-wrapped maleness oozing from his every pore, he could more than handle himself.

"You're going to Stone Cay?"

"Yes."

"To talk to the asshole on the phone."

"Hopefully not, no. To stop my sister from talking to the asshole."

"Okay." He straightened. "I'm doing this," he said when she opened her mouth. "You can kick my ass for it later. That's the deal. Take it or leave it."

She stared up into his determined face. He had badass attitude written all over him. He wouldn't back down. He never backed down. And suddenly, she didn't want him to. "Take it," she whispered.

Staying right where he was, he met her gaze evenly. Fiercely. "So we're a unit on this. On Sister Rescue 101. Right?"

"A unit," she agreed. *For now.*

"Until it's done."

She sighed. "Brody—"

"Until it's done."

He wouldn't budge. And no matter that she wanted to do this alone, she couldn't. "Okay, yes. Until it's done." Great. Yet another plan. How the hell did this keep happening to her?

With a short nod, Brody turned and left the suite without another word, and she let out a slow breath.

What had she just done?

Brody made a stop in Miami for fuel and Customs, then landed in Nassau at ten that night, just ahead of a mother of a storm that he was grateful to have missed.

Nassau, the bustling hub of the Bahamas since the ship-wrecking days of Blackbeard, wasn't really visible in the dark, but he'd been here before. The city always reminded him of any small Massachusetts town set down amongst palms and pines and iridescent sands.

Normally, calm waters and cooling trade winds were the trademark here, but not tonight. Tonight, the winds drove the treetops nearly to the ground, and though he couldn't see the water, he could hear it, whipped into a frenzy. The air was heavy, beyond muggy, and so hot that his skin steamed.

Or that might have been lingering temper.

He'd nearly missed her. If he'd sat around with his thumb up his ass at the cabin for another ten minutes or if Shayne hadn't stalled her . . .

Luckily, that hadn't happened, and here he was. Letting out a breath, he grabbed Maddie's overnight bag and his own duffel bag, and stood on the tarmac as the storm hit hard. When a bolt of lightning slashed down, followed immediately by a deafening crack of thunder, the lineman who was attempting to tie down the Lear shook his head. "Got in just in time, mate."

True. Brody had flown in worse, but not much. The clouds completely zapped out the stars and moon, and in air as thick as a down blanket, the rain came. Drenched within seconds, he looked up as Maddie came off the Lear. She'd changed into skinny jeans, boots, and a long jacket belted at her trim waist, the hood up over her head blocking her expressions from him.

She hadn't told him jackshit. Big surprise. He might have won round one, but she wasn't conceding the match. She'd have been just as happy to be alone on this little adventure, and given what a pain in his ass she'd been, he'd have liked nothing more than to let her be.

Except for one thing. Several, actually.

He could feel her nerves just beneath her cool surface, not to mention her fear.

And then there was the fact that he couldn't stand the thought of walking away from her, danger or not.

As a result, he was sticking to her like super glue.

Holding the handrail for support, she came down the stairs in rain coming down in sheets. A gust of wind blew the hood from her face, revealing how pale and wan she was, and looking just vulnerable enough to sucker punch him with her eyes alone.

It was stupid, asinine even, but suddenly, he wanted to hug her, baby her, which would have been as smart to his physical well-being as babying a spitting cobra. Wrapping his fingers around her arm, he guided her quickly down the last step.

"Thank you." She surprised him by not pulling away. Her hair blew in his face, her scent coming to him on the wind as the rain pounded both them and the tarmac, sounding like a pack of angry bees. She slid her hood back over her head as together, they ran across the tarmac.

Just inside the small metal hangar that served as the private sector of the airport, they shook off some of the rain and looked around. There was a single wood desk, behind which sat a mountain of a man smoking a cigar and eating a sub sandwich at the same time, all while gabbing on a telephone about some "fucking Cessna." Above them, the rain pounded the metal building, making it shudder and moan.

When the man hung up the phone, Maddie walked up to him. "Have you seen me already tonight?" she asked.

The guy blinked. "Huh?"

"Have you seen anyone who looks just like me come through here tonight?"

The guy took her in from top to bottom. "Lady, I've never seen anyone like you before. You're hot."

"Okay, thanks for that," Brody said dryly, pulling Maddie away from the desk.

There were several couches for waiting purposes, and beyond that, a vending machine stocked the usual heart attack–inducing items. Brody headed directly for it, taking Maddie with him. "Name your poison."

She curled her upper lip. "From there? No, thanks."

He pulled some change from his pocket. "You're a food snob."

"Yes." She eyed him as he bought himself three milk chocolate bars. "Seriously, where do you put all that crap?"

He patted his stomach, and she let out a low, disagreeing snort.

"And what does that mean?" he asked, wondering if he'd just been insulted.

"Like you don't know that in spite of your hideous junk food habit, you have the best abs on this side of the equator."

Un, no, he hadn't known that, but that she thought so made him grin like an idiot. "What about the other side of the equator?"

"Shut up, Brody. You inherited good genes, and you know it."

He didn't know how to tell her that the only thing he'd inherited was his mean gene. Oh, and his pickpocket abilities, which he'd honed as a youth. Yeah, that had come in handy. Thanks, dear Dad.

"Someday, you'll be old with a big belly," she said. "One that flops over your belt."

"Flops over my belt?" Now there was a disturbing image.

"I'm just saying, you'd better watch the chocolate. It's going to sneak up on you."

"Maybe I burn it off trying to help people."

"People who didn't want your help," she reminded him. Turning away, she walked toward the front desk, but Brody hooked her good arm and brought her back around.

"What?"

"Where to?" he asked.

Her eyes flickered, and she pulled her hood back up, hiding from him, goddamnit. "Getting a cab."

"To . . . ?" he inquired.

"About that. I've been thinking."

"*Shit.*" He bent down a little to see beneath the hood and looked her right in the eyes. "Save your time. You said we're a unit, and we're a damn unit."

"Until this is over."

"Damn A straight. So give me some more details."

"Okay." She shook her head as if she couldn't believe she was doing this. "I told you, I need to stop my sister from doing something stupid."

"Like making that 9:00 meeting on Stone Cay."

"Right. But I didn't tell you that it might get ugly."

"I've seen ugly before." At the doubt on her face, he arched a brow. "We're a unit, remember?"

"Only until we're back in the real world." She pointed a finger to the middle of his chest. "You remember that."

"Finally. We're on the same page."

"Why is this so important to you anyway?"

Hell of a question, one he didn't have a real answer for, at least none that he liked. "Because it's important to you. Now let's go."

"Brody—"

"Don't argue with your husband, woman."

"Oh, my God, stop saying that!"

He rented a car and got them on the road in the blackest, stormiest night he'd seen in a good, long while. Through the headlights and straining windshield wipers, they could see nothing but the slicked road lined with palms still nearly bent in half in the wind. "Anytime now, you're going to be happy I'm here."

She snorted.

He downshifted the piece of shit car and managed to keep them on the crazy road. "I'm serious."

"Okay, I'll let you know when I'm happy to have you here."

"You do that," he said grimly and outsteered a fucking golf cart on the road in front of them.

"Renting a car was a completely unnecessary expense."

"Yes, well, it's my expense, not yours." He tried to turn up the speed of the windshield wipers, but apparently, the highest speed was a snail's pace.

"Since when do you throw your money around? Usually, you're so tight you squeak when you walk."

He slid her a glance. "Hey."

"Admit it. You only rented the car because you can't stand taking a cab. You like the control."

"I do not."

"Then why wouldn't you let me make the arrangements? It's what I do for a living."

"I realize that. I sign your paychecks, remember?"

"I could have gotten you a cheaper car."

"No one could have gotten me a *cheaper* car. I needed more leg room."

"I meant a *better* car."

Okay, that may be. "The only other car was smaller. I needed more leg room."

"You need head room," she said. "How you ever get through a damn door with that big, fat head is beyond me."

"You're sweet."

She nearly choked on that. "Sweet?"

"Yeah. You only insult those you care about. Face it . . ." He shot her a look, waggling his brow. "You like me."

She stared at him. "You're crazy. And you still paid too much. Admit it—you like your control."

"Okay, I like my control. Now admit you like me."

"I like your damn fat head."

He snickered in triumph and kept driving. "You going to tell me where to any time soon? Or should I guess?"

"The docks. We need to stop Leena from taking a charter boat to Stone Cay."

Looking out into the nasty night, he laughed. "No one's going to charter a boat in this storm."

"Hopefully not. But I just want to make sure she doesn't try to go tonight."

No one would be going anywhere tonight. Not in this mess. But arguing with her was like beating his head against a brick wall. The brick wall of Maddie's stubbornness. So he drove her to the docks where she was told by two different charter guys exactly what Brody had already said.

No boat out tonight.

Brody drove them back toward town.

"A hotel," she said, resigned. Frustrated. "Five star. *Two rooms.*"

Yeah, he read that two rooms part loud and clear.

He pulled into a decent-looking inn because it was the first one they came to and paid for two rooms. Then he walked Maddie to hers, not missing the way she was rubbing her shoulder. "Sorry it's not a five-star hotel," he said.

"You are not sorry."

No, he wasn't.

The inn was decorated in shabby chic beach and was clean, his only requirement. "It's right on the beach."

"I'm not here for fun in the sun."

Which was a shame because under different circumstances— say, better weather and a better attitude on her part—he'd have enjoyed seeing her in an itsy bitsy bikini.

He opened the door to her room, eyes narrowing in on the shoulder she was still clearly favoring. The woman was hurting, and stubborn as a mule.

"My room key, please?" Holding out her hand, she waggled her fingers impatiently.

"Do you need ice?"

"I don't need anything."

Uh-huh. "Maddie—"

"My room key."

She accompanied this with another demanding wriggle of her fingers.

"Not yet." She wasn't getting rid of him that easily. "I'll be right back."

Her expression went wary. "Where—"

He shut the door on her, which gave him more satisfaction than it should have, then went to get her some ice, fairly confident that she wouldn't pull another Houdini on him since they were now a unit.

Even if only temporarily.

Chapter 13

The moment Brody was gone, Maddie sagged a bit. Keeping up the pretense of being fine had nearly killed her. She drew a deep breath, then carefully let it out, doing her best to regulate her heavily beating heart and shaky pulse.

Breathing didn't help.

Nothing would help.

Oh, God. She'd totally underestimated what coming back here would be like. The scent of the beach, the air, the tropical atmosphere that she'd once outrun but had never truly forgotten.

The storm blocked her view, but she looked out into the black night anyway, seeing in her mind what it would look like tomorrow—calm azure sea for as far as the horizon allowed. She knew elegant, posh resort hotels and casinos lined the white sandy beaches, which were mixed intermittently with weather-beaten motels and tourist trap shopping mazes, where she'd spent many hours as a young teenager working, saving.

Hording.

Planning. Always planning . . .

Nope, she didn't need to see the picturesque scenery; it was imprinted in her mind along with memories.

Some good, most bad.

Once upon a time, the island life was all she'd ever known. Her mother had had Maddie and Leena right here in Nassau. And up until the day she'd left them, Maddie had never understood how her world could crumble and fall.

Maddie didn't remember much about her mother, a fact that always disturbed her when she thought about it, so she didn't. But sometimes, like now, she wished she could see her mother's face more clearly in her head, that she could hear her voice.

That she hadn't left her girls behind.

Maybe they'd been difficult babies. No doubt, twins were hell on anyone. But if Maddie ever had kids—and just the thought made her want to laugh because she'd screwed up every single relationship she'd ever been in, so how could she ever have kids—she'd never leave them behind.

Never.

Ever.

But her mother had. And then their father had left them, too. Not by choice. No, death wasn't by anyone's choice, but gone was gone.

Leaving her and Leena with no one but Rick and a gang of thugs masquerading as gem dealers.

She and Leena had gone to school here, had played here as well. And had learned to lie, cheat, and steal here . . .

Feeling nauseous, she turned away from the window. If only she could turn from the memories as easily . . .

Now what? Brody would be right back. Damn it, this was all his fault. He'd given her the upper hand by being easier to manipulate when he believed her to be hurting and in need of taking care of, but suddenly, she didn't have to fake a damn thing, and couldn't have if her life depended on it.

Because being here made her feel like a victim.

She'd hate Rick for that alone, but there were so many other things to hate him for. Her entire childhood, for one. Losing Leena for another.

She felt sick, sick, at bringing Brody here. Putting him in danger . . .

Once upon a time, she'd actually hoped that they could have something. She knew she was different, that she didn't look like his everyday woman.

And he liked the everyday woman. He liked them sweet and kind and warm . . .

She wasn't those things, none of them. She was tough and driven and damn good at what she did, and yet . . . and yet he seemed to accept that about her.

She could love him for that alone.

Not that she could let herself. She had a sister to get to before Leena did something she would regret, and then there was that Plan, which unfortunately, did not include a big, tall, gorgeous pilot who made her feel things she'd never felt before.

Brody got ice—and also scored with another chocolate-filled vending machine—and let himself back into Maddie's room.

She was standing by the window, looking exhausted and unsteady enough that a soft breeze could knock her over. "Lay down."

"I can tuck myself in and get myself iced up."

"Really?" He moved closer. "Then what was earlier about? At the cabin, when you needed help out of your clothes?"

Guarded, she dropped her coat to a chair and sat on the edge of the bed. "Okay, you win. I need your help."

"What?"

"I need your help."

He cupped a hand over his ear. "I'm sorry?"

"I need your help! Are you deaf?"

"Nah, I heard you." He smiled at her. "I just wanted you to say it a couple of times."

With a sigh, she lay back on the bed. "You're a jerk."

"I know. Oh, and you're stripping yourself this time."

"Why?"

"Because my brain fails when I strip you." He waggled a finger at her shirt, a stretchy number that was hugging her curves and messing with his brain pretty badly. "Get moving."

"You're so romantic."

Brody opened his mouth and then shut it again, deciding not to touch that one with a ten-foot pole since it happened to be true. He didn't have a romantic bone in his body. Well, other than the one that wanted to, indeed, strip her and then kiss every inch of her body as he exposed it. But since what he wanted to do after that involved him stripping, too, he kept it to himself.

Then he heard the unmistakable hum of a cell phone vibrating from somewhere close. "You?"

"It's just my alarm. Can I have some tea?"

"Oh, no." He shook his head. "I've fallen for that one before."

"No, really." Her big eyes met his, all warm and soft and hurting. "I need some tea. I told you, I can't take my medicine without it, or it tears up my stomach."

"I thought you were done with the meds."

"I thought so, too."

He looked her over for a sign she was just fucking with him again, but she really did look pale and weak. "Okay, but if you're gone when I get back, I *will* find you." On that ridiculously empty threat, he left the room, then waited a minute, pressing his ear to the door.

He heard nothing.

Deciding to take her at her word, he made his way to the front desk, having to admit that a big hotel would have been nice for the room service alone. He asked for hot tea. The woman there took her sweet time making it, too. By the time he had a tray in his hands, he was nearly crawling out of his skin with impatience.

Once again, he swiped Maddie's room key, watched the lights flicker green, giving him the go-ahead, but when he turned the handle, the door didn't budge.

She'd bolted the door. "This isn't funny, Maddie. Let me in." When she didn't, he headed next door to his own room, walking directly to the connecting door.

She wasn't in her room.

His heart dropped into his gut until he realized the shower was running. Okay, so he'd overreacted. He sat on her bed and waited.

And waited, trying not to picture her in there, naked and soapy and wet . . .

Then he saw the cell phone on the nightstand, which immediately distracted him. With only a small zing of guilt, he flipped it open and checked her alarm. It was off. He moved directly to last received and dialed calls. Nothing he recognized. Then he got to text messages, where the last one stopped his heart.

Be late and Maddie pays, I promise you.

No longer feeling so patient, he knocked on the bathroom door.

Nothing.

A bad feeling curled in the pit of his gut right next to where his heart had dropped. He waited another minute and then decided the hell with this and broke in.

The room was filled with steam pouring over the top of the closed shower curtain. "Maddie?"

More of that silence.

Okay, so clearly they were going to do this the hard way, not that *that* was any big surprise. "I snooped on your phone and saw the text." With a quick jerk, he pulled the curtain aside. "And—"

And Maddie sat on the shower floor, head on her knees in rare defeat as the water pounded down over her, and the sight absolutely broke the heart still sitting in his gut.

Steam rose all around her but did not quite cover her. Nor

did her hair, plastered to her shoulders. Not looking would have been physically impossible, but still, he wasn't prepared for the visceral punch the sight of her gave him. "Maddie?"

She didn't move.

Resigned, he stepped over the edge of the tub and got in with her.

With a sudden gasp, she bolted upright, giving him a quick flash of her pale, shocked, horror-filled face.

And more. Way more.

Water ran over her in rivulets. Her eyes were wide, her mouth open in a silent scream, and two things hit him at once.

One, she hadn't been ignoring him—she really hadn't heard him coming in because she'd been asleep.

And two, he'd caught her in mid-nightmare.

Processing the information took a moment because she was naked, dripping wet, and extremely earth-shattering, heart-stoppingly gorgeous. Which is the only explanation he had for how she managed to wrap her foot around the back of his knee and tug so that his leg collapsed.

He fell like a ton of bricks to the floor of the tub, where he lay being pelted by the shower.

What the hell?

He blinked through the water raining down over the top of him to focus in on the very naked, very wet, very furious woman, hands on her hips, standing over him, glaring into his face.

Chapter 14

"Did I hear you say you snooped on my cell phone?" Maddie demanded.

"Yes." On the floor of the shower, fully dressed, drenched, Brody glared back at her. "And you neglected to tell me that if Leena doesn't make it to the meeting you're trying to stop her from making, *you* pay."

Maddie had no intelligent response, so she kicked at the inch of water in the bottom of the tub, splashing an already drenched man. She wanted to hurt Rick for the nightmare. She really needed to hurt him. Instead, she splashed Brody again.

"Hey—" He spit out a mouthful of water and came up on his knees, his shirt plastered to his tough body like a second skin as he held up his hands. "I'm not the bad guy here!"

Another kick of water helped, but her breath was still hitching, her body coursing with fury, hatred, adrenaline. Never mind the cell phone threat, she was caught on the stupid nightmare she hadn't had in years, but she'd had it now and she couldn't erase it from her brain.

She'd been sixteen again, back on that last night on Stone Cay, sleeping until she'd heard Leena cry out. Running through the compound trying to find her, running, running . . . desperate to find her—

"Maddie—"

She kept splashing him, and with an oath, a string of oaths really, he managed to surge to his feet and grab her, holding her against him.

But that just really did her in. She was so furious she saw stars, and yeah, way back in a corner of her mind, *waaaaay* back, she knew it wasn't Brody that was making her so crazy with fear and fury and guilt, but she didn't care. She couldn't care.

Her nightmare had reminded her of a time when she'd been young, alone, helpless, and in her head, she was there again. Memories, none good, had crashed down on her, pelting her, hurting her, killing her. "I can't—" She shook her head wildly. "I can't—"

"Sh-h." He softened his hold. "Shh, it's okay." He pulled her in against him. "It's okay, Maddie, you're okay."

But it wasn't. In spite of the hot water, she was cold, iced to the bone, and even worse, she couldn't control herself. Yet somehow, Brody's voice came through, achingly soft and so gentle she couldn't handle it.

"I've got you," he was saying, holding her to his big, steaming hot body while the storm raged both outside the building and within her. "It's me, Maddie, just me."

Pride and ego kept her struggling, but he just held her tighter. "Come on now. Stop."

"I can't." She fisted her hands in his drenched shirt, feeling that welcome heat of his body coming through, the comforting steady beat of his heart, and she gripped him for dear life. "I can't stop."

"I've got you now; you're not alone." He was holding her, his hands on her bare skin, his grip easy, soothing, firm.

He had her.

He really had her. And unlike any other time when she'd been falling apart, there was someone to catch her. It was then, reeling from that, still shaking from the dream, still bombarded by memories, still wanting to scream, wanting to fight, that she horrified herself by bursting into tears.

At Maddie's first sob, Brody's heart cracked right open. There was nothing more wrenching than a woman's tears, and that it was Maddie, strong, tough Maddie, made it all the more so.

Scooping her up against him, he turned off the shower and stepped out of the tub. Grabbing a towel, he tossed it over her the best he could and moved out of the bathroom. The main room was dark, but lightning lit it up, followed by a crack of thunder that rattled the window.

He set Maddie on the bed, planning on doing anything to make her stop crying, anything at all. He'd promise her the moon if he had to. And once he got her to stop, he needed to get her dressed, preferably in a suit of armor, because they were not going to the bad place again—that being the place where his brain ceased to function properly. And then when she was no longer naked or breaking his heart, he was going to make her talk. "Maddie."

He expected her to try to karate chop him again. Or maybe dive under the covers and pretend he didn't exist.

She was good at both.

Instead, with the only sound in the room being the driving rain and wind coming from outside, she curled toward him, pulling him down over the top of her.

"Mad—"

Her fingers shut him up, brushing over his mouth. Then she replaced those with her lips, while her hands ran down his arms, over his back, trembling, needing . . . It sucked him right in.

She sucked him right in.

Her mouth was on his, warm and salty, and somehow sweet, so damn sweet.

"Maddie—"

Or at least that's what he tried to say, but it was hard to talk with her tongue stroking his, not to mention the sheer, heart-stopping sensation of lying over the top of her while she was nothing more than a drenched, sleek, quivering form of mouth-watering curves. *Naked* curves. He couldn't possibly think straight. In the back of his mind, he knew she was trying to distract him, just as he registered it was working all too well, and then her hands tugged at his wet shirt.

"It's your turn to strip," she murmured, her voice all husky from her tears and barely audible over the sound of the storm raging outside.

Strip. He knew it was such a bad idea, but was getting caught up on the why. He had a reputation for being big and bad, but mostly, that was all attitude, and despite what women always said, they really didn't tend to fall for big and bad.

At least they hadn't been falling for him.

He'd had several relationships that had lasted longer than a few dates, but nothing in a long time, especially not this past year when he'd done little but work night and day to get Sky High Air off the ground.

So it'd been a while since he'd been naked, but he remembered how to get there. What he didn't remember, ever, was having a woman be so desperate for him that she was trying to climb into his skin, and it was just odd enough—especially for Maddie—to make him put his hands on her arms and pull back to look into her face. "You are Maddie, right?"

She went utterly still for one beat, then turned back into the wild woman with superhuman strength, but she was done catching him off guard, thank you very much. Pinning her to the bed, he stretched out over the top of her to hold her down. "Okay, it's you. I'm sorry, I—"

But she wasn't listening; she was busy trying to kill him again, so he threw a leg over hers, drawing her hands up over her head to get a better grip on her.

Which she absolutely did not appreciate. "Get off me or I'll—"

"Kick my ass?"

"I mean it!"

"A minute ago, you were kissing me like your life depended on it, and now you want to kick my ass?"

"A minute ago, you hadn't stopped to chat and then confused me with my twin sister!"

"I'll never make that mistake again," he promised and leaned in again so that their mouths were only a fraction of an inch apart. His initial shock at finding her in the shower had faded so that now he could go back to appreciating the situation.

That being him, fully dressed, drenched to the skin, plastered to her, also drenched and *not* dressed. He pressed his face to her neck, which was warm and soft, and inhaled, letting the scent of her fill his head.

"Kiss me again, damn it," she demanded.

She'd kissed him before, but now probably wasn't the time to point that out. Not with her wrapped around him, not with her voice still thick from the tears that had taken them both by surprise.

He wasn't a complete idiot. He recognized that she was most definitely back to distracting him, and you know what? Mission accomplished. At least for the moment, with her mouth racing across his jaw, her fingers working the buttons on his wet material, getting only halfway before she gave up trying and tugged. Buttons flew, and she yanked the shirt off his shoulders.

"I need to get there," she said. "To the kissing and then . . ."

He liked the sound of the "and then." She was soft and wet, and he was primed and ready to go, and had been for too long to count. She couldn't get his zipper down, so she ran her fingers over him, then tried to slip her hands into his pants, which he wanted her to be able to do, so he gave her a little room and then could still hardly breathe for what she did to him.

"Help me," she whispered.

"Whatever you want."

"Hurry."

Except that. "Is there a fire?"

"I like it fast."

Yes, and if she kept outlining him with her fingers, fast would be no problem. But he didn't want fast. Nope, he wanted slow and deliberate, so he could remember every little detail for the fantasies he was going to have about this for the rest of his life. So he grabbed her hand in his, brought it to his mouth to slow her down a minute.

Or two.

Or for an hour.

"That's not fast," she pointed out.

Normally, impatient would work for him, really it would, but not now, not with her. He rocked against her, pressing her back against the mattress, again burying his face in her neck, pressing his mouth to her skin, taking a little lick because he wanted a taste. He made his way up her throat to her jaw, then headed toward her ear because he needed a bit of that, too—

"Brody, damn it."

"Mmm-hmmm." He loved her ear. Small and delicate with all those sexy silver hoops.

She slid her fingers into his hair and he nearly purred, but then she tightened her grip, painfully so, and tugged. "Kiss me!"

"I was."

"Here! Like this!" And still holding his head by the ears, she tugged him up and locked her mouth on his. She used her tongue, which he also liked very much, and then, as if she needed to ensure he stayed with her, she arched up and wrapped her legs around his waist.

A move that pretty much guaran-ass-teed he wasn't going anywhere.

Ever.

* * *

This, Maddie thought with a helpless pleasure-filled sigh, this was what she needed. She needed it to keep Brody from thinking, from asking questions, from taking matters out of her hands, but more than anything, she needed it for herself, to forget, at least for a few minutes. She needed his mouth on hers, his hands on her body, needed it to even breathe.

Because he was her air. She'd die before admitting it, but fact was fact. In a world gone a little mad, he was her axis.

If she was being honest, he'd always been.

He knew how to kiss. Oh, God, he really knew how to kiss. She'd wanted him so desperately for so long that she was almost surprised that she didn't just burst into spontaneous flames from the feel of his mouth and hands on her, and when he stopped kissing her to murmur her name in a low, husky, sexy voice, she died a little.

More. She needed more.

He kissed her again, and she murmured in pleasure, feeling all her bones melt away. Oh, yeah, more of that, and she was willing to risk all to get it.

Her past.

Her present.

Her future.

Even her heart. Especially her heart. And she *was* risking her heart. Even knowing it didn't stop her. Nothing could. She was on empty here, on a rare low, with only fear and anxiety filling her tank, and he could make it all go away, at least for a few minutes.

Again, he said her name in that voice she loved, the one that said that every wild, crazy thing she was feeling, he felt, too. God, it'd been so long since a man had touched even a part of her poor, damaged heart. Too long.

Now, now, now . . . she slid her hand down his still damp chest between their bodies, going for the point of no return. This time, she was able to get a hold of his zipper, and the rasp of metal on metal filled the storm-ravaged silence around them. In the dimly lit room, their gazes met, his dark and heated, and she knew.

Oh, God, she knew.

No matter what happened to her here, no matter the outcome, she was going to have this moment with him. She was going to let herself be loved, and even more terrifying, she was going to let herself love him. "Hurry, Brody."

Instead, he latched on to her throat and sucked a little patch of her skin into his mouth, and as if her body was on a string, it arched up to him.

"I've been dreaming about this too long to hurry," he said. "Even for you."

"You've been dreaming of this?" Hands in his hair, she lifted his head to look into his eyes. "So why do you avoid me at work?"

"I don't mix work and pleasure." He slid his hand down her belly. "But we're not working now. . . ."

No. No, they weren't, and she let him kiss his way along her throat, his magical hands and talented mouth doing their thing, and his body, oh, God, his hard, toned body . . .

"No, we're not at work." Her eyes were crossed with lust. "But unless you hurry up . . ." She broke off when his mouth skimmed down her throat, over her shoulder, and directly toward a breast. "Oh, God."

And then he made his way to her other breast, taking a damn *year* to get there, igniting all sorts of fires along the way and he hadn't even taken off his pants yet. With each passing second, her heart further engaged, and it scared her. "Okay, you know what? You're taking too long. Oh, forget it. Forget all of it. Let me up."

Smiling into her eyes, his own dark and searing, he slid down her body, doing the opposite of letting her up. Nudging her legs open with a broad shoulder, breaking eye contact to take his eyes on a tour over her exposed body.

And she was exposed, just about as exposed as she could get. "Hey. I—"

He kissed her inner thigh, and she promptly lost her train of thought. "Um . . ."

He kissed her other thigh.

"B-Brody."

"Yes. That's my name."

She should have killed him when she had the chance. She'd get as many women on her jury as she could, no way would they convict her. With the last of her energy, she tightened her legs on his torso and tried to flip him.

He didn't flip. Of course he didn't. The big, bad Brody didn't go anywhere he didn't want to.

"Damn it!"

He looked into her eyes, grinned, and then flipped her, and then she was straddling him as she'd wanted, holding him down. "Or this way," he said agreeably.

"My way." She worked his wet pants off him. By the time she was done, she was sweating. *"My* way." And she crawled back up his body and guided him home.

"Jesus," he breathed. Smile gone, hands gripping her hips, he arched up, body tense and quivering. What happened next was as crazy as the storm beating up the inn.

The feel of him filling her was like nothing she'd ever felt. Before, in the shower, she'd felt barraged and battered with an emotional weight too heavy to bear. Nothing had felt right, but now, in this moment, all that was gone and everything felt right—amazingly, perfectly so.

Catching her hands in his, he tugged her down to his chest, kissing her. "Your way," he whispered against her mouth. "This time."

It wasn't until she began to move, until she was halfway to bliss, that she realized the truth—this wasn't her way at all. It was *the* way, the *only* way, and she had a feeling that no one else would ever be able to make her feel like this.

Knowing it, she faltered.

But not him.

Never him.

Lifting a hand to her face, he murmured her name in question, but she shook her head, then sped up the rhythm, needing him to take her to the edge, now, *now*, needing to take the plunge rather than savor this as she deeply, secretly wanted . . .

But her brain wouldn't shut down, and she couldn't . . . quite . . . "Damn it," she panted, frustrated, setting her forehead to his. "I can't—"

"You're rushing yourself." His hands went back to her hips to help guide her, his thumb stroking over her center, right above where they were joined, and just like that, he did exactly what she needed, he took her where she needed to go.

She had the feeling he always would, which was her last thought before she came, only peripherally aware of his low, rough groan as he followed her over.

He'd always get her there, always . . .

Chapter 15

At the sound of a cell phone somewhere far too close, Maddie stirred, then realized she was sprawled over the top of Brody's hard, warm body.

Not a bad way to wake up, really, though she couldn't believe she'd fallen asleep. Squinting through the room, dimly lit by the bathroom light that they'd never turned off, she read the clock. Two-thirty. She tried to shift away, but Brody's arms tightened, holding her in place. "The phone—"

"I've got it." Still holding her, he reached for his cell on the nightstand. "'Lo," he said, his voice deep and gravelly and sexy with sleep.

Sexy. So damn sexy. She wanted to rewind and repeat. God, she really needed a grip. But outside, the storm still raged, which meant she didn't have to get up yet . . .

"Yeah, I've still got her." Brody's eyes cut to hers as he listened. "What kind of question is that?" With a sigh, he scrubbed a hand over his face. "Yes, I'm taking good care of her." He listened some more, then shook his head. "No, Noah, we are not eloping. What the hell is wrong with you?"

Pulling free, Maddie rolled to her back to stare at the ceiling, ignoring the slight twinge of regret at the horror in his voice. No, they weren't eloping. They weren't even particularly getting along, unless it was in bed.

Where they somehow managed to get along pretty damn fine.

"I already promised to call you if we need you," he said. "Now go take a flight or a breath or something." He shut the phone.

She could feel him looking at her, now on the far side of the bed.

And looking.

He wanted to talk. She did not. She lay there, very still, thinking if she only waited, he'd fall asleep again. Because hey, that's what guys did after wild monkey sex—they slept.

After a moment, she slowly turned her head in his direction, and damn, didn't he look mighty fine all rumpled, sleepy-eyed, and naked.

And very awake.

The sheet had slipped, affording her a very nice view from his Adam's apple to his belly, which she wanted to lick like a lollipop.

And lower, too.

Being with him had been every bit as good as she had imagined. Fast, searing . . . perfect. When she'd come, she'd released all that terrible pent up tension. Now maybe she could use any lingering energy for something else entirely . . .

Like saving her sister's ass.

"You're going to fall off the bed," he noted.

"I'm good." She needed distance.

Lots of distance.

He was still just watching her with those mesmerizing eyes, scratching his jaw as if considering a particularly vexing puzzle, his fingers rasping against the growth of his unshaved jaw. Then he crooked a finger at her.

Come here.

No. No, no, no, that would be a bad idea.

Very bad.

But her brain apparently wasn't in charge because her body

obeyed, scooting close, and then his arms pulled her in, and then, oh, God, he pressed his face into her hair and inhaled deeply. "You smell good, Mad. You always smell good."

"Stop." Her voice was shockingly weak. *Fall back to sleep.*

He dipped his head down, pressing his mouth to her throat so that she could feel his lips move against her skin. "So damn good."

"Seriously." *Why wasn't he sleeping?* Maybe the bigger question was, *why wasn't she shoving him away?* Instead, she arched her neck to give him better access, loving how big and hard and warm he felt. After arriving here, she'd been cold, icy cold, but that had vanished lying next to him.

His hands swept down her body, urging her closer, then closer still so that she could feel that he was not sleepy, not even close. "We're *not* doing it again."

"Okay." One hand squeezed her bottom, then slipped between her legs, and she realized.

They were doing it again. "Brody—"

She'd have sworn she had nothing left in the tank, and yet when his fingers stroked her, she shivered in need and let her legs fall open. "I mean it. We're *not*—"

Another stroke, unerring and sure.

The man had talented fingers, and after yet another stroke, she admitted the truth.

She was going down with the ship. "Okay, maybe just one more time," she whispered, breathless as he worked his magic. Her fingers dug into his biceps as she clung to him, her world spinning, the pinnacle centering between her legs. "But only *once*."

He scraped his teeth over her shoulder, and she shuddered as his dark head made its way toward a breast.

"And it's going to be my way this time," she managed. *"Fast."* She tried to tug him over her, where she would have pulled him deep inside and had a go at round two, but he resisted.

"Not fast. We just did fast. We're going to take our time." He punctured every few words with a kiss as he began to move down her body. Her neck, her shoulder, the scar where the bullet had shattered her collarbone. He spent a long moment there, then just below, where the curve of her breast began . . . "I want to taste you, Maddie. Every single inch of you."

Oh, no. No way. If they weren't going to jump each other's bones and knock it out in a timely fashion, then—

He sucked a nipple into his hot, wet mouth, and she nearly arched right off the bed. In spite of herself, her body was responding. Her nipples were pebbled tight, and she was getting wet. *Again.* "Damn it, Brody."

He let her nipple pop out of his mouth and went for her other one.

"Brody Allen West."

"You're middle naming me?" Sounding amused but undeterred, he began kissing his way down her belly, his mouth hot and wet, not moving fast at all, nothing so easy as that.

She fisted her hands in the sheets at her sides. "Yes, and I'll do it again if you're going to drag this out."

Lifting his head, he smiled, pure wickedness in his gaze and voice. *"My* way," he repeated firmly.

Her stomach quivered at all the wicked, naughty promise in his eyes. But she couldn't go there emotionally. Couldn't. She was tapped out. Fast was all she had, so she pushed him aside and then climbed on top.

From flat on his back, he grinned up in pleasure at her and cupped her breasts.

She lifted up her hips to draw his most impressive erection inside her, but he pulled back and shook his head. "I'm not ready yet."

Arching a brow, she looked down at what was currently filling both hands. Impressive and quite ready.

"Yeah, that's because with you, I'm always hard as a damn

rock." Then, just as she had, he rolled her beneath him and held her there.

"Okay, listen." She tried a smile. "Maybe we should just go to sleep. I'm going to need to get a few hours before I stop Leena—"

"From what exactly?" He slid a finger into her, groaned at the heat and slickness he found, and licked her nipple. "That meeting, yes. But what's on Stone Cay?"

"The compound—" Her impending orgasm, the one barreling down on her like a freight train without brakes, was currently curling her toes and evidently, also loosening her damn tongue.

Not that Brody seemed to notice. He simply worked his unhurried way to her other breast, his fingers still driving her directly to bliss without passing Go.

"Compound?" he murmured against her skin, making his way south, leaving a hot, wet trail over her torso with his tongue. "Like a family compound?"

"Yes. Sort of. Brody—"

"So this Rick is . . ."

God, his fingers. He was in charge, controlling her like a puppet, and desperate to gain some of that control back, she gave as good as she got, stroking him, eliciting a rough, husky breath from him. In the interest of speeding this along, she did it again.

"Rick," he managed with what sounded like some difficulty. "He's . . ."

"Our uncle."

"A real asshole?"

"A real asshole," she agreed, arching up into his touch. His mouth was gentle, so damn gentle, as he ran it over her body.

"Did he ever hurt you?"

"No, he never dirties his hands himself."

He kissed a rib, and then another. "What does that mean?"

"He has his men do everything for him."

"I have to tell you, Mad. I don't think I'm going to like your family."

That tore a laugh out of her. "No. You won't. Now are you taking this somewhere or what?"

"Or what." He kissed her belly, then lifted his head and looked at her a long moment, his gaze softening. "Why would Rick threaten your safety?"

"It's complicated. Brody, we're in the middle of something here. In case you've forgotten."

"I haven't." His fingers proved that by dragging another soft gasp from her. "So what's your plan for after you get Leena?"

"Brody—"

"I know. I'm multitasking. Humor me." He settled a big, warm hand on her inner thigh and nudged it over as if she wasn't opened enough to him already. "God, look at you," he murmured. "So pretty."

She closed her eyes. "Stop with the sweet talk; you've got me. Now do me."

His thumb slid over her heated flesh, spreading her just a little. "You're all pink and glistening. And wet."

Words failed her as he played in all that wetness.

"Is it for me, Maddie? Are you this excited for me?"

His voice was low and thick and not just a little heavy with male satisfaction, which was both sexy and irritating. "Well, who else?" she asked.

"Maybe I want to hear you say it."

"Are you kidding me? I just said you've got me."

"Maybe a guy likes to know when a woman is hot for him."

She came up on her elbows to see him. He was all tousled and rumpled and damn it, sexy as hell. "Maybe a guy should just get on with it before she changes her mind!"

"Come on." He had the balls to smile. "You're not going to change your mind." With that, he leaned in and put his mouth where his fingers had been.

She managed some inarticulate response and gripped the

sheets beneath her, her hips arching right up into his mouth in shocked pleasure. Slipping his hands beneath her, he cupped her butt and in less than two minutes, had whipped her blood back into a frenzy. She was panting, gasping, an inch from meltdown when he pulled back. "You never answered my question."

Her heart was drumming so loudly she could hardly hear him. "I don't remember your question."

That earned her a cocky grin. "What does Rick have on Leena?"

He hadn't asked that one, she knew that much, but she wanted him to finish! "She works for him."

"Ah." Another slow, sure stroke of his tongue. "What does she do?"

"She's a jewelry designer for his gem company. Damn it, Brody!"

A soft huff of laughter brushed over her sensitized flesh. "Love the sound of my name on your lips. All hot and bothered and frustrated." Still between her legs, he kissed one inner thigh, then the other. "You should know, slow is really my thing."

"Your window of opportunity is closing down, big guy. I need my beauty sleep."

"Are you telling me you could actually go to sleep right now?"

"Like a baby."

"Really." His thumb lazily stroked over her, ripping a gasp of pleasure from her. His gaze met hers. "Tell you what, Mad. You go to sleep." And with a soft kiss to her hip, he went to roll away.

"Oh, no." Pulling him back, she let out a low laugh. "Finish what you started."

"Luckily for you, I always finish what I start." He gave another pass of his thumb. "Including in a few hours when we go find your sister."

"There's no we."

"Face it, babe." Bending his dark head, he went back to work, making her gasp again. "There's a we."

Damn the man. He could take her outside of herself like no one else ever had. "Brody, I need—"

"Me. You need me."

He was so damn sure of himself. And so damn right. "I'm going to—"

"Come," he whispered thrillingly, sucking her into his mouth. "You're going to come."

Yeah. Always right. With little to no effort, she burst, and then he was inside her once again, and she was pulling him down so that she could feel his heat, his strength, feel him nuzzling at her neck as she changed his slow, lazy pace to supersonic so that this time they both lost it together.

Lost . . .

Even as together, they were found.

Chapter 16

A few moments later, or it might have been a year, Brody let out a long, satisfied sigh. "Okay, so your way works, too."

He had his face against Maddie's throat, which smelled so good he took a lick. He hadn't found any more piercings or tattoos, which he had to admit surprised him. Unwrapped from the tough girl packaging, his badass Maddie was all warm and sweet on the inside.

"That wasn't fast," she said. "If I hadn't speeded things up, we'd still be at it."

He lifted his head, feeling pretty damn satisfied with his world, even more so when he saw the look on Maddie's face.

Her eyes were closed, but she was smiling. Her gorgeous, silky hair rioted all around them on the pillow, her skin dewy and flushed, and honest to God, just looking at her, his heart skipped a beat. "That wasn't fast enough? How is that possible? I've set new records for you."

Unimpressed, she lifted a shoulder. "Could have been faster."

He had to laugh. "How about I'll try harder next time."

At that, her eyes flickered open, and a set of sharp baby blues landed on his. "Next time?"

"You're telling me we're not doing that again?"

She didn't say anything to that.

How could she not want to do that again? She was still flushed and damp and glowing. She'd enjoyed herself. She'd come. *What wasn't there to repeat?* "How could something so good be bad?"

She slanted him a look. "You're going to be a guy about this, aren't you?"

"Apparently, yeah."

With a sigh, she sat up, tugged the sheet from beneath him, and wrapped herself in it, covering up that bod he could happily have draped around him forever. "I'm sorry I lost it earlier in the shower. But that helped a lot." She paused. "Thanks."

Thanks?

"It's been a long time for me. Which is why I . . ."

Okay, he liked that he'd been the guy she'd let break her dry spell. He liked that a lot. "Why you what?"

"You know. Went off so fast."

"Wait a minute." He thought maybe he'd just been insulted, but his brain hadn't quite gotten back on track, so he wasn't sure. "Are you saying any guy could have gotten you off that fast?"

Rolling her lips inward, she just looked at him.

"Hell, no." He shook his head. "You are not going to tell me that."

"It's not personal, Brody."

Hell, yeah, it was. "What just happened in this bed was not something that happens all the time." He was sure of it.

"My vibrator works its magic in six minutes." She lifted a shoulder when he stared at her. "Just saying."

"I was way better than a vibrator."

She laughed and went to get out of the bed, but her laugh backed up in her throat when he snagged the sheet at the small of her back. "Hey."

But he didn't let go, hell, no, leaving her two choices—get out of the bed naked or stay in it.

She stayed.

Craning her neck, she sent him the famous Maddie glare that had sent many people scurrying for cover. Never him, though. A sick part of him liked that look. It made him want to tug the sheet off and see what she would do about it.

So he did.

She squeaked and then rolled, executing a rather impressive dive off the bed to the floor, where she grabbed the forgotten towel, wrapping it around her.

And then, nose in the air, she strutted into the bathroom.

He lay back on the bed, tucked his hands behind his head, and waited. Vibrator, his ass. He was way better than a damn vibrator.

When she came out a few minutes later, wearing some sort of silky-looking pants and top that were shaped like sweats but skimmed and clung to her body in a way that suggested lingerie, her nose was still in the air.

"Going to get a nosebleed," he noted.

She put her hands on her hips and tossed back her hair. He wondered if she knew her nipples were hard and pressing against the silky fabric. Wondered if she knew that at just the sight, his mouth watered like Pavlov's damn dog. "You can reign superior all over the place," he told her. "But admit this at least—you're not hurting nearly as bad as you let me think."

"I took a bullet."

"Yes." His hands tightened reflexively into fists. He still couldn't even think about it without rage exploding through his body. "But you're recovering more than you let on."

"You wanted me to be weak."

"I wanted you to be honest."

"Honesty is not always the best policy. Especially in this case."

He stared at her, then shook his head. "We're going to have to agree to disagree there, babe. Now back to the important stuff."

"I'm done discussing my vibrator."

"The *other* important stuff. What exactly does Rick want Leena for so badly that he's willing to threaten you to get it?"

"You're like a bulldog. Anyone ever tell you that?"

"All the time. So . . . ?"

"Rick's my father's brother."

"And your father is . . ."

"Dead. Rick runs the fancy import-export gem company, bringing mostly unrefined jewels into the States. He needs Leena. Leena designs jewelry for those gems. Now if you could go to your room, I could get some sleep."

"What? No cuddling?"

She crossed her arms and shot him a get-real look, so he decided not to admit that holding her for the rest of the night wouldn't have been a hardship. "What else does Rick do?"

"Depends on who's asking. If you're Uncle Sam or the IRS, then that's it. If you're a company who buys unrefined gems to turn into jewelry designed and created on spec, then sometimes there's other things."

Ah. Now they were getting somewhere. "Such as?"

"Such as the occasional imitation gem that looks as good as the real thing but is worth a fraction of the promised item."

"There's probably good money in the swindle scam business, huh?"

"Undoubtedly."

"So Leena knew she was working the wrong side of the law?"

She sighed. "Aren't you tired?"

"Not in the least. But if you'd rather take those pjs off and show me the six-minute vibrator trick . . ."

The look she shot him threatened his family jewels. "Tell me this, at least. What does all of this have to do with you?"

"Nothing, really. I left Stone Cay when I was sixteen. But Leena recently decided to leave, too, and Rick . . . objected."

"Objected how?"

"Most of Leena's work is legitimate designs and creations."

"Most but not all."

She agreed with a slight nod. "Once in a while, he pressures her to do a job that isn't on the up and up. He needs her to set the gems. Both the real ones and the fakes."

"Why does she do it?"

"Fear."

He shook his head. "Not good enough."

"You've got a penis," she pointed out. "You don't feel fear like a woman can."

"Come on, Maddie. She has the law on her side."

Her expression didn't change, but he got a really bad feeling. "Okay, why doesn't she have the law on her side?"

"Ten years ago, she had a . . ." Something flickered across her face then, unhappy memories, and his bad feeling doubled. ". . . Disagreement with one of Rick's underlings."

"What happened?" Whatever it was, it was big.

"Manny came up dead the next day."

Yeah. Big.

"Rick linked Leena to the guy's death. He says he'll bring her up on murder charges if she leaves him."

"To which she said too bad, so sad and left anyway?"

"To which she caved. She was afraid, Brody."

Yes, and she wasn't the only one. Maddie had been afraid, too. Terrified. It was there in her eyes. "What sort of disagreement exactly?"

"Leena dated Manny. Once."

"What about the dead part? Did she do that, too?"

"No." Her voice was tight, certain. "No, she didn't."

"And so you stopping Leena from working now is going to accomplish what? Allow her to make her great escape while you put yourself at risk for someone who should have walked away years ago? Because she should know Rick isn't going to turn her in—it'll expose himself."

"You don't understand."

"Help me to."

"It's the middle of the night. I'm going to sleep."

"And then?"

"And then, I'm going to the docks to get my sister."

"And when Rick comes after you for stopping her?"

"That's a worry for another day."

"Are you kidding me?"

Tapping her foot, she stared at him. Silent.

But he was done with silence. "Am I going to wake up and find you gone, Maddie?"

"You're my pilot. How gone can I get?"

"There's always a commercial flight."

She wrinkled her nose and nearly made him laugh. She was a food snob and a plane snob.

"Look, you should really just wait here anyway. You don't need to risk yourself for Leena—"

"No. But neither do you." He rose to his feet and walked toward her. "But we're both going to." Snagging her hand, he gave a little tug, and when she looked questioningly into his face, he gave her hand a squeeze. "Not having to go isn't going to stop either of us from helping the person we care about."

She just stared at him. "You really are crazy."

"Already established, babe. Already established."

Chapter 17

Leena stood in front of Ben's New Orleans gallery holding the letter she'd written on the plane. It told him that she wasn't who he'd thought, that she was a fraud, every bit as much as the jewelry she'd made him, and that she hoped he could someday forgive her but that she wouldn't expect him to.

If he wanted to prosecute, she completely understood and understood she deserved everything that was handed out to her, but she'd promised him in the letter that someday, somehow, she'd compensate him for his loss.

Dawn had just turned the sky a pale purple, and the gallery was closed, but that worked. She didn't need to see him. For a moment, she stared down at the envelope that would give Ben the proof he needed to take her to the authorities if he chose. But if that happened and she went down, then Rick would, too.

She was okay with that. Heart heavy, fingers shaking, she reached for the mail slot, but suddenly, the door opened, and her gaze locked with Ben's.

Maddie woke up at dawn, wrapped up tight in Brody's arms. She could get used to this. But what the hell was he doing back in her bed?

His eyes were closed, his breathing deep and even. He had a scruffy jaw and bed head, and honest to God, just looking at him did her in.

But why was he here?

Lifting the covers, she took a peek. She was still in her pjs. Not Brody.

He wore the big zip, which she admitted, took a long, long moment to register. But being so damn gorgeous did not excuse him holding her close in a possessive, proprietary way that made her want to curl in against him even more. "Brody."

"Mmm-hmm." Eyes still closed, he wrapped her in tighter, snuggling his face against her throat.

She gave him a little shove that accomplished nothing. "What are you doing?"

He slid one hand inside her pj pants to cup her bare butt, the other slid languidly up her back, making her want to purr like a kitten. "Mmmm," he repeated.

"Wake up!"

Looking sleepy and sexy as hell, he opened his eyes. "Hey."

"Hey? Hey yourself. Why are you in bed with me?"

"Because you asked me to be."

"I did not." After they'd had all that inappropriate but amazing sex, she'd kicked him to his room. Hadn't she?

"Somewhere around three, you knocked on the connecting door and said you were cold."

Oh, God. She remembered now. She'd had the nightmare again, and she'd told him she needed his body heat. With a sigh, she got out of bed and headed for the window rather than risk giving into temptation and jumping his naked bod. Again. "I'm not cold now."

"Yeah. Getting that loud and clear." Behind her, she heard him get up and craned her neck, watching as he grabbed his clothes and walked naked into his room.

God, he was something to look at . . .

"Don't even think about leaving me behind," he warned.

Behind? He had a great one—

With an easy flick of his wrist, the connecting door shut, and her view was gone. Shaking it off, she turned back to the window.

The storm had vanished as quickly as it'd come, leaving a yawning blue sky and warm, salty air blowing in from the ocean over the town of Nassau. Time to track down Leena. She took a quick shower and dressed, then knocked on the connecting door for Brody.

He answered, looking a little grumpy and still, a whole lot sexy.

Damn it.

He checked them out of the inn, drove them back to the docks, and then carrying both of their small overnight bags, walked in brooding silence with her to check on charter boat availability.

There were three companies. One was closed, the other two open, with none of them having a reservation in Leena's name. Or any reservations, for that matter.

So Leena hadn't called ahead, which meant all they could do now was wait.

At least the salty air was warm and calm and filled with the cries of seagulls nabbing their breakfast from the dock railings.

"You okay?" Brody asked after an hour.

"Yes."

An hour later, he asked again.

"Where is she?" It was after eight now. It'd take thirty minutes or more to get to Stone Cay. If she didn't show soon, Leena would be late for Rick, something that just wasn't done.

"Have you called her?" Brody asked.

"Once or a million times."

In the time they'd been waiting, both of the available charter boats had gone out with paying customers, none of whom were Leena.

The third still wasn't open.

Brody stared out at the ocean.

Maddie sighed. "I guess she didn't come here after all—"

"Where is that boat from?"

Maddie focused in on where he was pointing, where she could see another charter coming in. "Hey!" she called to the captain on board. "Did you come from Stone Cay?"

"*Je ne parle pas anglais.*"

No English. And she had no French. "Stone Cay?" she asked, pointing out at sea.

He nodded and gestured them on board.

"The question is," Brody murmured, holding her back from jumping onboard. "Is he saying he'll take us there, or that he just came from there?"

"It doesn't matter," she decided. "She's not here. And if he took her there . . ." Pulling free, she hopped to the boat.

He followed. "Maddie, listen to me. For all you know, he was stuck there overnight because of the storm, and he's just now coming in."

"Which means Leena's been there too long."

"Maddie—"

"You don't have to come."

"*Fuck.*" He rubbed a hand over his eyes. "Do you have a plan?"

"I always have a plan." But she chewed on her lip, her mind racing. "Okay, I'm working on it." They paid for the ride, and Maddie watched the winding canals vanish behind them, the miles and miles of fine white sand beach fading away, as well as the towering palms.

It was beautiful, she thought. Far too beautiful to have such grim memories attached to it all. "I can't believe I'm going back."

She didn't realize she'd spoken out loud until she felt Brody at her side, arm to arm with her at the railing.

"That fun a place, huh?"

"You really shouldn't have come, Brody. I'm not all that nice when I'm around family."

"As opposed to the rest of the time?"

He was teasing her, but she shook her head. "I mean it. Leena got all the warmth and sweetness."

"You're not serious."

When she remained silent, he tipped his head up skyward, then with a softly uttered "hell," pulled her around to face him, then lifted her up against his chest so that her toes were dangling. Nose to nose with him, mouth to mouth, she opened hers to say something, except he stopped her with his lips. He kissed her hard and deep and wet, and she was shocked to find her arms entwining around his neck to hold on for more because oh God, did she want more.

She wanted it all.

She wanted everything they'd had last night and then again.

She wanted it because a small part of her wasn't at all sure if she was going to be able to pull this off, and if she didn't, she wanted something to remember. Wanted this to remember. So right there, with the sea breeze in her face and the salty, flowery scent of the islands all around, she slid her fingers into Brody's hair, holding on for dear life to the only steady thing in her entire world.

With a low murmur, he backed her to the hull and pressed up more fully against her, freeing his hands to cup her face, his thumbs sweeping over her jaw on either side as his mouth plundered, using his tongue, his teeth, his entire body to kiss her.

Unbelievably, everything faded away—the swells slapping against the sides of the boat, the cries of the seagulls, the murmur of the two fishermen also on board, the heat of the sun beating down on their heads . . . the fact that she was going back to a place she'd promised herself she'd never, ever go again—all of it simply faded away in the face of this, in the face of what she felt for Brody, of what she was afraid she could still yet feel.

His hands slid down her body and then up again with the familiarity of a man who now knew her every curve and nuance. That was new and thrilling, but then he was slowly changing the pace of the kiss from deep and hungry to something lighter, sweeter, settling his hands on her hips instead of letting them roam over her, stoking fires. Then, only mouths lightly touching, they just breathed each other's air . . . until finally, he lifted his head.

Ridiculously breathless, she stared at him. "What was that?"

"Me proving how warm and sweet you can be."

"That wasn't sweet."

"Felt like it to me."

"Your sweet meter is off."

"Maybe it's been off since you had me strip you out of your clothes at the cabin."

"Stop it."

He shrugged. "Or it might have been last night when I had you all wet and naked in bed."

"That was a fluke." She pointed at him. "I'm serious. No more thinking about wet and naked."

"Fine."

"Great."

"Yeah, great." But he let out a breath and shook his head. "Shit. That's not great at all. Not anywhere close."

Why that caused a little shiver of anticipation to race down her spine, she had no idea at all because she meant it. No more thinking it, no more doing it.

"Is that it? Stone Cay?" He was staring out at the faint outline of an island.

At the thought, her heart sank to her gut.

Stone Cay. "There it is." She concentrated on the choppy ride, waiting as the island got bigger and bigger—her first view of her childhood home in ten years.

The island was low lying, composed of coral and limestone. Its highest point wasn't even five hundred feet above sea level, and the island was covered in woodlands and surrounded by gorgeous, bright white beaches. The sea around it was shallow and clear for as far as the eye could see. As they moved closer, the subtropical exotic growth and flora became more visible. Lush, vibrant colors bloomed on the bushes and scented the air.

As there had been ten years ago, there was a dock with a wide, white beach sprawling out for several hundred yards before vanishing beneath heavy jungle growth. Straight back from the dock lay a road, obviously tended to but empty.

No sign of another soul, and certainly, no Leena.

Not good. Maddie hesitated, then got off the boat to look around.

"Maddie—"

"Hang on. I'm looking for—" Fresh tire tracks. But before she could say so, she heard an engine.

"Maddie." Clearly hearing it too, Brody jumped off the boat as well, just as a Jeep came down the road toward them.

Recognizing trouble when she saw it, Maddie grabbed Brody's hand and whirled back to the boat but skidded to a halt at a very unwelcome sight—the charter speeding off back toward open sea.

Maddie could only stand there and stare at it, feeling the bottom drop out of her stomach. "He wasn't supposed to do that."

"No," Brody said, calm. "He wasn't."

Calm was good. She felt his hand at the small of her back. "Breathe," he murmured in her ear. "You're not breathing."

No, she wasn't.

The Jeep parked, and the driver got out.

Standing at her side, gaze on the Jeep's driver, Brody kept his hand on Maddie's back. "Let's get this over with and get back to the fun stuff," he murmured for her ears alone.

"What's that?"

"Anything to do with getting wet and naked."

"Leena," Man In Black said.

Maddie blinked and glanced at Brody. Leena?

"You're late. You know Rick hates late." He looked at Brody. "Who's this, the husband?"

Maddie swallowed. "Uh—"

Man In Black raised a brow, waiting.

"Could—" Maddie licked her suddenly dry lips. "Could we have a moment?" She waggled a finger between her and Brody.

Man In Black nodded curtly and leaned back on the Jeep, arms over his massive chest, face impassive.

Maddie pulled Brody a few feet away for some dubious privacy. "He thinks I'm Leena," she hissed.

"Actually . . ." Brody glanced at the guy. "I'm not sure he thinks at all. You see the size of his neck? It's got to be ten times the size of his brain."

"Leena didn't come," she whispered, both relieved and terrified.

"Yeah." Brody cut his gaze to the empty dock. "But we did."

"Yeah."

"And the charter's gone."

Which really sucked. "Which leaves us at their mercy."

"Okay, I really hate the sound of that."

She did, too. "I have to be Leena." She looked at him. "It's the only way."

"*What?* No."

"Well, I can't be me!" she whispered harshly. "Don't you see? If I'm Leena, all Rick wants from me is some work, and then I'm free to leave again, assuming I convince him I'm not running away."

"Jesus. This is suicidal. You know that."

"What choice do we have? The boat's gone. If I'm Maddie, well . . . I think that might be a bit of a health hazard for me."

He swore beneath his breath. "Your life is too complicated."

"I told you!"

Brody looked over at MIB again. "Christ, I'm crazy for agreeing to let you do this."

They had no choice. None at all. Brody wore tan khakis and a white shirt. His eyes were a cool, give-away-nothing gray, and his wind-tousled hair fell carelessly across his forehead. Did he look like a husband? Her husband? She hoped so, because holy mother of God, he was who he was and didn't do pretense for anyone.

"I'm not going to screw anything up," he said, obviously reading her mind. "I know what we have to do."

Well, she was glad someone did, because she didn't. She was putting him directly in danger, and the thought wasn't an easy one. If anything happened to him, if anything at all went wrong, she'd never forgive herself.

Never. "Remember," she hissed. "I'm—"

"Yeah, yeah. You Leena. Me ball and chain. Got it."

"No." She was doggedly determined to make sure he had everything straight. "She's different than me. I'll be different. I'll be quiet. Demure."

"Your virtual opposite, you mean?" He put his hands on her arms and looked into her eyes. "I get it."

"Do you? Because Leena wouldn't marry a scowling badass. You need to act . . . beta."

"Beta?"

"Yeah. Easygoing. Laid-back . . ."

"That'll be new," he admitted.

"Can you try for . . . refined?"

He let out a low laugh. "I've never been refined, not from the day I was born in the gutter or the day I crawled out of it."

She stared at him as he put his sunglasses on his nose and said nothing else. "I'm sorry. I didn't mean to imply that you weren't—"

"Hey, no use fighting the truth, right? We both know what I am and what I'm not. Let's just do this."

Yes, they needed to do this. But she was realizing something about the tall, tough, enigmatic man in front of her. He wasn't one-hundred-percent badass at all, and that brief flash of vulnerability had just proven it. "Brody, about that refined thing—"

"Let it go."

"I'm really sorry—"

"Jesus." He took her hand. "What does let it go mean?"

Odd how she suddenly wanted to hug him, which would have to wait. For now, she squeezed his fingers, hoping she was imparting some comfort.

His big, warm hand closed on hers, but he said nothing, whatever he was thinking lost behind his reflective sunglasses. His hair was blowing back, his shirt billowing out, and she took a good long look, struck by what he was doing for her. Without question, he'd put himself on the line. He had doubts, lots of them, but that hadn't stopped him from being here for her.

And she had to admit, it was a bit staggering. Suddenly, she wished she'd spent all of last night in his arms, that at the very least, she'd kissed him for longer when she'd had the chance on the charter boat.

That she hadn't yelled at him.

Eyes on the man at the Jeep waiting for them, Brody lifted their joined hands to his mouth.

Had he read her mind and was offering genuine comfort? Or had he just begun the acting portion of the program and was simply playing her husband?

Then he turned his head, lifted his glasses, and met her gaze, his own steady and sure. "You okay?"

She swallowed the unexpected and slightly horrifying lump in her throat. "Always."

He smiled, the one she'd seen a thousand times over the past year. The one that said he was on top of his world and knew it, the one that said that on his watch, nothing would go wrong.

He was truly there for her, and for that moment, Maddie

couldn't seem to muster up Leena's persona, not to save her life. For that one beat, she was Maddie, just Maddie, and she could only stare at him, wanting him, caring about him, completely overcome with emotion and desperately trying to beat it back.

God, she needed a grip, a big one. "Brody?" she whispered.

"Yes?" His mouth quirked again. *"Wife?"*

Was it wrong that from deep, deep down came a longing and a yearning she couldn't explain, except that for the first time in her life, she liked the sound of that W word?

Wife.

Clearly, she was losing her mind. She looked out at the water. "This island, this compound . . . it was my childhood home."

"You've said."

"It wasn't a happy place."

He'd been eyeing MIB at the Jeep, but met her gaze, his own solemn and surprisingly understanding. "I'm getting that loud and clear."

She had no idea why she was going to tell him this. Maybe so he could really understand the need to pull this off, maybe because she had to explain the danger she was putting him in so that if he wanted to walk away, he could.

And that maybe he should do exactly that, walk away. "I don't know if my father was a bad guy or not. I was too young when he died, but Rick . . ."

"Bad seed. Got that, too."

"Yeah. And . . ."

"And . . ."

She shook her head. "And I should never have let you come with me."

Once again, he glanced at the man waiting for them. "Are you trying to warn me that it could get messy? Because I already figured that part out on my own."

It was why he'd come. That much was all over his face. "I wish I could give you an out."

Putting his hands on her arms, he looked into her eyes. "You really think I'd walk away to let you face this on your own?"

"What I think is that you should have."

"Yeah, well, think again."

She nodded, swallowed hard. "You should probably know, it didn't go so well last time I was here."

"Yes, but you're no longer sixteen and helpless. And you're no longer alone."

Amazingly enough, the truth of that helped.

So did he by just being at her side.

"Let's do this," he said, "and get back to the one aspect of our marriage that I can really get behind."

"What's that?"

"The good stuff."

Chapter 18

Maddie laughed as Brody had clearly intended. "The good stuff?" she repeated.

"Sure. You promised to love, cherish, and do good stuff. It was all in our vows."

"Huh." She knew what he was doing, trying to take her mind off the dangers facing her. I must have missed that part."

"You should have paid attention. You promised all sorts of things."

"Like?"

He waggled his eyebrow, and if they weren't facing imminent trouble with a capital T, she would have shivered in anticipation. "You really are crazy," she managed.

"Which isn't going to get you out of the vows, babe."

She laughed again, and he smiled, looking hot and sexy and cocky.

But it was pretend.

This was all pretend. Their lives depended on it. "Let's go," he said, taking their bags, slinging them over his shoulder, and reaching for her hand. Everything about him shouted alpha male.

He wasn't the only one. Moving back toward the Jeep, Maddie looked at Rick's man. He wasn't all that tall, but he was definitely built like a linebacker. Maddie didn't recognize him, but she recognized his type. All hired muscle and silent servitude.

And suddenly, she didn't have to fake the nerves Leena would have shown. Did Leena know this man? She had no way of knowing, but her sister was such a snob—a submissive snob, but a snob nevertheless—and as such, would have ignored all the hired help. Easy enough to imitate.

"Are you really married?" he asked her.

She didn't look at Brody. "Yes."

A smile split his mouth. "I won the pool then. Sweet."

"You . . . bet on me?"

"We all did. No one could see you hitched for real, but I thought it was way too inventive a lie for you, so . . ." He shrugged. "I win."

The familiarity was obvious. Leena did know this man, possibly well.

"Let's go," he said. "Rick hates to be kept waiting, you know that."

Be Leena. Her sister was quiet, yes, but she definitely had an attitude, always had. "Too bad."

The man sighed. "So getting married didn't improve your mood any." He gestured her into the Jeep, then eyed Brody with an expression that said, *and you put up with this why?*

Just grateful to have pulled off the first hurdle, Maddie slid into the Jeep.

"Given Leena's aversion to men," their driver said, "Rick figured it was just a bullshit excuse to be late, or to get more money out of him."

Maddie glanced back and nearly had a heart attack. He and Brody were having a stare down. MIB's dark lenses were over his eyes, and there was the obvious bulge of a weapon at his shoulder, but her "husband" didn't seem overly intimidated.

Oh, not good. Not good at all. Leena would marry someone quiet like herself. Meek. Reaching out for Brody's hand, she practically yanked him on top of her. "Baby, hurry up. It's hot out here. My makeup's going to run."

He shot her a look, but some of her fear must have shown because he slipped an arm around her shoulders and said nothing.

While all that he wanted to say crackled in the silence.

MIB slid into the driver's seat, watching them through his rearview mirror with great interest. "Trouble in paradise already? Shocking, Leena."

She wanted to snarl, but she wasn't supposed to be herself so she thrust her nose in the air and looked out the window in pouting silence.

Leena. She was Leena . . .

MIB put the Jeep in gear and drove them along the secluded beach, past the sparkling, clear azure waters, up the single hill on the island. Surrounded on both sides by the lush, colorful growth, they came out of the woods at a pair of stone and wrought-iron guarded gates that opened in silent invitation, leading to a long driveway arching up to the house.

Though house seemed far too meek a word for the 25,000-square foot complex that had cost millions to build and millions more to trick out with all the combined security and elegance Rick demanded. It was a simple yet sophisticated structure, done up in the epitome of rustic luxury. Exotic woods, glass, indigenous stone . . . no expense had been spared. Situated on the very top of the only hill, overlooking the secluded beach amidst coconut palms and seagrape trees, the place was admittedly breathtaking.

At the sight of it all, Brody stiffened next to her. Maddie glanced over at him, but he was facing the window, probably staring in shock at the ridiculous display of wealth the house represented. She'd admit the sight had to be impressive to someone who hadn't seen it before, but for herself, she only saw her past. When they pulled into the graceful circular driveway surrounded by abundant, flourishing landscape, breathing became difficult, if not all but impossible.

She was back . . .

MIB drove to the top of the driveway and cut the engine. The front door of the house opened, and a man stepped out.

Rick.

Oh, God. Could she really do this? Could she fool him? With no choice, they got out of the Jeep and moved up the stairs, Brody just behind her, his hand on the small of her back.

Rick didn't move. Medium height, medium build, with a small but welcoming smile, he shielded his eyes from the sun and waited as they came to him. Nothing about him suggested Evil Swindler, nothing at all. He was tanned from long days of the island sun, handsome even.

A soft, floral-scented breeze blew over Maddie, and she shivered. Nope, her uncle hadn't changed much in the past ten years. He still looked like a grown-up beach bum with sun-streaked hair, carelessly lean muscled build, and easygoing stride, until one looked into his eyes and saw the utter lack of warmth.

Yeah. Home sweet home.

Her heart was literally ricocheting off her ribs as she repeated one fact over and over in her head. You're Leena. You're Leena.

Leena was always all nerves. Nerves were good.

"Hello," Rick said in his quiet voice, the one that screamed I'm-in-charge.

"Rick."

He gestured to Brody. "So. What have you done?"

"I told you. I got married."

"Quickly, it would seem."

"Yes."

Rick nodded, and she took a breath. He'd bought her as Leena. He held out his hand to Brody, who was still bowled over by the surroundings or he'd realized quiet and meek was the only way to pull this off because he didn't say a word as he shook Rick's hand.

The only sound was a hum of insects in the flowers and the distant call of an exotic bird.

"Thought you didn't like the islands," Rick finally said to Brody.

"No. But the wife does."

Rick looked at "the wife." "You've not been gone very long. The last time you were here, you were still claiming you'd never marry, that you'd never settle down with one man."

"Things change."

Not looking convinced, Rick nodded again, still watching them both very carefully, and Maddie realized that she and Brody were standing several feet apart, not touching at all, giving off vibes that did not exactly say newlyweds. Damn it. Rick knew Leena, unfortunately well. Leena had always held a healthy fear of men, especially big, badass-looking men like Brody. This was never going to work unless Maddie could convince Rick that Brody was really just a pussy cat. Scooting closer, she slipped her arm around her "husband," feeling buckets of tension in that big badass body. "We're very happy."

But Brody didn't look happy. He looked the opposite of happy, and Maddie slid her hand down from the small of his back to his butt, which she pinched hard.

Brody turned his head and slid her a look.

She forced her sweetest smile, making up a story on the spot. "Brody was my dentist." She hugged him while he just looked down at her, silent. "He fixed my crown, and the rest is history."

"You married your dentist," Rick said slowly.

"His business is booming. Everyone needs a dentist, of course, and good ones are hard to find."

"You married your dentist," Rick repeated. "A *dentist*."

"Well, he only works one day a week since his trust fund kicked in."

"Ah." Rick's tone suggested that he finally understood. "Trust fund."

"Oh, no, it was his kindness, his sensitivity that got to me," she gushed, setting her head on Brody's chest with a dreamy little sigh. "Not his bank account."

"Sure." Rick nodded, looking amused. "And his bank account had nothing to do with it."

"Of course not. He's sensitive and compassionate." Wow, listen to her gush. "We're going to have babies."

Brody's eyebrows nearly leapt off his face at that one, and Maddie couldn't even look at him anymore. "The point is," she said after controlling herself by biting her tongue hard, "I don't have to work."

"So you mentioned." Rick's voice stayed even, but his eyes hardened. "Except that you and I have an agreement. You *will* continue to fulfill your end of this agreement, designing and creating for me as needed." He shot another look in Brody's direction. *"Confidentially."*

The morning was warm, hot even, especially in the island sun, but Maddie's blood ran cold. His meaning was clear. He must not be made to feel a need to divest himself of her husband. "Brody isn't into jewelry," she said, hoping she didn't sound as desperate as she suddenly felt. "Not at all."

"I see."

"He's really not." Hopefully, he believed that, which led her to the next problem. Rick wanted her to do a job, probably create an item from a design and then set a gem for it. Only it'd been ten years since she'd even watched Leena do such a thing. She had no idea if she could pull it off.

No idea, and no choice.

"Was your sister at your wedding?" Rick finally asked.

Oh, God. "M-Maddie?"

"You have another sister I don't know about?"

"Of course not. I just . . . " Mind whirling, she smiled sadly. "We haven't been in touch."

Rick just looked at her.

"We're no longer that close." She struggled not to fidget, to continue looking him right in the eyes, but man, it was really hard to do that and lie through her teeth. "So no, there's been no contact."

Another long, uncomfortable beat. The tension was thick, so much so that she could hardly breathe through it. Rick didn't seem bothered by that fact in the least. She was. Silence from Rick had always bothered her, and this one went on so long she nearly waved her hand to make sure he was awake.

But he was awake; he was just waiting for her to crack. Leena cracked, and cracked often. It was what she did. "Okay, there's been the occasional contact," she admitted.

"So you lied to me?" He asked this in the same quiet tone that suggested her answer had no importance at all, but she knew better.

"Omitted," she said. "Not nearly the same thing as lying."

Rick's mouth tightened. "I'd like to talk to Maddie, Leena."

Oh, God. "That's not necessary."

"I think it is. We have things to discuss, her and I." He snapped his fingers, and the two goons who'd been standing behind him like statues vanished, presumably to go contact Maddie.

Who was standing in front of him.

"She's probably pretty busy," she said, trying to think over her panic. Brody hadn't been kidding—her life was complicated. "You know, living her life."

"She'll make time to talk to her family. To maybe visit if things don't work out here during your visit, Leena."

Oh, shit. He'd just given her a whole bunch of information she didn't want, such as if she, as Leena, screwed up, Maddie was going to pay.

Well, no way in hell she was giving herself up to him. She valued her new life way too much for that. She valued Brody's life too much for that, and she stepped even closer to her "husband." For show, of course.

But also for the sheer comfort in having him there, big and reliable, and at her side.

On her side.

He immediately tightened his grip on her, running his hand up and down her arm in silent comfort.

He was here for her, right here. The marvel of that was never going to get old. "Why don't I get to work," she said. *Before your goons go and find out that Maddie is standing right here in front of you.*

"You're in a hurry?"

"Well, I do have a honeymoon to get back to." She leaned her head against Brody's chest and felt the solid, comforting thump of his heart. "I'd like a charter here waiting for me when I'm done."

"All right." Again, Rick's gaze flickered to Brody. "The notes are in your workroom. And so are all the materials you'll need." He gave Brody another long, considering look. "I assume you'll still work completely alone, without distraction, as you've always insisted. Maybe your husband would like to go back to Nassau and wait for you there. I can arrange for deep sea fishing or any number of activities—"

"No."

This from Brody himself in a voice of steel. His eyes matched. "I'm staying."

Oh, crap. Why didn't he just pee on her to mark her as his territory? Turning her back to Rick, she shot Brody a look of warning.

He ignored it. "I'm staying with my wife." He smiled down at her. Sweetly. Kindly. So much so that she had to blink.

She'd seen him smile, of course. With genuine affection and amusement for Shayne and Noah, with triumph when he'd rebuilt any of a hundred different planes. And then there'd been that smile of wicked intent just before he'd put his tongue between her legs and taken her to a whole new world of pleasure just last night, but she'd never seen him smile like this. Like she was the love of his life. It was a bit . . . dazzling, and she had to remind herself that this was all for show. She turned to Rick. "He's staying."

Looking none too happy about that, Rick nodded and gestured them inside. "Let's get on it then." He gestured to a new Muscle Guy, who had two inches on Brody and no neck at all and looked as if he was a steroid-for-life kind of guy.

His name turned out to be Tiny Tim, and he led them into the foyer of the house. The décor had been updated and changed since Maddie had seen it last, now done up in a ritzy beachy decadence.

She could hardly breathe. Everywhere her gaze touched filled her with memories—sliding down the front sweeping arch of a banister and hitting the huge white tiles in the great room where she'd broken her arm. Hiding behind the two marble sculptures and knocking one over. Pretending to be an ice skater in her slippers along that cool, smooth floor . . .

Tiny Tim held up a hand to halt their progress and whipped out a metal detector. Okay, that was new to the Welcome Home process. Wielding the thing like a weapon, he walked around the back of Brody, or tried to, but Brody simply turned with the guy, keeping him face to face.

"Looking for weapons," Tiny Tim said and gestured for Brody to turn around.

Maddie squeezed Brody's fingers hard enough to bruise her own, and after an indescribable look in her direction, he, indeed, turned, facing her while the goon searched him for weapons.

"Now face me," Tiny Tim demanded. "Arms out."

With a grim tightening of his mouth, Brody turned, lifting his arms as directed, letting the guy thoroughly search him.

Finally, Tiny Tim gestured him aside and turned to Maddie. Her turn, and she had a knife in her boot and a gun in her bag, both of which would light up the detector like a Christmas tree.

Thoughts whirling with ready-made excuses, she held out her arms, but to her surprise, the guy set aside the metal detector and stepped close, a gleam in his eyes.

He was going to pat her down by hand.

Okay, this could work. Because unless he asked her to strip, he was going to miss the knife. But then he put his hands on her, and not exactly gently or with care for her personal space, and over his bent head, she locked gazes with Brody.

Such temper shot from his eyes that she nearly flew backwards from its blast. He took a step toward her, and just like that, her life flashed before her eyes. *Don't*, she mouthed.

He stilled with obvious difficulty, his body tense enough to shatter.

Oblivious to the silent battle, Tiny Tim stood in front of her, his meaty paws patting down her hips, her legs . . .

Jaw ticking, Brody jammed his own fisted hands into his pockets, probably to keep them from closing around Muscle's throat as Maddie continued to silently beg him to behave himself and stay still.

Muscle didn't so much as glance at Brody, but Maddie knew he had to be incredibly aware of the sheer fury resonating off of her "husband," whose eyes were promising her that if Tiny Tim took this any further, he *would* take action.

Oh, God. And what then?

But Tiny Tim finally finished getting his jollies feeling her up and straightened as she took a breath. Okay. Okay, they were nearly done here—

Except not, because then he settled those hands back on her waist, gliding them upward, heading with wicked intent toward her breasts.

Brody's eyes narrowed to slits, and he took another step toward him, but by some miracle, Tiny Tim's phone chirped, and he turned away to answer.

Maddie let out a slow, careful breath and took a quick glance at Brody, but before she could say a word, Tiny Tim turned back, slipping his phone into his pocket. "Follow me," he said gruffly, not even glancing at Brody as he took them to the huge, curved staircase.

Miraculously still armed, Maddie followed with Brody in the rear. She didn't speak to him, mostly because she knew from living here all those years ago that the place was under surveillance. Most common areas of the grounds and house were under camera surveillance, with only the bedrooms and bathrooms off limits.

"Where are we going?" he asked, not knowing about the sound system, his voice filled with a lethal calm and absolutely no quietness or meekness about him.

"To Leena's room," Tiny Tim said. "Where you'll stay until you're needed."

"And Leena?"

"She'll go to work."

Brody didn't say a word, but his opposition to this plan practically bounced off the walls as if he'd shouted.

Silent and doubting her own sanity, Maddie let Tiny Tim lead them up the stairs to Leena's bedroom. The place was spotless, as always, and Maddie wondered if Rick's housekeeper Rosaline still worked here. Once upon a time, Rosaline had been the sole soft spot in this entire place, always kind and gentle with Maddie and Leena, their only true female influence. Maddie wondered if it was possible that the woman had put up with Rick all these years . . .

Next to her, Brody was taking it all in, the elegance and sophistication, the museum quality art and furniture, his expression going more and more grim. At the top of the stairs and down a wide hallway, Tiny Tim opened a door, gestured them in. "I'll be back for you in a few," he said to Leena, then left.

Silence settled over them. In Maddie's case, it was heavy with the weight of the memories from being back in Leena's childhood bedroom. She wasn't surprised to find that nothing much had changed, not the pale yellow and white lace or the expensive Victorian furniture Leena loved.

Brody moved through the room, his big shoulder nudging the corner of the dresser so that a vase perched there nearly toppled off. He neatly caught it, then as if he felt like a bull in a china shop, set it back with exaggerated care, letting out a low breath as he backed away from the dresser. "That thing is probably worth more than my car. Hell, everything in this place is worth more than my car."

His tone was light, but nothing about his body language said light, and certainly nothing about the fire spitting from his eyes said it either.

But he was right about the value of the vase. Everything in here was valuable. Or invaluable. It was how Rick liked things.

Almost robotically, she stepped toward a pocket door just beyond the dresser.

Sliding it open, she felt the full force of the blast from her past as she stared into her own childhood bedroom.

Chapter 19

Brody took in Maddie standing in that inner doorway, shoulders stiff, body practically shimmering with tension, and wished like hell he'd never let them get this far. She was clearly fighting demons, and damn it, he wanted to slay them for her, but he didn't even know what exactly they were.

His kick-ass warrior concierge had a helluva lot more secrets than he'd imagined.

The house around him had secrets, too. He'd never seen anything like this place. The art on the walls alone could have funded a third world coup. And then there was the furniture, the rugs . . . hell, even the air had class.

He'd always looked at Maddie and seen that class and told himself a million times to keep his hands off. And he had, mostly.

Until last night.

And now he was here, playing at being her husband.

Husband. But even that wasn't as terrifying as Uncle Rick or his goons.

No, nothing about this was going to be easy, not if one more person threatened or touched Maddie.

Especially touched.

Maddie was gripping the doorjamb in fists gone white, her

shoulders and spine so stiff he was surprised she didn't just explode on the spot. He wanted to say her name, her *real* name, but he didn't dare, not here. "Are you okay?"

"Sure."

She was a liar. Beautiful, strong, amazing, but a liar nevertheless. He might not be privy to half of what was really going on here, but the other half had been pretty damn clear. Maddie as Leena needed to do this job and keep it under wraps and out of the hands of the good guys, or Rick was going to go after Maddie.

A threat. Christ, he hated threats.

But what he hated even more was the look of sheer misery radiating off of Maddie. They might be The Princess And The Peon here, but he wasn't stupid. Being back here was killing her. He wanted to drag her ass out of here and keep her safe.

Always.

Only, that wasn't really an option. In fact, he had few options at all at the moment, which only served to make him feel all the more helpless, an emotion he especially hated and always had. Moving close, he set his hands on her shoulders, not surprised when she tensed. "Just me," he reminded her, but stayed on guard because with Maddie he never knew. She could dropkick him. She could slug him.

She could kiss him.

He personally wouldn't mind door number three but didn't see that happening, so he remained alert.

Reaching back, she gave him a little go-away elbow.

But he wasn't going away. Instead, keeping his hands on her, he peered over her shoulder into the room she was staring at so intently. Another bedroom, not yellow and white and girly, but blue with stark white trim. The furniture was pine and wrought iron. Very expensive and very Spartan and completely empty of all personal belongings. But he didn't need personal belongings to know what he was looking at.

Maddie's childhood bedroom with all its elegance and class.

Yeah, they'd grown up worlds apart, that was for damn sure. Tilting his head, he looked into her face, a virtual frozen mask of inscrutability. She was giving nothing away, but she didn't have to, the self-loathing was escaping out her pores, and this bothered him more than anything he'd learned in the past two days.

Leena stood frozen in horror and humiliation on the steps to Ben's art gallery as Ben looked through her as if she was nothing to him.

Less than nothing.

He was everything she remembered and more, including being the best-looking man she'd ever met. Not magazine gorgeous, but *real* guy gorgeous with the shaggy hair that he'd finger combed at best, faded jeans and a T-shirt, both splattered in paint, neither hiding his graceful, athletic body, the one that fueled her deepest fantasies in the dark of the night.

Once upon a time, his smile had been the only thing that could somehow reach deep inside of her and spread warmth where she was always cold.

But he wasn't smiling now.

"Is that for me?" he asked in his quiet Irish voice, gesturing to the envelope in her hand. When she didn't answer, he reached for it, but she had at least enough wits about her to take a step back.

Yes, the letter was for him. Of course it was, but the thought of him reading it in front of her was way too much.

Seeing him was too much. How had she thought she could do this?

She'd missed him incredibly but she'd also hoped never to see him again because she couldn't handle watching his face when he learned the truth about her.

No, that she most definitely couldn't handle. On the flight, she'd realized that to do this, she needed anonymity, she needed to be gone, long gone.

Or she couldn't do it at all.

Motionless, unable to do anything, including walking away, she stared at him as he came down the two steps.

Run, she told herself, but her feet didn't budge.

Slowly, he reached out, but instead of grabbing the letter, he took her free hand, then startled her by leading her up the steps and into his gallery.

"I can't stay," she managed, still letting him pull her inside.

"Okay." Watching her as one might watch a deer stuck in the headlights, he very slowly and carefully took the letter out of her hands.

And she let him. Oh, God, she let him because apparently she really needed to completely and totally humiliate herself.

"I wasn't sure I'd ever see you again," he said.

She hadn't planned on it either. . . . She really shouldn't have come inside. She had no business being here . . . "Ben, I've got to—"

"Wait." He kept his grip on her. Not hurting her, never hurting her, but not letting her go either. Eyes on hers, he tore the envelope open with his teeth, then let it fall to the floor so he could read the letter while still gripping her hand.

Two more times, she tried to pull free.

And two more times, he simply tightened his grip and held her at his side as he read.

Silently.

Without a single hint on his face of what he was thinking, he took in the words from the very depths of her heart and soul, the words that bared her to him like nothing else ever had. When he finally lifted his gaze, it was dark and unreadable. "So you did know about the gems," he said. "I wondered."

Sick at heart, she nodded.

"You knew they'd been switched, and you didn't tell me."

Again, she nodded.

He looked at her for an interminably long beat. "So I guess

my next question is, why shouldn't I nail your gorgeous ass for swindling?"

All the other times she'd seen or talked to him, there'd been a natural warmth about him, a light welcoming warmth that radiated such easy, sexy charm that she'd helplessly responded to him.

Not now.

Now he was holding back, no sign of that warmth anywhere.

She'd never seen him like this, so absolutely void of any expression on his face. She'd done that. She'd hurt him. But just as she opened her mouth to try to make him understand, two men stepped inside the gallery. They were big and beefy and dressed all in black, and with a sinking feeling, she instantly recognized them as two of Rick's men, Ed and Saul.

Ed looked straight at her as he shut the door behind him. "Hello, Maddie. Been following you."

Maddie?

"Good thing you finally used your credit card. Thank you for that."

Right. She'd used Maddie's card to fly here . . . but that didn't explain why they were following Maddie.

Saul glanced at Ben, then spoke directly to Leena alone. "You're coming with us back to Stone Cay."

"What? Why?"

"Insurance."

Oh, no. Oh, God. Suddenly, she got it. There was only one reason to need insurance. To need Maddie. Rick needed her to make Leena behave.

Which meant . . . he thought he had Leena on the island, but that meant he had Maddie.

And how had that happened? The whole thing was enough to make her head spin, and a sick sense of panic swirled low in her belly. "I'm not going anywhere."

Not letting go of her hand, Ben shifted a little closer to her, and she felt the heat and strength in his body as it brushed hers.

Saul shook his head at him. "We just need Maddie."

But Ben didn't back off. "She said she's not going anywhere."

"Look, man. We don't have a beef with you, so don't give us one. She's coming with us."

"No, she's not." Ben's Irish accent came out thicker now. The rough brogue sounded icy and dangerous.

Saul sighed and pulled out a gun.

"No," Leena gasped, jumping in front of Ben. "Stop! I'll come with you."

"No," Ben said again, yanking her to his side.

"Oh for fuck's sake." Saul looked less than thrilled. "Seriously, dude. Let go of her."

Ben didn't, and Saul aimed.

"No!" Leena cried. "Don't shoot him. I don't even know him—"

"Shut up." Saul studied Ben.

Not cowed, Ben studied him back, not nearly as terrified as he should be. "You're not taking her," he repeated.

Oh, God. "What part of shut up didn't you understand?" she hissed to him out the side of her mouth.

"You know, I think he's right." Saul's eyes narrowed thoughtfully. "We'll take 'em both."

Ed shrugged.

"No—" Leena started, but Saul pointed at her chest.

Ben squeezed her hand tight, silently telling her to take her own advice and shut up.

Why was this happening? When she'd left Maddie at the cabin yesterday, everything had been fine. What had made Maddie go to the island as Leena—

Oh, God. There was only one reason Maddie would have gone to Stone Cay. She believed Leena had gone back, and she'd gone to save her.

Well, now Leena would save Maddie. Somehow.

* * *

Brody watched as Maddie turned away from her childhood bedroom. She moved to Leena's bed, rifling through her bag without saying a word, then hands full, walked right by him and into the bathroom.

"What are you—"

The bathroom door shut.

Okaaaay.

"Getting ready," she said through the door. "And you should, too. The sooner I do this, the sooner we're gone."

Again, he looked down at himself. He hadn't worked on any planes today, he hadn't done anything but shower, argue with her, come here, and then argue some more, so in his opinion, he was ready enough to go anywhere. "I'm fine. I'm ready." For what, he had no clue, but he sure as hell was ready.

Maddie opened the bathroom door, stuck out her head, eyed him from head to toe, and then shook her head and shut the door.

He looked down at himself but saw nothing wrong. "What the hell was that?"

"Nothing."

Yeah, right. He put his hands on his hips and scowled at the damn door. He really hated having conversations with doors. "If there's a problem with the way I look—"

Once again, she peeked out. "Not the way you look. Never the way you look."

His gaze locked on hers, and for a moment, he got a little lost in that statement, not to mention the blue of her eyes.

"I like the way you look." Her voice sounded just a little husky and a whole lot sexy.

Or that might have been wishful thinking on his part.

"Which," she said, "I'm pretty sure I proved last night when I jumped your bones."

Maybe not so much wishful thinking, which felt pretty damn good.

"It's your face," she said.

He put a hand to it. Yep, still there. "What's wrong with my face?"

"You scowled when we set foot inside this place. You've been scowling ever since."

"Yes, that's what happens when some asshole put his hands all over you instead of using the metal detector."

"It was fine."

"Are you kidding me? He just did it as an excuse to feel you up, and you expected me to just stand there and let it happen."

"Yes, I did."

This, like so many other things, boggled his mind. "Why? Why would you want them to do that to you?"

"Why would I want—" Eyes flashing, she broke off and yanked him into the bathroom. Slamming the door, she flipped on the shower and the sink and flushed the toilet. Then in the noise of all the running water, she came right up to him and pushed him back against the door so that their bodies bumped. His mind immediately went from frustrated to lust in zero-point-four seconds, and then she went up on tiptoes and put her mouth to his ear.

Oh, yeah—

"It *had* to happen."

When the words sank in, he blinked.

"I didn't want him to use the metal detector on me," she whispered, then stepped back while he just stared at her.

And that's when the truth sank in. Of course. She'd smuggled in a weapon, possibly two. When he could speak, he hauled her back up against him and put his mouth to her ear because while he might be slow, he was not a complete idiot. "You think the room's bugged?"

"No, but just in case," she whispered. Hunkering down, she unlaced her boot, during which time his brain hiccupped and went to another place. He couldn't help it, so help him

God, he couldn't, but kneeling at his feet the way she was, it felt . . . erotic. Unintentionally so, yes, but he couldn't seem to stop thinking about sex, as inappropriate as that was. If she so much as lifted her head, her mouth would be just about even with his—

"See?"

He stared down at the boot she'd removed and the knife that lay inside.

At the quick rap at the bedroom door, they both jumped. Maddie slipped back into her boot just as the door swung open to reveal a small, dark-haired, olive-skinned woman in her late forties wearing black trousers, a white blouse, and an apron.

"*Hola*, Leena." The woman's voice was cool, but oddly enough, her eyes were warm. "You've come home and brought a man. This I had to see for myself." She looked over at Brody, taking him in with a careful sweeping gaze. "I'm Rosaline."

"Brody West."

"You married my Leena."

He looked at her "Leena." "Yes."

Maddie hadn't said a word. In fact, she'd gone still as stone, just staring at Rosaline, which was such an oddity all in itself, Brody took another look at his "wife."

She was surprised.

And pleased, very pleased. It was in her shiny eyes and the flush in her cheeks.

"Of course I've come home." Maddie's voice sounded thick with . . . emotion? "I always do."

Not seeming to notice Maddie's barely suppressed joy, Rosaline sniffed derisively. "I suppose you have laundry."

Maddie swallowed hard, and if Brody didn't know better, he'd say she looked overcome. "Don't I always?"

"Yes, you—" Rosaline suddenly went as still as Maddie, staring at her for a long beat before slowly lifting her hand to her mouth. "Oh," she breathed softly. "Oh, you're not Leen—"

Maddie crossed the room in quick strides and gripped the woman's arms, shaking her head.

Rosaline appeared to be blinking back her own tears as she cupped Maddie's face. "Oh, look at you. Look at you."

Speechless, Maddie nodded, and Rosaline pulled her in for a hard hug. They stood there like that for another moment, then Rosaline pulled free and surreptitiously swiped at her eyes. "I have work."

But neither shifted away, both clearly moved. Finally Rosaline made another quick dab at her eyes with her apron before quietly leaving, shutting the door behind her.

Maddie let out a low breath, closed her eyes for a moment, then turned back to Brody. Once again, the knife was in her hands. "Rosaline's been the housekeeper here for many years, and I—I missed her."

He nodded, then looked at the gleaming, sharp as hell-looking knife in her hands. That she'd had the guts to smuggle it in, that she'd even thought they might need it told him volumes, mostly all the stuff she'd left out about this little family reunion.

Then came another knock.

Maddie's gaze met his. "That's not Rosaline this time." She slipped the knife back into her boot, calmly and quietly flipping off the water before straightening and facing him. "Show time," she said. *"Husband."*

Chapter 20

Leena's workshop was at the cellar level. Maddie had never spent much time in the huge, expansive space built beneath the house, but Leena had. It was where she designed and created, and to this day, Maddie didn't know how she'd spent so many years down here with no windows and no hint of whether it was night or day outside in the real world.

Tiny Tim had brought her down here, along with Brody, who had flatly refused to wait upstairs in the bedroom.

Rather than argue with him, Maddie had forced a sweet laugh and had hugged him tight. "Oh, honey," she'd said gaily for Tiny Tim's benefit, waggling her eyebrows suggestively. "You should stay in the room and regain your strength for later."

"Ah, man," Tiny Tim had groaned. "Come on. Don't talk like that around me."

"Can't help it." Maddie rubbed up against Brody like a cat in heat. "Why don't you leave us alone for a little while?"

"Good idea," Brody said, hands going to her hips. "Go away, Tiny Tim."

Rick's man pulled Maddie free from Brody's grasp. "She has a job to do. She'll do it."

Brody pulled her back to his side.

"Dude," Tiny Tim said warningly.

"Dude. Back off."

Instead, the muscle-bound MIB stepped closer and once again, reached for Maddie, who actually slipped a hand into her purse for her gun, because this was it—she was going to have to protect Brody right here, right now—but then Tiny Tim backed off and took them to the cellar, and things were okay.

At least as okay as they could get for the moment.

Now Maddie stood in the middle of the workshop, surrounded by the stone walls, commercial lighting, and all the top-of-the-line tools and equipment filling the place, feeling what was beginning to be the norm emotion for her today—panic.

She stared down at the huge metal table spread with several different drawings, all of the same design, a timeless, classical 18k gold, pearl, and gem pendant, the gem—a large sapphire—being the whole reason for this operation.

Beyond the worktable was another with parts laid out for her—18k yellow gold sheet, 18k yellow gold round wire, gold bezel, and the gems themselves—not the original sapphire but a most excellent replacement.

At her disposal were all the tools required, and Maddie took her first pause.

She was really going to have to do this.

She took in the goggles and face shield, the pin vises, hammers, ring clamps, the saws and files and pliers, the rest of the layout tools, and so much more and did her best not to take a big, obvious gulp.

"If you need anything," Tiny Tim said, jerking his head to a white telephone on the wall. "You know the drill. Just pick that up."

"I'll need food," Maddie said, doing her best Leena impersonation. "Good food. All fresh."

"I'd think being married would take the spoiled out of you."

"Think again. That is, if you can think."

Tiny Tim sighed.

"Don't forget, fresh."

"I told the boss to get Maddie for this one," Tiny Tim muttered. "I told him, sure, Maddie would just as soon rip your throat out as be nice to you, but at least she wasn't a princess. No one listens to me."

Maddie turned away from the tools to look at him with narrowed eyes. "Maddie hasn't been here in years."

"Damn shame, too. She was a lot less work than you. No offense," he said to Brody.

Maddie shook her head. She didn't remember this guy, not at all. But he clearly remembered her. She glanced at Brody, then at Tiny Tim again. "So you remember Maddie?"

"You know I do."

Careful. "How would I know?"

"Oh, like you don't remember how she'd crank her music late at night. It drove you crazy. You'd yell and scream, and she'd just stand on her balcony and stare at the sky for hours, that music blasting loud enough to rattle the windows." Tiny Tim smiled in fond memory. "With her light on behind her, we could see right through her pjs."

Maddie had to speak through clenched teeth. "And you know that because . . ."

"Because me and the guys would fight for space below on the pool deck."

Her stomach executed a triple gainer, and it took her a minute to speak. "Perverts."

He grinned broadly. "Ah, come on. Maddie knew. She had to know."

"She *didn't.*"

"She wanted us to watch."

"Are you kidding me?" She felt disgusted. Disgusting. Her fingers clenched on the hammer in front of her as a hot hatred filled her for this place and the people in it. "She was sixteen. A kid. Practically a baby—"

"Maddie was never a baby. She was always thinking, always trying to get a step ahead of the boss."

"Her uncle. Who should have been protecting her. Us," she added when his eyes narrowed in surprise. She was breaking her cover, and in that moment, she didn't care. She wanted to kill him.

Brody came close, slipped an arm around her. "Honey? You getting low blood sugar again?"

Honey. That broke her concentration, having Brody call her honey. "Yeah." God, she needed air. Or something. "Food."

Tiny Tim gave the martyr sigh again. "Same old demands."

Leena. You're Leena . . . Maddie needed to believe it. She also needed a grip, a big one, especially with Brody all ears, soaking up bunches of information that she hadn't wanted him to have.

Tiny Tim shrugged, apparently unconcerned about the hammer in her hand or the urge she had to smash it over his head. "Pretty damn ungrateful. Rick fed and clothed you both for years, kept a roof over your heads when he could have sent you away."

"There was no one to send us to."

"Exactly. He kept you out of the goodness of his heart. And that wasn't easy. You two were a handful, especially your sister. She was wild and out of control."

"She was *not* out of control."

"She required a strict hand."

There was a difference between a heavy hand and abuse, but she wasn't going there. Not with Brody suddenly looking ready to do some violence of his own. "I have work to do."

"Yeah." Carefully, Tiny Tim took the hammer out of her hand and set it down. "Maddie was most definitely different. She'd have had the balls to come at me with that thing. She had a set of cajones, that girl. Not to mention more curves on her bones than you." He looked her up and down. "Though that's changing a little bit now. Guess marriage is agreeing with you." He reached out to touch, and two things happened simultaneously: Brody straightened to attention, and Maddie smacked Tiny Tim's hand away herself.

"Don't touch," she said through her teeth.

"Married," Brody said through his.

With a last careless shrug, Tiny Tim left.

The tension didn't. In fact, the silence was oppressive. Pretending she didn't feel it, she pulled the stool out from beneath the worktable.

"Well, wasn't that a nice little walk down memory lane for you."

Not fooled for one instant by the calm cool in his voice, she sat at the stool and resisted setting her head down on the table and giving in to a moment of self-pity.

She didn't do self-pity.

Ever.

Spreading out the designs, she didn't look at him. She didn't need to in order to sense his escalating tension and anger. It was in his careful control of his every movement.

"You okay?" he asked.

Lifting her head, she met his gaze.

He'd asked the question softly, but she could tell he was doing his best not to tear something apart.

"Yes." She had no choice but to be okay. The two of them were locked in down here; she knew that without checking the door.

They'd remain here until Rick decided she'd done enough work for the time being, or maybe he wouldn't send anyone for them until she was completely finished.

Or maybe he'd figure out she wasn't Leena and he wouldn't come at all. Yeah, she was okay . . .

Except she wasn't. She was the opposite of okay, really, because she couldn't breathe and the walls were closing in on her.

Brody took a step toward her, but she held up a hand to ward him off.

Because she was fine.

Suffocating but fine.

"Fuck this," she heard as if from a great distance, and then two strong, warm arms slipped around her.

She closed her eyes. A silly defense, she knew. Silly, and pathetic, but she still couldn't breathe. "Brody?"

"Yeah?"

"Promise you won't say I told you so."

"Why would I say that?"

"Because I'm going to say something." She set her head on his chest. "I'm glad you're here."

Cupping her jaw, he tilted it up to his, and then those pewter eyes were holding hers, his fierce and determined. "I won't throw that back in your face until this is over."

"Fair enough."

"You're not breathing."

"Trying."

"Try harder."

She did, and he waited patiently, nodding when she managed. "Okay, then. Let's get this over with."

It was exactly what she needed. If he'd given any more sympathy or worse yet, pity, she'd have probably fallen apart.

And he knew it.

Knew her.

God, she could really fall for him.

Damn it.

Slapping his hands away, she stepped back and faced the table. She had work to do.

And a plan to get back to.

If she ever found Leena, that is . . .

"You can do this."

Yeah. He stood just behind her, so strong and sure.

So capable.

Fitting so effortlessly into her life the past two days. Walking away from him was going to be the hardest thing she'd ever done. But she'd face that when she got there. With new resolve, she reached for the bezel and gold sheet and got to work.

Chapter 21

Wearing goggles and a thick apron, Maddie hunched over that worktable for four hours, and for most of that time, Brody watched her, stunned by the amount of work involved in creating a piece of jewelry.

About an hour in, Tiny Tim brought a tray of fancy finger sandwiches that were nothing but a bite each.

He'd have rather had McDonald's.

"Trust me," Maddie told him at one point, the goggles magnifying her baby blues to huge proportions. "This really shouldn't be taking this long."

Meaning Leena could have done it faster. But certainly not better for Maddie paid excruciating attention to detail, and he supposed she had to. It had to look professional. Better than professional.

It had to look designer.

Brody didn't envy her the job, but he sure as hell wished he could help because he was not used to standing around with nothing to do but worry.

"Nearly there," Maddie told him. "I just have to solder the bezel and ornamental border onto the gold sheet." When she'd done that, she reached for a small handheld saw. "And cut around the border so the edges aren't visible from the front."

She tapered the backing sheet so that it flowed smoothly into the round wire border. "The stone is translucent," she murmured, head bent over her work, goggles in place, tongue caught between her teeth in concentration, "so the light can enter the stone from behind." She stopped and shook her head at herself as if surprised to find she'd remembered more than she'd thought.

"You ever think about cutting some corners?" *And speeding this process up?* he continued to himself.

She tipped her goggles up to her forehead and slanted him a look. Her shiny auburn hair was standing straight up above the oversized, thick goggles, and there was just something about the way she sat there looking like a tech geek that revved his engines.

Unbelievable, but even here in the middle of deep shit trouble, she did him in.

"You can't cut corners," she said.

He arched a brow, implying that yeah, she could, and maybe she should. After all, maybe if she did some shoddy work, Rick's little game would be exposed. And how in the hell that would be a bad thing was beyond him. Leena would be incriminated, but surely, she could come up with some sort of a plea that the law would buy.

And yet he could tell by the look on Maddie's face that it wasn't a gamble she was willing to take.

Finally, Maddie stepped back from the worktable and dusted off her hands. She stood there a moment and let out a long breath, then moved to the white telephone on the wall. "Done," she said into it and hung up.

Tiny Tim showed up in less than five minutes.

"Charter boat," Maddie said. "Now."

Tiny Tim shook his head. "Wind's up. Got an advisory. The boat'll be here at seven AM but not before."

That was not good news.

They were led back to Leena's room, with Brody sticking

tight to Maddie, his hand on the small of her back. She shot him a look, but he didn't give a shit. Until they were out of here, and by that, he meant off this fucking island and back on the continental US of A, he was peanut butter to her jelly.

Because no way in hell was he giving anyone another chance to touch her, feel her up, or so much as insinuate violence.

He was done with all of it. Done with pretending to be quiet and meek, done with pretending not to care when people leered at her, done with pretending not to know that this entire compound was filled with criminals. Bullshit, all of it, and he was getting her out before anything happened.

As they crossed the main living room toward the stairs, they saw Rick sitting on an artful but probably incredibly uncomfortable love seat with a woman on either side of him. All three were in bathing suits, holding drinks, laughing.

Rick's gaze landed on Maddie, though he didn't say a word to her.

Nor she to him. At least not with her mouth, but her eyes said plenty. Mostly *I hate you* and *die a slow painful death*.

Rick smiled.

And Brody actually shivered. Jesus, this place was really creeping him out, and he hadn't spent his first sixteen years here. He could only imagine what it was doing to Maddie and how she felt.

When they were alone in Leena's bedroom, Maddie went directly toward the bathroom, kicking off first one boot, hopping on her bare foot to pull off the other, making sure the knife stayed hidden. Reaching in, she grabbed the knife, letting the boot drop, moving with great purpose.

"What are you doing?"

Ignoring the question, she slid off her myriad of silver bracelets, leaving them on the dresser by the bathroom door.

"Hello?"

She didn't even look at him.

"Goddamnit." He grabbed her arm just as she would have slammed the bathroom door on his nose. Pulling her around to face him, he looked into her eyes and found the answer to his unspoken question. No. She was not okay.

She pulled free, and he let her because he was not interested in a wrestle session. At least not unless they were off this island and naked.

Very naked.

Without a word, she walked into the bathroom and once again, turned on the shower and the sink and flushed the toilet. She pulled off her necklace. "I'm taking a shower."

Okay. He could understand that. Except . . . "I thought there's a chance we're being watched."

"Not in the bathrooms." She ripped off her top, then leaned in to whisper in his ear. "You should know, I have plans for tonight."

Her words didn't register for several heart-stopping seconds due to the fact that she was wearing a bright pink bra edged in black silk, complete with a bow between her breasts, breasts that were full and creamy smooth, threatening to spill out with her every movement as she reached up to pin her hair on top of her head.

"It shouldn't take long," she added.

Since most of his brain cells had ceased to function, he was definitely working with less than a full deck. "What shouldn't?"

Her hands went to the button on the waistband of her skirt. "I'll show you later."

"Now's better."

She looked at him as if he was a very stupid man, then put her mouth back to his ear. "I'm going to break into Rick's office and try to get proof of his illegal activities to take with us in the morning."

Christ, that was a spectacularly dangerous idea. He hated this. Well, he loved the stripping part, especially how that gorgeous, willowy, curvy bod was shimmying out of that skirt, but hated everything else. "Maddie."

She dropped her skirt.

His jaw nearly fell as well. It made no sense—he'd already seen her naked. Hell, he'd kissed every inch of her naked, and yet here he stood, rooted to the spot, instantly galvanized by the sight of her in her underwear like he was a horny teenager who'd never gotten lucky except by his own fist.

Her panties were little boy-cut shorty shorts, matched the bra, and like everything else about her, just about did him in. Low on her hips and cut to a deep V in front, they dipped low enough to give him heart failure, and that was before she turned her back on him to check the water temperature, bending over the tub to do so, revealing the back, which rode up so high that half of that gorgeous, mouthwatering ass was revealed in all its perfection.

And she was perfection. His secret fantasy. Actually, maybe not so secret as he stood there probably drooling and most definitely hard enough to strain the button fly on his jeans. He pulled her in close under the guise of wanting to kiss her. "Let's just get out of here in one piece."

"There's no boat until morning anyway. Now move. I have to get this off me."

Nothing marred her skin except the surgery scar across her shoulder. Nothing but creamy, smooth skin and long, sleek toned muscles, all put together in the most feminine, sexy package he'd ever seen. "What off you?"

"The ickiness." She reached up and unhooked her bra, letting it fall to the floor. Turning to face the water, she stuck her thumbs into the sides of her panties and slid them down as well.

And whatever brain cells he'd managed to retain went *crack, snap, pop* and promptly fried themselves.

Oblivious, she stepped into the shower and grabbed the soap, which she proceeded to rub between her hands and then briskly spread over her body. Up and down her legs, her arms, her belly, ribs, and those perfect breasts. Leaning in, he whispered, "Snooping could get us killed."

"No." She whispered, too, so low he had to stay close, getting wet. "He needs me. Well, me as Leena. He won't kill her."

Since he could think of several things—*hundreds* of things— that could be just as bad as not killed, this wasn't exactly a comfort.

She was still vigorously rubbing that soap over herself as if she really could eradicate whatever memories were torturing her by skinning herself alive. Admittedly mesmerized by the sight of that gorgeous flesh all wet and soapy, he had to shake that off. "Your skin is getting red."

She didn't stop. The solution was simple enough. Kicking off his shoes, he tugged off his shirt and shucked his pants.

All for the cause.

She looked up again when he stepped into the shower with her, her gaze taking him in, slowing in the region of his chest, his abs, and then a little lower, which stroked his ego.

Water sluiced over the both of them, blessedly hot and hard enough to pound away some of the stress of the day. She scooted back to give him some room but that's not what he wanted, not when she was shiny and slicked up, bubbles and water pouring over those breasts, down her belly, between her legs.

He wanted to be between those legs. Wanted to feel, wanted to look, wanted to taste—

"Not here," she said, reminding him of where they were.

Yeah. He didn't want to taint what they had with this place either. Instead, he drew her in, kissing her softly as he took the soap out of her hands.

Maddie looked into his eyes for a long moment, the water raining down over them, and Brody would have sworn he was looking right into her heart and soul, the moment so real and deep it was almost as good as sex would have been.

* * *

Brody came instantly awake in the dark when the warm, soft body wrapped in his arms tried to slip away all stealthlike. He had to give her credit—she was good, wriggling down his torso with hardly any movement at all, just a whisper of the sheets, but he was better than good.

He'd always slept extremely lightly, especially in places he hated, and Stone Cay with all its opulence and riches topped his list. He let her nearly make her escape and then tightened his arms on her.

She went still as stone.

He waited and was rewarded when she lifted her head and met his gaze in the dark.

"You're up," she said.

Instead of answering, he slid his hands down her back, cupped her extremely cuppable ass, then went for her thighs, pulling them up to his hips so that she straddled him. From there, he gave a slight rock of his pelvis.

Her gasp revealed that she understood he was indeed . . . up.

Very up.

"I have to go," she said.

Right. Clearly, it was time for the breaking and entering portion of their evening. But it didn't escape his notice that she didn't move away.

"Really have to go—"

He kissed her, then pulled back. "*We* have to go," he corrected, and with a fond sigh for the long life he might have lived if not for this stupid plan, he got out of bed with her.

Chapter 22

Leena and Ben were taken to the airport. Saul manhandled Leena onto Rick's Cessna, then gave her a hard shove into her seat. When he left her there alone for the first time since she'd stepped foot into Ben's gallery, she hurriedly reached into her pocket for Maddie's phone and turned it on, quickly reading through the texts Maddie had sent until she understood exactly what was going on.

Maddie thought Leena had gone to Stone Cay, and believing that, she'd raced after her to protect her. Because that's what Maddie did, protect Leena. Only now, because of it, her life was in jeopardy.

And so was Leena's.

There was only one thing to do. Besides panic, that is. She somehow needed to make sure Ed and Saul continued to believe she was Maddie. It was the only way. Otherwise, Rick would hear about it from Saul and Ed, and he might hurt the real Maddie.

Head spinning, Leena put the cell phone back in her pocket. Wave after wave of guilt crashed over her, but before she could drown in it, Ben received the same treatment she'd gotten and fell into the seat next to her.

Then they were alone in the back of the plane. Just outside,

she could hear Ed and Saul talking amongst themselves, waiting for their pilot.

And though she didn't want to—God, she so didn't want to
see his hatred—she glanced over at Ben.

Eyes narrowed, jaw tight, he was looking out the window.
Even furious and slightly roughed up as he was, he was still
the best-looking man she'd ever met.

And soon, thanks to her, he was going to be the best-looking
dead man she'd ever met. "Ben."

His gaze slid her way. His mouth was bleeding, and he already had a bruise forming alongside his jaw. He hadn't come
easily, and she wanted to cry. This was her fault. All her fault . . .
"I'm sorry," she whispered. "So damn sorry to get you into this
mess."

"What mess is it exactly?"

Oh, God. She'd wondered how long it would take him to
ask. "It doesn't matter. But I'll get you out of it, I swear."

His scathing look said he doubted that. "Why are they calling you Maddie?"

"Maddie's my twin sister."

"And they think you're her?"

She looked at the opened door, but no one was paying them
any attention. "Yes, and pretending to be her is very important, so you have to be sure not to call me Leena."

He was quiet a moment, his eyes focused on her while he
considered that. "Why?"

"It's complicated."

"Try me."

"Being Maddie right now is keeping me from being dead."

"Why would they want you dead? You're invaluable to their
operation, to the swindling of their clients."

Regret and sorrow for what she'd done to him nearly strangled her. She hated that he thought that of her. "They don't
want me dead, but my sister, who is pretending to be me."

"Clear as mud."

"I know. Ben, I'm sorry. I'm so damned sorry. I was just trying to fix things, and I made it all worse."

He just looked at her, so furious, so absolutely heartbreakingly
gorgeous. "Seems easy enough to fix things," he said, sounding very Irish. "You just change employers."

"Yes. Except Rick . . . doesn't like the idea of me leaving
very much."

He processed that a moment. "So what does Maddie have
to do with this? Does she do what you do?"

"No. She left Stone Cay a long time ago and never looked
back. Until . . ." Her throat tightened so that she could barely
speak. "Until she thought I was in danger there, and then she
came running." *God.* "This is all my fault, and I have to fix
it."

"How are you going to do that?"

"I don't know. I wasn't going to go back there. Not ever
again. I was going on the run, but I decided to make a stop first.
To you," she whispered when he just looked at her. "I had to
try to make you understand. But now, Maddie . . ." Finishing
the thought nearly killed her. "She's in danger."

"I still don't get why you came to me."

At that, she opened her eyes and looked into his quietly intelligent gaze. "I—"

"*Hey!*" Saul stuck his head in the plane and pointed at
them. "You two! Shut up!"

Their pilot climbed in then and started the plane. Leena
looked at Ben, but he'd turned back to the window, her answer not important.

Brody followed Maddie down the dark stairs of the big
house. It was two in the morning and felt like it. After the long
flight last night, their off-the-charts sex for several hours, then
the stress of watching Maddie go through her own personal
hell of being back here, he could hardly move.

Not Maddie. She'd dressed all in black—black jeans, black

form-fitting, long-sleeved top, black boots with that knife in one of them.

His own kick-ass Bond girl.

She'd wanted him to stay in the room, and he'd told her over his dead body. He still couldn't get over her trying to protect him. *He* was protecting *her*. She just hadn't gotten that part yet. He watched her turn a corner and followed, admitting to himself that she might never get it. Other than when she was naked, that is. Then she seemed to get him just fine.

In any case, she was certainly in no hurry to let him inside her head or to reveal any more of herself to him than she had to.

Which had always been his own MO when it came to women, so why the hell he was brooding about it was beyond him. He should be wanting to get back to that no touch policy, but actually, that was the furthest thing from his mind.

The hallway was completely dark, so much so that he had to stop because he couldn't even see a hand in front of his face. Then suddenly, Maddie's fingers wrapped around his wrist and tugged. He heard a door quietly shut, and then a flashlight came on, flickering over a huge room decorated in the same lavish over-the-top style as the rest of the house.

"Rick's office," she said. "I'll make it quick."

Yeah. And hopefully, they'd not run into any watchdogs in the form of six-foot men with no necks who'd taken too many steroids.

"Look." She flicked her light around the room, pausing at the large desk, upon which sat a laptop. "Maybe that's Leena's."

"Seems too easy."

"Yeah, but—*what the hell?*"

Something in her voice told him it was bad, and when he looked, it was confirmed.

It *was* bad.

Behind him, on the far wall of Rick's office, sat a bank of monitors. Security monitors, all in black and white. There were exterior shots, presumably showing all the entrances and exits of the compound, and then there were the interior monitors, some from downstairs reviewing various rooms such as the den and living room and along the hallway. There were the stairs, the upstairs hallway, and every room along it, including . . . ah, *fuck* . . . Leena's bedroom.

And bathroom.

The shower was empty now, and off, but it'd been neither a little while ago, and even as he thought it, Maddie's fingers started tapping on the computer beneath the bank of the monitors. "Ten years ago, there weren't monitors in the bathrooms," she said.

"That seems to have changed," he said, sounding perfectly calm but actually perfectly pissed.

"Yeah." Her voice was grim as her fingers worked, and then suddenly, the bathroom monitor flickered and changed.

Rewound.

And yeah, there it was—him in the shower with Maddie, standing face to face with her beneath the water. Their mouths were moving, but all that could be heard was the rush of the water, none of their words. Good to know that plan worked. He had his back to the camera, naked and wet, bare ass and everything.

Brody remembered that part distinctly because it was where Maddie had told him "not here." At the time, it'd been hot as hell, standing there with a soapy woman, and under any other circumstances, even just watching would also still be hot as hell.

But this . . . this was an outrageous invasion of privacy, and the thought of anyone else's eyes seeing it filled him with fury.

Not a new feeling for him here on Stone Cay.

The movie kept playing, probably because Maddie stood there, finger on the keypad, as stunned as he.

On the monitor, he hugged her to him. He watched her arms go around his shoulders, grip him tight, then gently push him away.

Then his black and white self brilliantly shifted to expose

Maddie full frontal, her gorgeous face tilted up, eyes closed as the water ran over her.

Needing to rip the monitor off the wall, he stepped forward, but Maddie reached out and slapped a hand to his chest, holding him back, her gaze still glued to the screen.

Reluctantly, he once again watched, struck by his black and white expression—he was looking at Maddie with everything in his eyes.

Just seeing it brought it back, how he'd felt in that moment. Apparently for her, too, because next to him she swore, and with a tap of her fingers, the images were gone.

There was a beat of silence.

"I should have known. I'm sorry, Brody. I'm deleting the whole thing." She said this tightly as her fingers moved swiftly over the keyboard. "The entire night. Hold on."

He was clenching his jaw so tight he was surprised his teeth didn't shatter, but then all the monitors went blank, and she smiled grimly. "Look at that—there's been a little mishap. Okay, a major one. All the security monitors are down."

"For how long?"

"I'm thinking until they can get a tech here to fix it, which means a boat, which means it won't be until after we're gone. But there's no guarantee." She reached for the laptop. "I'll be quick."

Brody paced behind her, one ear cocked for the slightest sound, his gut twisted with stress and the need to protect this woman at any cost.

"There's nothing here," she said after a moment, sounding bitterly disappointed. "Nothing I can take with me."

"Shut it down then; we're done."

"Yes," she said, agreeing with him for once, though the victory felt hollow because she was quiet, too quiet, which meant he had to rein in his own urge to go postal. If she was going to be coolheaded and calm, then fuck it, he'd be coolheaded and calm, too. Being taped while in the shower? No sweat. He wasn't even going to blink.

Hardest thing he'd ever done.

"You look all calm," she said. "But I know you've got to be just as pissed off as I am."

That she knew him, that she'd admit it completely disarmed him for a moment. Disarmed and charmed. "Yes." He let out a breath. "Very."

"I'm not sure what to do now."

This admission was even bigger, and he reached for her hand. "We can't leave until dawn."

"No."

"Then I think you know exactly what you want to do next."

"Yeah. I know you think it's stupid to search, but . . ."

He hated buts. Unless it was her *butt*. Her bare butt—

"But I have to get some proof of Rick's activities. If I don't and he follows through with his threats, it won't be Leena going to jail." She let out a breath. "It'll be me."

"For what?" he asked in disbelief.

"If I tell you, this conversation is going to deteriorate pretty quickly." She turned away. "In fact, your feelings for me are going to deteriorate pretty quickly."

"Not possible," he said flatly, turning her back to him. If she thought she'd be going to jail for killing Rick, then no way because *he* was going to be the one to do it. "Tell me."

She let out another long breath. "Leena didn't kill Manny. I did." And with that, she headed to the door.

Maddie got as far as reaching for the door handle before Brody managed to grab her hand and halt her progress.

She couldn't blame him—she'd just dropped quite a bomb. She'd hoped to never have to tell him about killing Manny. She'd hoped to never have to tell anyone.

Brody just stared at her, the air weighted with his disbelief and shock. "What did you say?"

"I killed Manny."

"Come on." He didn't want to believe her. "Seriously?"

"Yeah, seriously." He probably hadn't slept with very many murderers. She understood that, too. He wanted answers; of course, he wanted answers. He might have grown up rough, but he had morals and values, and right about now, he had to be wondering at hers.

She'd wondered herself, many times. She *had* killed Manny. Nothing could change that, not more time and certainly not discussing it, so she went to move away again, but he caught her arm.

"Wait." Backing her to the door, he cupped her face, tilting it up to look into his.

She put her hands on his wrists to tug clear of him but somehow ended up holding on because he felt like the only steady thing in a world gone a little crazy. "Searching," she said. "We're supposed to be—"

"In a minute. Tell me about Manny. Leena was dating him?"

"She liked him. As in she was sixteen and she had a sixteen-year-old silly crush on a twenty-two-year-old thug."

"Let me guess. And he took advantage."

Clearly, he'd been here on Stone Cay long enough today to know what kind of men they were dealing with. "On our sixteenth birthday, he brought her wildflowers, and she liked that so she kissed him. On the cheek. Thinking that was a come-on, he kissed her back. She liked that, too, and that night, she left her bedroom door unlocked so he could come up. She just wanted more kisses, not thinking about the fact that he'd expect more than that."

Brody let out a breath. "I'm not going to like the rest of this story, am I?"

"When Leena said no more, Manny didn't want to stop."

"Yeah, I was right," he said tightly. "I'm not going to like this story at all."

"He got a little rough, so she ran out of her bedroom to the top of the stairs, looking for me. She was crying, and her night-gown was ripped, and I—" Maddie shook her head, remembering it so clearly she could still taste the tropical rain that had been on the air that night, still smell the scent of blood.

Manny's blood.

"He was going to rape her." She remembered the feel of the kitchen knife in her hand, how easily she'd gripped it, how it had felt watching Manny turn to her when she'd called his name. "I'm not sorry. In fact, I'd do it again if I had to; I'd kill him all over again—"

"Shh," Brody said and yanked her close, hugging her tight. "Don't say it. Not here."

In his voice was fear, for her, and she nearly broke right then. "I have to get proof, Brody."

"Yeah, we do. Would Leena have kept a laptop in her workshop?"

"Maybe. I didn't think to look before."

"Let's look now."

Let's.

That was a word she hadn't used often, or accepted, but the sound of it right now was like a balm to her bruised soul. "You should wait here. You don't have to—" She broke off at the look on his face, fierce yet solid.

No, he didn't have to do anything, but he was coming with her regardless.

"We'll need a cover in case we're caught," she said.

"We're on our honeymoon. Honeymooners like to do it in every room." He accompanied this with an extremely husband-to-wife look that made her knees wobble.

Pretend. They were pretending to be on their honeymoon.

They didn't run into anyone, for which she was grateful, but they did find the workroom locked.

Maddie pulled a set of keys from her pocket.

Brody just stared at her. "How did—"

"Stole them from Rick's office. I know. I'm going straight to hell."

"Are you kidding?" He pressed his mouth to her temple. "You're an angel."

Well, that was a new one. She'd been called many things, but an angel? Never, and it seemed that every minute that they were together was only making it all the harder to remember that they had a good-bye coming, a big one.

The far wall of the workshop housed a floor-to-ceiling shelving unit filled with things that had given Leena inspiration over the years: books, boxes of cosmetic jewelry, stacks of pictures . . .

"Your sister's a pack rat." Brody came up behind her, his hands settling on her waist. "You doing okay?"

She nodded even though she wasn't, not by a long shot.

He rubbed his jaw to hers. "You're not breathing again."

No. Not breathing. There wasn't time for breathing. Knowing it, she dropped her forehead to a shelf and absorbed the feeling of him pressing up against her from behind.

That was nice, very nice, but she still wasn't going to breathe easy until she got them both out of here—

A sound came from the other side of the door, and she jerked upright. "Did you hear that?"

Behind her, Brody went still as stone. "Shh," he breathed softly.

It came again.

Oh, God.

There was no lock on their side of that door, so they hadn't been able to generate privacy for this little B&E mission, but Maddie had her own wits for protection, not to mention the knife in her boot and the gun she'd taken from her purse and stuck in her waistband.

They were a second away from being discovered, which was a hell of a time to realize that Brody's brilliant idea of saying that they'd taken the honeymoon mobile didn't seem too brilliant.

Not when they were both still fully dressed. "Your shirt," she hissed. "Give me your shirt!"

While he tugged it over his head, she yanked on the sleeve of her own shirt, revealing a bare shoulder and nearly a breast in her haste to make it look like they were in the throes of passion.

That was as far as she got before the door handle slowly turned.

Chapter 23

Too late for panic, Maddie knew, painfully aware of the door creaking open. With her life passing before her eyes, and Brody's, too, with his hard thighs pressed to the backs of hers, she struggled to look turned on, completely in the moment, because that's what honeymooners did, right? They had wild animal sex everywhere, never in a bed, so it should seem rational that they'd be down here at her workstation, jumping each other's bones.

Or so she hoped.

All they had to do was make it look good, real good. Turning her head, she sought Brody's mouth with hers, sliding her tongue into his open mouth, absorbing his murmur of surprise while arching back against him, rocking her bottom to his crotch.

As the door opened, Brody's hands dropped from his waist to her hips, squeezing gently before one hand slid to her belly, his fingertips spread so wide they nearly touched the undersides of her breasts.

Not good enough because someone was watching, maybe trying to decide if they should be brought to Rick . . .

"Here," she panted, trying to sound sexy in her panic, but sounding more like a porno queen, and a bad one at that. She arched her throat so that the back of her head was cushioned in the meat of his shoulder. The movement arched her back, too, filling his hand with her breast as she ground her bottom into his crotch. "Yeah, oh yeah, just like that . . . Brody, baby, tell me you have a condom in your pocket."

Voice low and husky, he nipped at her jaw. "For you, baby, I've got anything you want."

Acting. They were acting. Trying to prove they were so hot for each other that they'd left her bedroom to make it somewhere else, maybe a whole bunch of somewhere elses, just because they could. She knew it, so why did her nipples harden? "This room makes what?" she asked breathlessly. "Room number three?"

"Don't forget the bathroom."

Where they hadn't been acting . . . "Right. Four. You're such a stud."

The sound he made might have been a snort. Turning her head, she nipped his jaw. *Don't make me laugh.*

His hands tightened on her. "Maybe the kitchen next," he murmured. "There are utensils in there for all sorts of things, especially bad girls like yourself."

Funny. Wasn't he so funny?

Were they still being watched? She didn't dare look. "You don't need utensils. You've got all I need, baby."

"Do I now?"

"Yeah." And he had all she could ever need now.

His gaze slid briefly to the door, then back to her, filled with such fierce protection and anger that she knew that yeah, they were still being watched. Worse, she knew that if anyone caught that look on his face, they'd know he was capable of being a huge threat, so she hooked an arm around his neck and tugged his face down to hers, taking his mouth with hers to keep his expression hidden.

Anything to keep him safe, even if it meant kissing him, and kissing him . . . which of course, was no sacrifice at all because man, the guy could kiss . . . long and deep and hot, and the feel of his tongue dancing to hers was making her wish they were alone, back at her place or anywhere other than here.

How long could they do this? And what would happen if they stopped? Not willing to take the chance, she let the show go on. The Brody and Leena Show. "Here," she whispered huskily—a tone she didn't have to fake—and bent forward over the desk, shooting him a come-get-me smile over her shoulder, using the excuse to peek at the door.

Yeah. Still a big, beefy shadow standing there.

Eyes smoldering with temper, and also a heat that stirred her up pretty good, Brody wrapped himself around her, using his free hand to swipe the desk free of the tools in front of her. They clattered to the floor, and as a gesture, even a pretend gesture, it made her knees weak. If only they didn't have an audience. If only he could unzip his pants, pull down hers, and push into her—

God. It definitely was no hardship pretending to be lost in the throes. Brody had kept her completely covered, but opening his mouth over hers, he let his thumb come up and over her nipple, back and forth.

God, she wanted this to be real. *Needed* it to be real. "Brody—I can't stand." To prove it, her knees buckled.

He slid down to the floor with her, out of sight of the door. Heart pounding in her ears from adrenaline, fear, and a lot more, she gripped onto him and put her mouth to his. "Are we alone?"

He took a peek. "Yeah." Sinking all the way to the ground, he leaned against a leg of the desk. "Jesus," he breathed and then again, more softly, shoving his hair back with hands that weren't quite steady. "Stud?"

"*Utensils?*"

He managed a smile, but it was fleeting.

Her hands weren't any steadier than his as she righted her clothes, her body still hot and sweaty and definitely on overdrive. "That was close. And I'm all hot and bothered. I need another shower."

"Too bad. You're not taking one until we're out of this fucking *Alice in Wonderland* nightmare."

And once they were, she'd be busy finding her sister. Following the grand Plan.

He was watching her carefully. "What?"

"Nothing."

"Oh, there's something. Spill it. You don't see us taking this thing back with us to Sky High?"

Yeah. Yeah, she did. That was the problem. But it wasn't going to happen, unfortunately.

"What was your original plan, before you and your sister got your signals crossed?"

"Brody—"

"Ah, Christ. Tell me you weren't going to just run away." He stared at her. "You were." He pushed to his feet, staring down at her. "You were just going to leave your place, your job, the people in your life. Shayne, Noah . . ."

Him.

But he didn't say that; he just shook his head in disbelief. "Come on." Turning back to the room, he began searching again.

She got to her feet and joined him. They worked in silence, and as they decided a few minutes later, in vain.

Defeated, they left the workroom. Not stopping at the kitchen, utensils or otherwise, they headed straight for Leena's room.

Maddie had no idea if the surveillance cameras were back up and running, but knowing it was a possibility, she didn't say a word. Didn't have any words to say anyway.

But it was nearly dawn now. They could go to meet their charter boat for their ride to Nassau.

"Get your things," Brody said. "We're getting out of here."

When she didn't respond, he tugged her close, bending a little to look directly into her eyes, his own a little hot, undoubtedly because she'd failed to tell him about her plan.

"We're leaving," he repeated very softly but with unbendable steel in his voice. "We'll find another way to deal with what we need to deal with."

"Brody—"

"No, I mean it. I'll help you find another way; you're just going to have to try something new and trust me."

Trust him. A promise that just might be even more terrifying than anything she'd faced so far, and that was saying something.

Brody didn't take a deep breath until they'd set foot down on Nassau's shores. He took Maddie directly to a huge, luxurious five-star resort, not even wincing when he handed over his credit card to be abused because he wanted that look of failure off of her face yesterday.

Then, and only then, could he deal with how furious he was at what she and Leena had planned to do.

Maddie stood in the center of the lobby looking out the huge windows toward the ocean as he waited for their room key, and when he got it, he walked up to her.

"I can't believe Rick actually let us go," she said.

Brody either. "At least you've given your sister a head start. Rick won't need her again for a while."

"Hmm," she said noncommittally and followed him to the elevator. "Why are we staying here?"

"You said you wanted to take a shower."

She stared at him. "Are you telling me you just paid nearly a thousand dollars for a five-star suite so that I could take a shower?"

"Yeah."

She just stared at him some more as if maybe he was the best thing since sliced bread, so he moved in close, lifting a hand to her jaw. With his thumb, he stroked her skin, not liking how pale she seemed or the purple bruises beneath her eyes. "Let's call it a present. From me to you. Okay?"

"I want to give you a present, too."

"Yeah? Then abandon your plan. That could be a great present. The best present. The king of all presents ever."

They got off the elevator to walk to their spacious, gorgeous room. Maddie checked her cell phone for at least the hundredth time, waiting fruitlessly for a call from Leena. Then she looked at Brody.

The despair in her gaze killed him, and he discovered standing there, exhausted himself, feeling more than a little raw and unsettled, he needed to touch more than her face, so he pulled her into his arms.

"I could have gotten you killed," she whispered.

"But you didn't. I'm still very much alive and well."

That she even allowed his hug told him more about her mental state than anything she might have said. She simply wrapped her arms around his waist and set her head against his chest with a long, shuddery sigh. "Brody." It did something to him, her holding on to him. It cut through all the uncertainty of his feelings for her, the ones he'd simply set aside rather than face, and told him the truth.

He had it bad for her. Caressing her back, he felt her willowy body curl into his like a heat-seeking missile as she let out another long breath.

How could she walk away from this?

"I'm afraid it's not over," she whispered.

Yeah. Him, too. He was afraid it'd never be over between them. And he was afraid that was okay. Really okay.

"Rick isn't going to ever let it go."

Right. Rick. Not him. Got it. Staring grimly over her head out the picture window that revealed the gorgeous day in the making, the ocean dotted with whitecaps and sailboats, he waited until he could speak evenly. "It'll be over soon enough."

He'd see to it.

"I didn't want you to come here with me."

"Yeah. You've mentioned that a time or two."

"I didn't want you to see any of my past."

He understood that, too. What he didn't understand was how such an amazing woman had come out of those circumstances, and at age sixteen. She hadn't said; she'd been careful not to say, but he could only imagine what it had been like for her growing up under the care of Rick Stone.

It had to have been pure hell. Knowing it, picturing it made him want to go back there and do something about it. Even thinking about doing it gave him a rush of satisfaction that faded when Maddie let out another of those sighs that seemed to reach right in and grab him by the throat and not let go.

"I want Leena to be safe," she said. "But I don't think she is. I just feel like she's in danger."

"We'll find her. Back at Sky High, we'll use all our resources, and we'll find her."

She nodded but didn't say anything.

She'd made plans to walk away . . . He was still having a helluva time processing that. But they'd been together now, both in bed and out of it, and things had changed. At least for him. Just standing there holding her, feeling her face burrow into the crook of his neck so that her lips were touching his skin, made him ache.

And also hard.

Nice show of self-control. But when it came to her, he had none. Knowing it, he let his mouth brush her temple. He told himself he was offering comfort and nothing more and managed to keep his hands light and easy on her back to prove it. That was him. Light and soothing.

But then she slid her hands beneath his shirt, putting her chilled fingers against his heated flesh, digging into the muscles of his back as if he was her anchor.

Feeling distinctly unsoothed, he got a little harder.

Clearly feeling his reaction, she pressed more fully against him, her breasts to his chest, her thighs to his, going for more of that comfort he told himself he was offering. God knew, she

probably needed it. Hell, after the past twenty-four hours, *he*
needed it, the simple comfort of knowing she was okay and
safe and out of harm's way.

This hug, that would do it. Yes sirree, that was all he was
going to do. Keep hugging her.

"Brody," she whispered in a sort of breathy tone, shooting
his comforting theory all to hell.

"Yeah?"

"You're . . . strange."

"Um, thanks?"

"No. I mean . . ." She hesitated. "This is strange."

"Actually, it happens every time you touch me."

"I don't mean that—" She actually laughed. "I like *that*."
Okay, good. That was good.

"I mean you make me feel . . . soft."

He stroked her skin. "You are soft."

"Yeah, only with you." She said this with marvel. "Brody?"
"Yeah?"

"Is that shower in there big enough for two?"

"For a grand, it sure as hell better be."

That choked another laugh out of her, chasing more of that
haunted misery from her eyes, and he smiled in relief, in affection, in . . . hell, so goddamn much he couldn't even begin
to name all the emotions coursing through him.

She couldn't possibly walk away, not now . . .

"Do we really have time before we fly back to Sky High?"
Her hands came around his sides, his ribs, sliding up to his
chest, bringing his shirt with them. "I know how you are about
time." When she got the hem of his shirt up past his pecs, she
leaned in and pressed her lips over his heart.

Killing him . . .

"Brody?"

"We have time," he managed as she opened her mouth and
flicked her tongue over his nipple. "When getting naked with
the woman of your dreams is on the table, there's always time."

Her breath huffed against his skin. "I'm the woman of your dreams?"

"Dreams. Nightmares. Pick one."

She laughed again, and the sound was so sweet he buried his face in her hair. "Listen, I've never really been much for worrying about other people's feelings . . ."

"No," she agreed, still kissing his chest, making her way over his collarbone.

"But you've had a rough night and—"

"Yeah." Lifting her head, she locked gazes with him. "So?"

"So maybe this isn't what you need."

"It's exactly what I need." She pushed him until his hands fell from her. Another push had the back of his legs hitting the high mattress of the bed, piled with that luxurious thousand-dollar-a-night bedding.

One last push, and he fell back, and then she was crawling up his body and he couldn't remember what he'd been about to say, not when she pulled off her clothes and then his and not when she straddled him.

Gripping her hips, he thrust up into her, his body already so tight he knew it was going to be over before they started if he didn't slow her down. "Maddie—"

"If you say you want to go slow, I'm going to hurt you."

He let out a half laugh, half groan, but it backed up in his throat at the look on her face. Stark need, and a good amount of desperation. She needed to lose herself, if only for a minute.

A fast minute, apparently.

She needed him. He'd never been needed by anyone a day in his entire life, and he realized something else—he liked it.

Grabbing his hands in hers, she entwined their fingers and bent over him. "No."

"I didn't say anything."

"No to anything but this."

Yeah, he was okay with that. Arching up, he caught her mouth with his. He let her take him fast and hard, and only when she'd burst beautifully all over him, did he make his move.

"What are you doing?" she gasped as he rolled.

Still inside her, he tucked her beneath him. "Guess."

She gripped him tight. "Again?"

"Yeah."

"Oh, God." Her breath caught in her throat with an audible click. "Brody . . ."

He loved the way she said his name. He really did. Loved the way she looked at him as if he was doing it for her, as if he was the only one who could do it for her.

"What do you suppose it says about us that the only place we get along is in the sack?" she asked breathlessly.

"It says that we should stay in the sack."

She let out a short laugh and arched into him. "Okay, but—"

"If you say you want to go fast, I'm going to hurt you . . ."

"You won't. You won't ever hurt me."

And wasn't that the bottom line, and his own truth. His lips a breath from hers, he shook his head, then kissed her softly. "No, I won't. I'll never hurt you, Maddie."

She opened her mouth to say something to that, maybe something sharp and just a little mean as she tended to do when he got beneath her skin, but he kissed her again and began to move with a slow, achingly perfect rhythm until they were both breathless, panting for air, gazes locked on each other with a blistering intensity such as he'd never known . . .

"I can't believe . . ." She sounded so sincerely baffled. "I don't get it . . ."

Neither did he. He wasn't a repeater, and he knew damn well she wasn't either, and yet here they were, repeating and repeating . . .

One of these times, any minute maybe, they'd get it out of their system, but for now—

"God," she breathed, her hips moving faster, then faster still. "Brody . . . I'm going to—"

"Do it. Come—"

Her muscles contracted before he'd finished the word, milking him as she went over, and as he'd discovered about himself, about them in general, he could do nothing else but helplessly follow.

A few minutes later, when his toes had uncurled, Brody managed to summon enough energy to nuzzle at Maddie's neck. "Hi."

Looking dewy and sated, she opened her eyes. "Hi."

"So we've come to an understanding about the fast thing," he said. "Slow is better."

"Actually, I'm still not sure."

When he opened his mouth to protest, she kissed him quiet. "We might have to keep working at it. You know, until we come to a compromise."

Liking the sound of that, he stroked a finger along her jaw, tucking a strand of hair behind her ear. "Compromise has never been my strong suit."

"Tell me about it."

"Hello, Ms. Pot, you might recognize me. I'm Mr. Kettle."

"Hey, I compromise plenty."

"How is vanishing a compromise?" he asked.

She rolled away to her back and stared at the ceiling. "It was never about you. It was before you, in fact."

"It was two days ago."

"Before this." She gestured to their naked bodies. "Before we *knew* each other."

"Well, at least you get that much about us."

Her gaze swiveled back to his.

"I do know you," he said quietly. "I get why you're so tough, for instance. And resilient. And . . ."

Her eyes narrowed. "And . . . ?"

"Strong. Capable."

"I thought maybe you were going to go in another direction and say stubborn and unbending and selfish."

"Stubborn and unbending, yes. Not selfish. Never selfish."

She swallowed hard, as if moved by his words when she didn't want to be. Not his stubborn-ass Maddie. She didn't want to be moved by him at all.

Join my club, babe. He didn't want to be moved by her either, and yet she broke his heart with every breath. "You know what I think?"

"You can think after what we just did? Because I'm pretty sure I blew most of my brain cells."

"I think," he said again, "that you've never had anyone in your corner before."

She just looked at him.

"Am I right?"

"I've never needed anyone in my corner." She rolled off the bed. "And you did not pay a fortune for this room to lie here and talk. Let's check out that shower."

"After you tell me your new plan. There's a new plan, right?"

She sighed.

"Christ. What is the plan, Maddie?"

Now she tightened her mouth.

"Are you kidding me?"

"And you call *me* stubborn."

"I'm still in your corner," he said. "I'm here, and I'm sticking."

"No one asked you to."

"I know." He slipped out of bed and lifted her in his arms, heading toward the thousand-dollar shower. "It's part of your charming personality."

She slid her arms around his neck. "What is?"

"Your undeniable inability to ask for anything."

She stared up at him for a beat, then set her head on his shoulder. "You say the nicest things."

Chapter 24

Leena and Ben were instructed to buckle into their seats. "This is ridiculous," she said to Rick's men. "You can't take me as a prisoner to my own home."

"Stone Cay isn't your home anymore." This from Ed in the shotgun seat. "Hasn't been in years."

Crap. In her panic, she'd nearly forgotten they thought she was Maddie. "Well, you can't take Ben there against his will. You're kidnapping an innocent man."

Saul buckled himself in. "He chose to come. That's not kidnapping."

"He changed his mind!"

Saul looked at Ben.

Ben looked back coolly. Calmly. And with just enough attitude that Leena felt terrified for him.

"Look, he's crazy," she said. "Don't listen to him. We're not even together." She was desperate for them to let him go. Shaking with it. But she had to be Maddie, and Maddie didn't shake. Maddie wouldn't show her fear. She'd kick ass. "I demand that you let us both go."

Ed rolled his eyes in Saul's direction before turning back to Leena. "Rick wants to see you."

"For what?"

"He needs to talk to you. See, he thought maybe you were interfering with Leena's interest in her job."

"What?" Oh, God. "I'm not!"

Ed and Saul just shrugged.

"Please. Let him go." Leena turned to Ben. "Tell them. Tell the truth, and they'll let you go. There's no reason for you to have to go to Stone Cay." No reason at all . . .

Ben looked at her for the longest moment, into her eyes, his touching each of her features before he slowly, unbelievably shook his head. "I'm not going to lie for you, Maddie."

Oh, my God. *What the hell was he doing?*

Leena and Ben were taken out of the Jeep and led through the house that for nearly all of her life, had been the only home she'd ever known. They passed through the large living room, surrounded by the wealth and elegance and sophistication that Rick's dealings had purchased, and she wondered how she'd ever enjoyed it here. It was as if her eyes had been shut for years, but they were open now.

This wasn't her home, and it never had been.

They were taken to Maddie's old bedroom, and the minute they were left alone, she whirled on Ben. "Why did you do this?" She knew that all of the house was under camera surveillance except the bedrooms and bathrooms, but she didn't trust Rick. She knew she needed to be careful what she said, but she couldn't help herself. "They might have let you go if you'd only agreed with me."

"You think I should have just let them take you all by yourself?"

"Yes!"

His gaze on hers, he shook his head. "Then I wouldn't have known what happened to you."

"What do you care? You would have been free!"

He didn't answer that. Frustrated, petrified, she paced the floor. "It makes no sense. Taking you makes no sense."

Ben didn't say anything to that, either. He just looked out the window into the black night. His jeans were loose on his body and still splattered with paint. His T-shirt was vintage and fit him in a way that would have made her want to touch . . . if she hadn't been preoccupied with being so absolutely terrified for him.

In some deep recess of her mind, she recognized that this man made her feel things that no other did. Not that it mattered at the moment. Not that it would ever matter if she didn't manage to get him out of here safely. She glanced at him. "I'm sorry I got you into this mess," she said to his strong, solid back. "So damn sorry."

He stood there, shoulders broad and strong, hands in his pockets, giving nothing away of his thoughts, not even a hint. "I don't need you to be sorry."

She wondered what he did need, but didn't have the nerve to ask.

"And taking me makes perfect sense, really."

"How's that?"

"More leverage with which to manipulate you. The only problem will be, of course, once Rick sees me. He'll take one look and realize I'm no stranger, not to him and not to Leena." He turned to face her. "But unfortunately, to Maddie I would be."

She stared at him as the truth sank in. And it no longer mattered if they were being watched or not because he was right. "You met Rick in person? When? He rarely meets clients in person."

"And yet I met you in person."

"Yes, but that was only because . . ." She broke off, blushed. She'd flown to him under the guise of needing to talk to her client, an excuse that had worked with Rick at the time but had been nothing but a big, fat lie. "Never mind."

The truth was, she'd flown to New Orleans to meet with Ben because she'd been attracted to him from the very start, to his voice, to the way he strung his words together, to how he seemed so laid-back and easygoing, so intelligent and yet utterly approachable.

And genuine. Kind and warm and genuine.

There had not been enough of that in her life, and she'd homed in on it like a bee to honey. Meeting him had only deepened her crush, and it had been a crush. A deep, heart-yanking crush. In person, he'd been even more dynamic than she'd expected, and her visceral reaction had shocked her.

She wanted him. Mind, spirit, and even more shocking, physically.

He'd been completely clueless, of course, and one-hundred-percent professional. Together, they'd pored over her design, talking for hours and hours.

And then he'd taken her to dinner. And over sushi and candlelight, over laughter and more easy talking, she'd done the unthinkable. She'd fallen.

Hard.

And then she'd had to go back to Stone Cay to make his design a reality and screw him over.

That she'd done so was her own personal humiliation and shame, and she'd take that to her grave.

But Ben would not be taking anything to his grave, not if she had anything to do about it.

He was regarding her from unfathomably deep eyes. "I contacted him after I discovered the swindle," he said.

Her mouth fell open. "You *what?*"

"Did you think I wouldn't? That I would just let it go and not care about the fact that I was robbed?"

"Most do," she admitted. "All do. Because his clients are all of questionable wealth to begin with. So far no one's wanted to admit they were a victim."

"I was referred to him by a relative," Ben said quietly, "of questionable wealth. I don't know what came over me to actually use an acquaintance of his, and believe me, I'm extremely sorry I did, but I won't be a victim for anyone."

Certainly not for her.

The message was loud and clear.

"The problem is, of course," Ben said, almost thoughtfully, "I'm now an expendable complication."

Leena swallowed. She was afraid he was right, but the thought of Rick doing anything to Ben did something to her. It revealed her backbone, and she pointed at Ben now, stabbing a finger into his chest, which was hard and ungiving.

How the hell did a rich artist get so damned buff? "Nothing's going to happen to you. Do you hear me?"

"Hard to miss. You're shouting." He rubbed his chest. "And ouch."

"I mean it. You're going to be okay."

He let out a low laugh at that. "Sweetheart, look around. I've been taken and brought to what is for all intents and purposes a deserted island. I'm already pretty far from okay, and I have a feeling it's not going to be the last of it."

Oh, God. He was right. What could she do?

If only Maddie really was here. She could think incredibly quickly on her feet, but thinking quickly had never been a particularly strong suit of Leena's.

At the knock on the door, her heart thumped hard against her ribs, and she glanced at Ben.

He lifted a shoulder.

They were pretty much helpless, and he knew it.

Before she could make a move, the door simply opened and Rick stood there.

He smiled at her, but it wasn't a very nice smile. In fact, it curdled her blood, and she took a slight step in front of Ben.

The gesture was not missed, not by Rick and especially not by Ben, who stepped out from behind her with a fulminating don't-you-dare look on his face.

But he had no idea what they were up against. Not really.

Unfortunately, she did.

"Greetings," Rick said.

"Rick—"

He held up his hand to silence her, his sharp gaze locking on Ben. "Ah," he said. "Interesting. Hope you're enjoying your visit to Stone Cay, Mr. Kingman."

"Considerate of you to ask." Ben's eyes flashed fury. "Considering that first, you insult me by swindling me out of a family heirloom, which I want back, by the way. And now you bring me here against my will."

"Sorry about that second part. A most unfortunate accident. You will be returned to your gallery soon enough."

Ben's eyes narrowed. He didn't believe it.

Neither did Leena.

Rick pulled out a two-way radio and spoke into it. "Have Ed and Saul sent to my office. They've managed to bring me the wrong sister. Which means it was Maddie we had here the first time. Explains the security cameras breach, yes?" Then he turned to Leena. "You're going to call your sister. Tell her we're having a family reunion, and her presence is required. *Again.*"

Leena shook her head.

"No? Then tell her you need her help."

"But I don't."

"Actually, you do, but that's neither here nor there at the moment."

"You should have just let us go!" she cried. "It would have been smarter to just let us go!"

At that, his eyes cooled, nearly freezing her skin on the spot. "Call Maddie, Leena."

When she hesitated again, he calmly pulled out a gun and pointed it at Ben.

She immediately opened her cell phone. *Maddie's* cell phone.

"Atta girl," Rick said approvingly.

Chapter 25

Maddie and Brody made it back to Sky High Air, where everything seemed so normal it was hard for Maddie to adjust. She walked into the lobby with the inviting leather couches, the tall, leafy plants, the huge maps spread over the walls. The scent was distinctive—jet fuel and oil—the sounds as familiar as breathing. She could hear a jet engine roaring, the thunk of a candy bar falling from one of the vending machines, a lineman yelling to another . . .

Home. She was home.

Too bad it wasn't to stay. She had to find her sister, and in that vein, pulled Leena's cell phone out of her purse to turn it back on from her flight.

It immediately vibrated, which had her heart racing. She retrieved the voice mail—from Leena!—but the fear in her voice reactivated Maddie's.

"I'm on Stone Cay," Leena said.

What?

"I'm here to . . . um, visit."

No way. Whatever reason Leena had for being there, it wasn't to "visit."

"Anyway, it's been so long since we've all been together, and Rick was thinking you might come back. For a family reunion sort of thing. Yeah. So . . . see you soon."

Okay, this was bad. Maddie shut the phone, her brain racing.

Rick was on to them.

Somehow, he'd found out he'd had Maddie there on the island instead of Leena. Even worse, Leena was now bearing the brunt of his rage by herself. Now Rick wanted Maddie back on the island, and the only reason for that had nothing to do with a family reunion.

A family funeral, maybe, but not a reunion.

Brody came up to her, rifling through a stack of phone messages. "We've got a problem in maintenance," he said. "Vince is freaking out, so if you need me—" He broke off, catching the look on her face. "*You* need me."

From the corner of her eye, she could see out the window, across the tarmac to where Vince, their mechanic, stood in front of the maintenance hangar, waving wildly for Brody. "I'm not first in line."

"Maddie—"

"You'd better hurry. He looks apoplectic."

Brody's mouth went grim. "So we're back to that already."

"Well, we are in the real world, right?"

"And what the hell does that mean?"

"In the real world, we're not married." She had no idea why she said that or why the words brought her a little pang. She'd never wanted to be married and in fact, had promised herself she'd never give any man that much power over her.

She wasn't safe with anyone having power over her. It was why she was the one who always walked away.

Always.

"In the real world," she said, "we're not a unit. We're not lovers. In the real world . . ." In the real world, they spent their time bickering and butting heads at work. They didn't see each other outside of it. "We're not even friends."

His eyes never wavered off her face. "In the real world, things change—" His cell phone buzzed. At the same time,

Vince stuck his head inside the lobby, giving Brody a hands up that said, *what's keeping you?*

"Popular man," she said softly. "And you've really got to go." She turned to walk off, but of course, he grabbed her arm and pulled her back around.

"I have a feeling you have to go, too," he said tightly. "Am I right?"

"We can't do this now, Brody. You have a job."

"And you?"

"I have other things."

"Goddamnit, Maddie. Don't do this."

She had to. She couldn't let him go back with her, not when this time, Rick was on to them. He knew he'd been fooled, and he would not be happy, or kind.

Not that he was ever either of those things anyway, but it *would* get ugly. No way in hell was she going to risk Brody's well-being *again*. But she was going to risk her own this one last time.

For Leena.

All she had to do was get there, get Leena out, and then they were home free. She'd worry about the particulars later.

Brody hit the ignore button on his phone, yelled something to Vince, and then turned back to Maddie, still holding on to her arm. "Why do I have the feeling that if I so much as turn my back, you're going to go do something rash and stupid?"

"I think I resent that."

"You mean you resemble that." Two line guys came in from the tarmac, also looking for Brody. "Goddamnit." He turned to Maddie. "I need ten minutes, okay? Give me ten minutes to see what I can postpone and what I can't, and then we'll go over our options."

"*Our* options?"

"You are not going to do whatever it is you're planning to do all by yourself."

Oh, yes. She was. Stupid or not, she had to. There was no choice.

"I mean it, Maddie."

"I can see that you do." She craned her neck around his huge shoulders to see Vince pacing. "Now you really have to go. You've wasted enough time on me."

"Not a minute of that time with you was wasted." But he relented. "Ten minutes. Be here, Madelyn Stone."

When she didn't answer, he swore the air blue, whipped his cell phone out again, and punched in a number. "Shayne, where are you? Damn it, that won't help me." He hung up on Shayne and punched in another number. "Noah, I need you. Now. Yeah, lobby."

Less than ten seconds later, the lobby door opened, and Noah came in from hangar one, smiling wide at the sight of them. "I just got in," he said. "And Christ, you two are a sight for sore eyes. We're overbooked and understocked and—" He broke off and divided a look between them. "Okay, what's up?"

Brody grabbed Noah's hand and put it on Maddie's arm. "Vince has an emergency. The line guys have an emergency. I gotta go. Watch her for me, okay? Do not let her pull a disappearing act, and trust me, if you blink, she will."

Noah's brow vanished into the hair falling over his temple as he turned to Maddie. "What's going on, Mad?"

Maddie rolled her eyes. "What's going on is that your partner thinks he's the boss of me."

"Just hold on to her," Brody commanded, thrusting a finger in Maddie's direction. "Do not let go for one second, or she's going to go do something colossally idiotic."

Noah nodded agreeably. "Sure. I'll just kidnap our favorite employee, hold her against her will, and then hand her back over to you like she's your hostage. Is there anything else illegal you'd like me to do while I'm at it?"

"I don't have time for your jokes, Noah, not now."

"Who's joking?"

Brody sighed, looked heavenward as if seeking divine intervention, and when it didn't come, laid a long look on Noah. "Life or death," he said very quietly. "Hers."

"Brody, stop it." Maddie did not intend to bring another person into the living hell that was her life, even if it was Noah, one of her favorite people on the entire planet. No way, no how.

But at Brody's words, all kidding fled Noah's face, and he brought up his other hand, holding both of Maddie's arms now.

Maddie sighed.

"Thank you," was all Brody said, clearly relieved, as he loped off.

"This is ridiculous," Maddie said to Noah. "He's completely overreacting."

"See, that's the thing. Brody never overreacts." Noah brought Maddie in close and hugged her. "Which you already know. Now what the hell did you get yourself into?"

Maddie didn't answer. *Couldn't.* From over Noah's shoulder, she watched Brody stride away from them out the door to the tarmac with Vince, those long legs churning up the distance as if it was nothing. Sure. Strong. Capable. He was all those things and more, so much, much more.

"Maddie?"

"You wouldn't believe me even if I told you."

"Try me." When she didn't answer, Noah pulled back and looked into her face. "Not too long ago, my life was so fucked up I couldn't see straight, do you remember?"

She let out a breath. "Yes."

"Right after the crash."

A plane crash where he'd been the pilot. A crash that had killed his passenger. He'd nearly not recovered from that, and remembering it now, remembering his pain and how she'd felt it as if it'd been her own, her throat tightened. "I know."

"You got me through that. You and Shayne and Brody."

It hadn't been easy. They'd bullied, babied, nagged, and just about begged Noah back from a deep, dark abyss. But he had made it back.

"You helped me, and now you'll let me help you," he said firmly.

"Noah." Touched, scared, and just a little overwhelmed, she pressed her forehead to his comforting chest. "I can't."

"That's what I said to you. Daily. You never listened, not once."

She let out a half laugh, half sob and then annoyed at herself, swiped at a tear. "I have to do this without you."

"How about Brody?"

Oh, God. "I have to do this without him, too."

"Does he know that?"

"He knows we're not going to go anywhere with our . . ."

Noah arched a brow, waiting.

"Attraction," she said carefully.

"Are you sure about that?"

No. God, no. "Yes."

Looking unhappy but not arguing with her, he turned her toward her desk, the one she hadn't sat at for six long weeks.

The last time she'd been in that chair, she'd been shot, and she stared at it for a long moment.

"It's a new chair," Noah said quietly.

Behind her desk stood a man she'd never seen before. He wore a Sky High pilot's uniform on his tall, rangy body, and he was leaning over a petite, harassed-looking woman pecking away at the keyboard.

Maddie's keyboard.

"Jason and Kim," Noah told her. "Jason's the new pilot, the one who you almost took with you instead of Brody, and Kim's your temp."

"I don't get it," Kim was saying. "I don't get how I managed to schedule you for two flights at once. I'm sure I didn't do that. The computer must have made a mistake."

Jason shook his head. "Computers don't make mistakes. And yet now we have a Hollywood director who needs to get to San Francisco pronto and some Wall Street exec pacing a hole on the tarmac wanting his flight to New York, and both are expecting me."

"I know!" Kim's fingers hunted and pecked and hunted some more, but she looked miserable. "Maybe one of them will wait?"

"Sky High isn't a place that they come to wait."

"I agree," Noah said, dragging Maddie closer. "I'll take the San Francisco flight. Jason, you take New York."

Jason nodded and with one last frustrated look at Kim, headed toward the tarmac door.

Noah glanced at Maddie and gestured with his chin at the computer, a question in his eyes.

She sighed, knowing she wasn't getting out of here before Brody got back anyway. "Maybe I can help," she said.

Kim blinked at her. "Who are you?"

"Your miracle for the day."

"Seriously?" With a relieved laugh, Kim all too gratefully relinquished the chair.

Noah, Maddie noted, didn't leave her side. "You don't have to babysit me, I've got this."

"Uh-huh. And until Brody gets back, *I've* got *you*."

Maddie's fingers flew over the keyboard. "You have a flight is what you've got."

"If I know Brody, and trust me, I do, he'll be here in oh . . ."— he glanced at his watch—"four minutes, to make sure I haven't fucked up and let you out of my sight."

Maddie rolled her eyes, then tuned him out, loving the feel of her computer, which she'd missed like she might have missed a limb if she'd lost one. She had to stop herself from opening every file, from checking every piece of equipment right this very minute to assure herself she was really back in her chair, in her place.

Where she belonged.

The phone rang, and it was for Noah. She handed it over, ignoring how absolutely right it felt to be back in charge, even if only for a moment, and then felt her cell phone vibrate with an incoming text. With Noah still on the landline, she carefully turned so that he couldn't see her phone or the text from Leena.

Don't come. Go with The Plan.

Leena didn't want Maddie to come. She probably was terrified about what Rick would do to them. Just the thought of all Leena wasn't saying was enough to make Maddie's heart pound with a sick sense of impending doom and dread, not to mention anxiety. She put a hand to her chest over her thudding heart as if she could ease the ache while the fear pingponged back and forth in her belly.

No way was she going to vanish on Leena. Not in a million years. She was going to go back to Stone Cay.

Again, she glanced at Noah, who was still on the phone and fully engrossed in his conversation. Perfect. She brought the schedule screen up on her computer and scanned for available planes.

There were plenty.

What they didn't have was a pilot. Each of them was booked. Brody was right about one thing—Sky High's business had doubled in the time that she'd been gone. The guys were flying themselves into an early grave. No wonder they'd hired an extra pilot. They could use two or three more.

And if she came back to work here, she'd see to it. No one was going to get overworked and exhausted on her watch.

Except she wasn't coming back to work. Not letting herself go there, she pulled up the evening's schedule. They didn't usually schedule at night, unless specifically requested by a client. She could probably try again for Jason after hours, under an assumed name, staying hidden until they were in the air. Once upon a time, Bailey had done just that to Noah, and she'd gotten away with it for long enough to get to where she needed to go.

Except they were on to her now. She could fly commercial or . . .

Or she could tell Brody.

Yeah. Even she knew that was the right answer, and wasn't that just the crux. She rubbed her temples and breathed for a few moments while trying to talk herself out of the insanity of that.

But he'd asked to be a part of this. He wanted to be a part of this, and she'd promised him that they were a unit until it was over. Just because he didn't know it wasn't over didn't release her from that promise.

A small voice, a very small voice, whispered that it would be nice to not be alone in this . . . to trust . . .

Brody didn't trust easily. She knew that. He'd grown up rough, with no one to count on but himself until Noah and Shayne had come into his life. And still, he kept a part of himself back.

Except he hadn't with her.

He trusted her, and all he'd asked for in return was her trust back. "Goddamn him." She stood up, intending to tell Noah not to worry—she wasn't going anywhere without talking to Brody, but when she turned around, Noah was gone. In his place, leaning back against the wall, arms and legs crossed as he studied her, stood Brody.

He pushed away from the wall. "I have to tell you, it feels damn good to have you back in that chair."

"Yeah. See, that's the thing." She drew a deep breath. "I'm not back."

His eyes went flat. "Tell me."

She let him listen to Leena's voice mail, then showed him the text. His head bent over hers to read it, his jaw dark with a couple of days' worth of growth, his mouth tight, his body protectively close.

"Damn," he breathed.

Yeah. Damn. As in damn, he smelled good. Damn, he looked even more amazing.

And damn, just being this close to him made her ache deep down in her chest cavity as if her heart was rolling over and exposing its underbelly.

But she needed to get over herself because any second now, he was going to realize what she planned to do, and that would be the end of her just standing so close to him, absorbing his heat, his strength, his innate masculinity that had her in a state of constant awareness.

At her involuntary little sigh, he lifted his head and searched her eyes for a long moment. "You should know," he said, "I like her don't come idea. That's all I'm going to say on that."

She felt her surprise cross her face.

"What?"

"I expected you to go all caveman and beat your fists against your chest, demanding I stay here."

He raised a brow. "Beat my fists against my chest?"

"Yeah. Maybe even drag me off by my hair to your cave to keep me with you."

He let out a low laugh. "Drag you off by the hair?"

"Oh, like you've never done the Neanderthal thing."

"I have definitely not dragged you off by your hair to my cave." Watching her speculatively, he rubbed a hand over his chin, the five o'clock shadow rasping. "Although it's a very interesting fantasy."

She choked out a laugh at the sudden heat in his eyes. "You really do surprise me," she admitted.

"And you me. Constantly. You want to go back."

"Yeah."

But she intended to do it alone.

Chapter 26

Brody knew exactly what Maddie wanted to do. She wanted to go back to Stone Cay alone. Short of pulling that whole knuckle-dragger thing she'd accused him of, he wasn't sure how to proceed. "I need to talk to Noah. Give me a minute," he said and pointed at her. "And you should know, I'm keeping my eyes on you."

She rolled hers but didn't move when he walked to Noah, who was in the center of the lobby. From where Brody stood, he could still see Maddie. She was glaring at him, and he didn't care. "I need a few more days off," he said to Noah. "And I need a plane tonight."

His partner didn't blink at the scheduling nightmare, but they both knew it was going to hurt. Their clients wouldn't be happy. And for the first time in memory, Brody didn't give a shit.

This was more important. Maddie was more important. She intended to vanish on him again, and this time, he couldn't be so sure he'd get lucky enough to catch up with her.

"Which plane?" Noah asked.

"Something fast. The Lear, if it's available."

"I think it is. Is she okay?"

"Fuck. I don't think so, no."

"You're on it?"

"As much as she'll let me be," Brody admitted.

"She's a tough cookie, she'll—"

Maddie walked up to them, and they both stared at her. "So. Do I need a magic handshake to join this club?"

"We weren't talking about you," Noah said quickly.

Brody looked at him.

"We weren't," Noah said, sounding like a guilty kid.

"Uh-huh." Maddie gave them both a long look, but especially Brody, who wanted to squirm.

He never squirmed.

"I'm going home," she said. "I want to get a change of clothes."

"I'll take you." Brody put a hand to the small of her back and turned her away from Noah, who he shot a dirty look.

Noah lifted his hands innocently.

Brody nudged Maddie to the front doors. That she was letting him take her home didn't ease his mind. She'd ditch him at the first opportunity, and he knew it.

They drove to her condo complex in silence. "Thanks," she said before he could turn off the engine of his car, leaving him to park and catch up with her, which he managed to do at her front door.

When she found she couldn't shut it without taking off his foot, she sighed. "I promised I wouldn't do anything stupid."

"Yes, but I believe we have different definitions of stupid." And though she had a hand on his chest to hold him off, he simply pushed and stepped inside.

Which earned him another sigh. "I'm a big girl, Brody. I'm just going to shower, eat, catch a quick catnap, and then . . ."

"Yeah. It's that 'and then' that I'm worried about." He tried a smile. "Besides, a shower sounds nice. So does eating, and I especially like the nap part."

Her eyes narrowed. "I'm not sleeping with you."

"No problem. We can find something else to do in your bed."

She stared at him, clearly at a loss for words, which he could honestly say he hadn't seen happen to her very often.

"Do you really think sex is appropriate right now?" she finally asked.

He shut the front door behind him, just in case she had ideas about pushing him out. "Sex is always appropriate."

"Brody." She let out a low laugh. "Even setting aside the ridiculous amount of ways I'm attracted to you and you to me . . ."

Setting it aside? He wasn't sure he could do that.

"You're not here for sex. I know it, and you know it. You're here to watch over me."

Guilty as charged. "We could have sex while I'm watching over you, if that makes you feel better."

She didn't laugh, but she did shoot him a half-bemused look. "How many times do I have to tell you, I don't need a babysitter?"

He stepped close, at the moment honestly wanting nothing more than to just hold her. "How about a friend then?"

She hesitated.

And he took another step. "Or just someone who cares about you." He leaned in so that his mouth brushed against her temple. "Someone who wants to make sure you're okay."

Her eyes drifted shut, and she didn't move away. In fact, her body swayed toward his. "This is just some misguided hero complex," she murmured.

Letting out a low laugh, he lifted his hands and slid them along her jaw, letting his fingers sink into her hair as he tilted her head up to his. "No. It's not. It's me caring about you."

"I . . . I honestly didn't know you cared this much."

"Then you've not been paying attention."

Her eyes filled with a mix of uncertainty and the urge to turn away and pretend this wasn't happening between them. He himself was not sure what *this* was, but he did know ignoring it was the easy thing to do.

He never took the easy route.

"Before these past two days, we spent a lot of time ignoring each other," she said.

"You ignored me. I never ignored you. You are one unignorable woman."

"That isn't even a word, unignorable."

"Trying to tell a story here."

"Sorry."

"Then we spent two incredibly intense days together—"

She lifted her head. "Actually, that doesn't count because adrenaline sort of magnifies—"

"Maddie."

"Right." She mimed locking her mouth and throwing away the key.

As if that would work. "And now you're going to take off." He drew in a breath, but it didn't help. Shaken, he dropped his head, pressing his forehead to hers and took a breath. "Just take off. And I could lose you."

She turned away.

And he tried not to panic. "So that's still the plan."

"Yes."

Jesus. He tightened his grip on her. "What about our plan? To be a unit?"

"Don't worry. That wasn't the real world. I won't hold you to anything."

At an utter loss for words, he just stared at her. "What is it with you and the whole real world thing? Maybe I *want* to be held to something. You ever think of that?"

"No. Listen, I'm too tired for this." She pulled free. "I told you about Leena's message because I do understand that we're more than boss and employee. I just don't have time or brainpower to figure out what exactly that more is. So go home, Brody. Get some sleep. You have a wicked schedule over the next few days."

"I have nothing more pressing than this."

"This being . . ."

"Getting you what you wanted—showered, fed, and some sleep." And then, using a patience that was rapidly going thin, he ushered her down her own hall to the bathroom. When he heard the shower go on, he turned to the kitchen. His cooking skills were limited, but he was a master at takeout, so he ordered a pizza to be delivered.

He went back to the bathroom, stood with his hand on the handle, debating with himself.

Go in and make sure she was okay, or stand guard outside the door in order to keep his hands off her . . .

She'd locked it. Not that that would have stopped him if he'd been needed, but apparently, he wasn't. Which left him standing there, listening to the shower like a man who cared far too damn much, and wasn't that just a bitch.

His cell phone buzzed. "Hey," he said to Noah, ear cocked for any excuse to break into the bathroom. "Didn't I just talk to you?"

"Yeah."

Brody waited, but Noah was not forthcoming with the reason for this call. "Is there something you needed?"

"Sort of."

Brody sighed. There was no rushing Noah. Ever.

"Are you okay?" Noah finally asked.

"Why wouldn't I be?"

"Don't know."

"I'm fine."

"Okay, good. Fine is good." But Noah didn't hang up. "You with Maddie?"

The shower was still on. She was in there, wet. Soapy. Warm and glistening . . . "Yeah."

"She okay, too?"

"Yes, she's okay, too. Could you get to the point?"

"I would if I knew exactly what was happening."

"I promised you I'd call if I need you guys, and I meant it."

"Okay." But he paused. "I was just worried that you might get your heart stomped on, tough as that organ is."

The abrupt change of subject made him blink. "Huh?"

"I know Maddie shot you down. She told me you two weren't going to go anywhere with your attraction."

"And how does that translate to her shooting me down?"

"Because there's no way you shot her down."

"Nice." Inside the bathroom, the shower went off. "Listen, my heart's fine." Sort of. "And I have to go."

"What are the two of you doing?"

Well, he had no idea what Maddie was doing, other than driving him crazy. As for himself, he was keeping her gorgeous ass out of trouble. Keeping her safe. Because he could do that. And if while he was at it, he got his stupid heart broken, then he deserved that for opening it up in the first place. "Honestly? I have no fucking clue what we're doing."

That was new. Normally, he knew. He always knew. He did whatever had to be done. It was what he did with women, and he sort of figured Maddie had the same policy with men. Get in, do whatever came to mind—which in this case, covered a lot of ground—and then get out.

Only he didn't want to get out . . .

"Okay. Listen, man, just don't get hurt."

Brody found a laugh. "A woman can't hurt me."

"Right. Be careful. Take good care of her."

"I intend to." Brody closed the phone and looked at the door. He'd do whatever it took. That was *his* plan. And then . . . hell. And then he'd get over her.

And himself.

Face tight with rage, Rick held Leena by the throat, her feet dangling off the ground by several inches. "You turned me in."

Leena clawed at his hands around her neck as her oxygen was cut off. "No! I didn't. I wouldn't!"

"If I'm going down, Leena, you're going down with me."

"No!"

Rick merely tightened his grip, and with her last breath, Leena screamed.

And then suddenly, it wasn't Leena, but Maddie. Maddie *being held off the ground, gasping for air, unable to draw any into her lungs to scream—*

"Maddie. Maddie, it's me. Come on now. I've got you."

Still choking, her hands to her own neck, Maddie opened her eyes. She was curled into a fetal position in her own bed, dusk robbing the early evening of light. Brody was on the bed with her, fully clothed, on top of the covers, leaning over her. His mouth was grim with concern, his eyes leveled on hers. "You're okay. I've got you. You're home, you're safe."

Heart still racing, she clutched at him, and he fell on top of her. She welcomed his weight because he was familiar. Big, strong. Hers.

She had no idea where that thought came from because he wasn't really hers at all and never would be. "Brody?"

"Yeah." Rolling to his side, he pulled her in. "Just you and me. No one else."

With a shaky exhalation, she relaxed against him. Or tried to. After her shower, he'd put her in bed, brought her pizza, then sat like a vigilante while she ate it. Then he'd tucked her beneath the covers. That had been the last thing she remembered before nodding off.

But clearly, despite her explicit instructions, he'd never left.

Somewhere in the back of her mind, she knew she should point that out, but she couldn't find the breath for that at the moment, couldn't find the breath for anything. She gingerly ran her fingers over her throat. "It felt so real."

He let out a long breath and tightened his arms on her. "It wasn't."

No. The only real thing at the moment was him. And suddenly she knew—like Leena, she wanted her good-bye. *Needed* her good-bye, and she pressed her mouth to the side of his throat. "You smell good. You always smell good."

"Maddie—"

She shoved up his shirt and kissed the center of his chest. "Here, too." She inhaled deeply and sighed. She'd gone to bed in nothing but her towel, which she wriggled out of now.

"Maddie—"

"Are you going to turn me down?" Naked now, she hugged him, pressing her bare breasts to his torso.

With a groan, he tried to pull free. But it was too late—she'd felt his reaction to her. "You want me."

"Yeah," he said, his voice a little husky. "You need to ignore that. Some parts of my body have a mind of their own."

"Maybe I don't want to ignore it."

"That's not what you told Noah."

"I didn't tell Noah I didn't want to have sex with you." Bicycling her legs, she kicked off the rest of her covers, then went to work on Brody's clothes.

He didn't stop her. "I take it you're over your bad dream."

"If I said no, would you make it all better?"

Pushing the hair from her eyes, he looked at her, really looked, and like always, she got the feeling he saw more than anyone ever had. "I'd try."

"Then no," she whispered. "I'm not over it."

"Come here," he whispered back, even though she was already against him, and he pulled her closer, then closer still, then proceeded to make good on his promise, skimming a hand up from her belly to her breast, playing his fingers over her nipple while his other hand slid between her thighs.

He was still looking into her face, letting her see what she did to him. She had no idea why that gave her a small rush, no idea at all, but she wriggled a little, eliciting a rough groan from him, and then she was the one groaning when he slid into her. With his arms wrapped around her, his tongue sliding to hers with the same rhythm that he was moving within her, and she realized something. He was making it all better, making her better, and when she was panting for air, gasping small, wordless pleas, rocking against him on the very edge, he murmured her name. Just her name in his voice that tore right through her defenses and snuggled into her heart.

And that was it for her, that was all she could handle. She burst, and he was right with her.

Just as he was always right with her . . .

Brody opened his eyes and found himself all alone in Maddie's bed. He glanced at the clock on the nightstand—only half an hour had passed. "Maddie?"

Silence.

Goddamnit. Leaping out of bed, he was simultaneously punching Leena's cell number into his cell and stumbling around looking for his clothes when a sound in the doorway had him whipping around.

Maddie stood there, wearing jeans and a halter top in the exact color of her baby blue eyes, a mug of tea in her hands, watching him with wry amusement.

Butt-ass naked except for the pants he held in one hand and the cell phone in his other, he dropped both, put his hands on his hips and glared at her.

Her eyes smiled.

"Not funny."

Now she laughed out loud. "You should see it from my perspective."

"You're standing there looking at a naked man and laughing. How in the hell am I supposed to put that in perspective?"

She laughed again, and he just stared at her, realizing she did not do that nearly enough. It transformed her face, made her seem even younger, and frankly, stole his breath. "I thought you'd left," he admitted.

"I know." Her smile slowly faded. "I almost did. But the truth is, I couldn't do it to you."

Relief filled him, but it was short-lived.

"I couldn't just leave without telling you."

"Maddie." He struggled to remain cool and calm when he really wanted to do that whole dragging-her-off-to-his-cave thing. "You know it's just a trap."

"Yeah," she agreed. "But I'm still going."

"*Shit.*"

"I have to, Brody."

"Fine. What's the plan?"

"I'm going to wing it."

"Terrific." He hated winging it. "I'm going with you."

"Why? We're not a unit, not—"

"Don't say it. Don't you dare say we're not a unit in the real fucking world. Because we are. Especially when it comes to being stupid." He strove for lighter. "Seriously, if you go solo now, you'll just hurt my feelings."

"You told Noah that a woman can't hurt your feelings."

A slow churning panic began low in his gut, along with the knot that had been there since she'd been shot, goddamnit. Because standing there stripped down to just the man and nothing else, the truth hit him in the chest with the force of a Mack Truck.

Noah had been wrong. He wasn't going to get his heart stomped on.

It'd already happened.

Somehow, he'd come to care about her more than his carefully constructed world, more than his planes, more than his next breath. "I didn't mean what I said to Noah about the whole not being able to get hurt thing."

"No? Well, I always mean what I say, and I told you from the very beginning this wasn't real."

"Okay, I have no idea how we got so off track here, but you have to promise me that you won't do anything foolish without me."

She sipped her tea and said nothing.

"Maddie."

"Why?" she asked.

"Why? What kind of question is that?"

"A valid one. Why does all of this matter to you so damn much?"

He stared at her, let out a low laugh, and shoved his fingers in his hair. "Because."

"Because? Your answer is because?"

"Because . . ." Ah hell. He had nothing left to lose. "Because I love you, damn it."

Her eyes went wide as saucers, and she took a step back, nearly falling on her ass in her haste to put distance between herself and the crazy naked guy. She smacked up against the wall and held on to it like a lifeline. "*What?*"

"Yeah, and I can see that just makes your day."

"Are you kidding? I just told you that this wasn't real, and your response is I . . . I . . . I—"

"You can't even say the word?" he asked incredulously, clutching his clothes to his suddenly aching gut.

"What is more unbelievable is that you can." She set down her tea, picked up his pants and threw them at him. "Don't look at me like I'm an alien, all right? It's nothing personal. I just don't put much into that word, that's all." She found his shirt and threw that at him, too, which he caught after it hit him in the face.

"What does that even mean, you don't put much into the word. It's a pretty damn big word."

She tossed him his shoes. "Forget it."

"Are you kidding? I can't forget it."

"Okay, fine." She straightened her spine. "It means I don't love you back." Then she softened, her eyes misting. "I'm sorry."

But not sorry enough, apparently, because she didn't take any of it back. "Wow," he said, staggered. Destroyed by words. He'd never have believed it possible.

"Not personal," she repeated more softly, turning to the door. "I'm assuming you no longer want to come with me."

"Oh, I'm going."

Slowly, she craned her neck his way. "Huh?"

He smiled grimly at her shock. Had no one ever stuck with her through thick and thin? Through pissiness and foolishness? "Hell, yeah. I'm going."

She closed her eyes and then opened them and nodded her head.

He nodded his back and then watched her walk out of the room. Standing there holding his clothes, he shook his head. He had no idea what he'd expected to happen here, but it hadn't been to blurt out his feelings, and it sure as hell hadn't been that she'd throw those words back at him the same as she'd done with his clothes. He hated that she'd so easily dismissed the words and the emotion behind them simply out of fear because for him, they were as real as the air in his lungs.

Unfortunately, he was breathing that air all on his own.

Chapter 27

Leena was tired of pacing her bedroom. Tired of Ben watching her pace. And she was especially tired of being afraid. She let out a frustrated, shaky breath and took another lap around the room. "Tired of it," she muttered.

"Tired of what?"

"Following the advice of a crazy guy. For letting him ruin my life. For getting us in this situation. Pick one."

"I'll take all three for a hundred, Bob."

Yeah, she'd really screwed up. "Mostly, I'm tired of letting my life live me."

"There are always choices," Ben said, still watching her pace.

"Yes." She wanted to tear out her own hair for being so damn slow to understand that very fact. "And it's my own fault that I never made my own, but that's going to change." She pivoted, nearly plowing into him because he'd stepped into her path.

"How's it going to change?"

She stared up into his face, his beautiful, strong face. "I'm working on that."

"I guess it won't be easy. Leaving this lifestyle."

"Look, you don't need to beat me up, okay? I'm doing it enough for the two of us."

His eyes never left hers. "Are you?"

"Yeah." She tried to move around him, but again he blocked her path, this time putting his hands on her arms to hold her in place.

"I'm not staying for the cushy lifestyle," she said. "I know you probably don't believe me. You have no reason to, and I deserve that. I deserve a lot of things, but like you said, it's about choices. *My* choices, so get out of my way and let me think about the ones I need to make."

She expected him to scoff or show more anger.

But he surprised her. Gentling his hold, he leaned in and kissed her. In that single moment, he awoke every single nerve ending she owned, but the all too brief glide of his lips to hers ended far too soon, and with a slow blink, she stared up at him, stunned to the core. "What was that?"

"A reminder that it's all wide open for the taking."

"What is?"

"Your life. It starts now, so go for it. Take it wherever you want. You just need to decide where that is."

And suddenly she knew. "I want to take it to a place where I have more seconds in which to live it," she whispered.

Her reward was a heart-stopping smile. "Sounds like a great plan to me."

Maddie stepped onto the tarmac and faced Brody, who'd readied a plane for her. He stood there in the setting sun, the evening breeze brushing over him, looking bigger than life, utterly competent, and very on top of his world.

That's all she wanted, damn it—to be on top of *her* world. "Brody—"

"We're not going to go over this again, are we?" Without waiting for an answer, he took her hand and walked with her toward the Lear, but before she could board, he pulled her around to face him. "A couple of things first." He spoke quietly, firmly, badass to the bone. "We *are* a unit, you and me."

When she opened her mouth, he put his fingers to her lips. "I get that scares the living shit out of you. You're going to have to get over it. I love you, Maddie. You'll have to get over that, too."

Well, if that didn't root her to the spot. Heart pounding, she lifted her hand to his wrist to tug his hand from her mouth but he shook his head. "I love you, damn it, and one of these days, maybe you'll let your guard down enough to believe it. But for now, let's get this over with." With that, he lowered his hand, waiting for her answer.

She found her throat almost too tight for words. He loved her. Oh, God, he *loved her*. Her heart felt so much she didn't know if she could take it.

"Okay?" he repeated with far less patience.

"I . . . need a moment."

"No." He turned to the plane, his shoulders seeming tense. "If I give you a minute, you'll be long gone. You can take your moment later, when it's over. Then, I promise, you can argue with me all you want."

"You don't mean that." She had to clear her throat, still bowled over by those three little words he tended to throw around. "You hate to argue."

"With you? I live for it. Now let's do this."

By the time, Brody stepped off the charter boat onto Stone Cay and turned to offer a hand to Maddie, dawn was streaking across the Bahama sky. The only sound was the water slapping loudly against the sides of the boat in the dewy morning air.

They hadn't spoken much more than a few words to each other on the flight to Florida then on to Nassau and now here. Actually, Maddie hadn't spoken to him.

He'd pretty much opened up his chest, exposed his heart, and let her run it over with a steamroller a few times, and she'd gone mute.

She stepped off the charter with absolutely no expression

on her face. He had no idea what she was feeling because she'd been careful not to show anything, which pissed him off. A guy says I love you, the least a girl could do is react one way or another.

But she'd retreated within herself, and he realized she probably wasn't even thinking about him, but looking ahead to what they were going to face.

He got that, he really did, but it'd have been nice to factor in her thoughts as well.

Tiny Tim got out of the Jeep waiting there for them. "Took you long enough." He eyed Brody before looking at Maddie. "So you're the one who got married? You cost me five hundred bucks in the pool."

"Ah, that's a damn shame because I'm easily worth a thousand."

Tiny Tim's eyes darkened. "You're definitely Maddie."

"Most definitely," Maddie agreed.

At her attitude-ridden tone, Tiny Tim's jaw tightened, and Brody got a very bad feeling. Damn it, a showdown.

But after a second, Tiny Tim jerked his head toward the Jeep, indicating that they should get in.

Maddie didn't move. "Where's Leena?"

"Waiting for you."

Maddie looked at Brody, and they exchanged an unsettled gaze, but Maddie shrugged and got in the Jeep.

What choice did they have?

Brody followed, and then they were being driven along the pristine white beach, all too quickly turning up the road toward the compound.

There'd been another storm, which had left the sand churned up. In the Jeep, they were knocked around a bit by the bumpy ride, and Brody's shoulder brushed Maddie's.

She looked over at him.

Her eyes were unreadable, her mouth tight. And given how

they'd spent the past hours, which was mostly in silence, what she did next shocked him to the core.

She took his hand in hers and squeezed. He stared down at their joined fingers, hers narrow and smooth and capable, his big and work-roughened and just as capable, and squeezed back. Lifting his head, he met her gaze.

One corner of her mouth turned up, and leaning in, she set her head on his shoulder.

He hugged her close, offering comfort, offering whatever she needed, but it turned out she needed nothing.

"You shouldn't be here," she whispered. "Damn it, you really shouldn't be here."

"That makes two of us."

She sat back, looking frustrated and just scared enough to unnerve him, a feeling that intensified when they were brought into the house where instead of being taken to Rick or even to Maddie's room, they were immediately brought to the cellar workroom.

And shoved inside.

The ensuing click of the lock indicated that yeah, they weren't attending any family reunion.

Chapter 28

As the echo of the lock died away, Maddie sighed, her voice cutting through the pitch black cellar. "This isn't good."

With the lights out and no windows, Brody couldn't see his own hand in front of his face. "Not good at all," he agreed tightly.

"Okay, any time now."

"Any time now what?"

"You can say I told you so."

Goddamn this dark. Reaching out in front of him, he tried to get his bearings but felt nothing. "How about I save the I-told-you-so for when it's more satisfying to be right. Like when we're out of here. *Where the hell are you?*"

"Here." Her voice sounded lower now, as if she'd sat on the ground.

"Where the hell is 'here,' and what are you doing?"

"Taking off my boot."

For her knife, no doubt. "You don't have two of those things, do you?"

"No. Listen, I don't want to freak you out . . ."

"Oh, I'm not freaked. I'm as calm as Zen. I'm a fricking Buddha. What is Rick up to do you suppose?"

"I'm not sure. People who cross him, they tend to . . ."

"What?"

"Pay."

"Pay as in found in the bottom of a lake with concrete shoes pay?"

When she didn't answer, he let out a breath. Yeah, concrete shoes. He was so happy he'd asked. "You do realize this is like a bad seventies flick, right? The family patriarch who coerces his helpless nieces into doing his bidding—"

"Niece."

"Excuse me?"

"Niece as in singular. Leena did his bidding, not me."

He heard her going through what sounded like drawers. "What are you doing now?"

"Looking for something, *anything*."

"Another knife would be nice. Or a gun."

More rustling. "You don't know how to shoot."

"Under these circumstances, I think I'd pick it up pretty quickly."

She let out a huffing laugh that didn't sound at all full of amusement, and then suddenly, she was back at his side. How the hell she'd been able to maneuver around in the utterly complete dark, he had no clue. Just another secret to the life of Maddie Stone.

"I'm so sorry," she said.

"For not listening to me or for giving me a headache from bashing my head against the brick wall of your stubbornness?"

"For everything. For how this turned out—"

"Hey." That sounded an awful lot like a good-bye. Oh, no. *No.* "Bullshit to saying good-bye, we're not dead yet."

"Also, I'm sorry for lying to you. If I could take anything back, it'd be that."

"You mean when you tried to come here without me?"

"No." She came to stand right in front of him. He could smell her shampoo, then felt her hand on his arm. "I lied when I said I don't love you."

Well. If that didn't stun him into silence.

"Brody? Did you hear me?"

"I don't think I did, no."

"I said . . ."—she got closer and louder—"that I lied when I said I didn't love you!"

Wow. That sounded just as amazing the second time, and in spite of everything, he felt a ridiculous smile split his face.

"*Brody?* Did you hear me?"

"Yeah," he admitted. "I just wanted to hear it again."

She smacked him in the chest. It didn't hurt, but he nabbed her hand and tugged her close, cupping her face in his hands. "Maddie." His throat felt rough as sandpaper, and his voice reflected that, but he was both unbearably moved *and* pissed off. "No fair tossing those words at me now just because you think we're going to die—"

Before he could properly finish that thought, whatever it might have been, the door to the cellar opened, and a rectangle of light flooded in from the hall. Brody quickly sighted several no-neck thugs, each of whom tossed someone into the cellar and slammed the door.

The lock sliding into place rattled through the silence.

"Hello? Is anyone here?" came a voice that sounded just like Maddie.

"*Leena,*" Maddie gasped, and given the rustling and the low, muffled murmuring, the two of them had located each other, a feat utterly beyond Brody.

"I'm sorry about the cell phone switch!" one of the twins cried.

"But not about taking off?" the other demanded. *Maddie.* "Or how about running The Plan without me?"

"That was for your own good," Leena told her.

"How is that even possible?"

"I was trying to preserve the life you'd made for yourself! And I had it, too, Mad. We were both home free until you came here."

"Oh, this is *my* fault now?"

"Ladies," a guy said, but neither sister was listening.

"It's no one's fault, but don't worry. I'll fix this." Leena sounded stubborn. A family trait, apparently. "It's *my* turn to fix things."

"No," Maddie said firmly. "I've got a plan—"

"I've got a plan—"

"How about *this* plan—we get the hell out of here," Brody said.

"Sounds good," a mystery guy agreed. "A voice of reason."

"And who are you?" Maddie demanded.

"He's with me," Leena said. "It's Ben. He was with me when Rick snatched me."

"Brody wasn't snatched," Maddie told her. "He bullied his way along."

"I came along," Brody said. "Because you were going to be stupid about it."

"Oh, so he calls the woman with the knife stupid," Maddie said to the room.

"I didn't call you stupid. Your plan is stupid. And don't even bother yelling at me. You can yell at me all you want when we get off this island."

"Count on it," she promised. "Okay, a new plan. I've got a knife and a gun, so—"

"Wait a minute." Brody reached out for her. Finally got her. Fisting his fingers in her shirt, he yanked her close.

When she tried to knee him, he did as she'd done to him the other day—he pinched her ass.

"Hey!"

Oops. Wrong sister. "Sorry."

"You pinched my ass!"

"What?" Ben asked. "He did what?"

Brody felt around for the right sister. The one who drove him crazy. Snagging her, he held tight. "I'll take one of those weapons."

"Leena has tools in here. We can all arm ourselves, right, Leena?"

This was tricky in the dark, but Brody somehow ended up with a hammer, though he'd managed to hold on to Maddie as well. "You have a gun and a knife, and I'm stuck with a hammer?"

"I realize that goes against your Boy Code of Ridiculous Ego and Controller, but I'll protect you."

"Give me one or the other."

"Fine." She slapped the knife into his hand. "No stupid heroics, do you hear me?"

"Loud and clear, and back attcha." He tightened his grip on her. "Did you really say you love me?"

"Actually, what I said was, I lied when I said I didn't."

"Jesus. Was that in English?"

She fisted her hands in his shirt. "You said no good-byes, not like this."

"Maddie—"

"Listen to me. I want to know you're going to fly another day, okay? I want to picture you standing in the lobby of Sky High with your iPod making you deaf before your time, buying candy bars by the dozen out of the vending machine, dating any of those fancy schmancy bimbos you favor—"

"Dating?"

"Real world, remember? You're going back to it."

"That's right," Leena said. "That includes you too, Ben. Now this is *my* fight, so all of you, stand back."

"No way in hell," Ben said tightly.

"Ditto," Brody said just as tightly.

But the decision was taken out of all of their hands when the door opened and light flooded into the room.

"Clearly," Rick said from the doorway, "we have a little problem."

No one answered. No point when they all knew they were the little problem.

"My men wanted to deal with you," Rick said, "since you've made fools of a couple of them."

"Not that difficult to do," Maddie muttered.

Rick's eyes narrowed. "I plan to give them their wish. But I wanted a private moment first. You two . . ." He divided a look between Leena and Maddie, clearly unable to tell them apart. "You banded together to trick me."

"We wouldn't have if you'd just let us go," Leena said.

Rick eyed her standing on the other side of the shelving unit from Maddie and then shifted to Maddie. "Dammit. Who's who?"

Neither answered.

"Fine." Rick lifted a gun. "I'll hire another designer."

Brody's heart all but stopped.

Maddie's eyes flashed. "You're not going to shoot your own flesh and blood."

"Try me."

No one tried him. No one moved.

"Now," Rick said with far less patience, "will the real Maddie step forward, please."

Brody didn't dare look at Maddie and give her away, but he did send her a mental DON'T EVEN THINK ABOUT IT.

Again, no one moved. For Brody's part, he didn't even breathe.

Rick stepped farther into the room.

Ben was beside Leena. Brody was where Maddie had left him, between the door and the work area, which meant he was closest to Rick.

With a hammer in one hand and a knife in the other.

Giving him a wide berth, Rick passed by, heading toward the sisters. "Come on, Maddie. Be brave. There's going to be a tragic accident."

"You're going to die?" Leena asked hopefully.

"Oh, no." He smiled, and the temperature in the room dropped ten degrees. "It won't be me. Maddie's going to drown."

At that, Brody fingered the knife. Throwing it across the room was a maneuver effective only in the movies, so he needed to get closer.

"Terribly tragic, of course," Rick lamented. "Leena'll be so distraught." He waited for one of the twins to give herself away. "You'll stay here and work for me, of course. You girls have been so busy fucking with me, I never did get to tell you. I'm expanding our design and spec business."

"You mean swindling business." This from Maddie.

Rick acknowledged her words with a little bow of his head. "So you can see why it's best if our designer is here full time."

Brody just gripped the handle of the knife and did his best to bide his time. And breathe.

"Maddie will step forward now," Rick commanded softly, no longer smiling. "Or would you rather I call in Tiny Tim, who'll figure it out for me."

There was only one way Brody could think of for Tiny Tim to do that, and that was by stripping down the twins and checking for that birthmark on the back of Maddie's thigh. Yeah, this was going to get ugly quick, and clearly, Maddie knew it because she stepped forward.

Brody immediately moved to stand next to her, but Rick stepped in his path, blocking him, lifting the gun and pointing it right at his chest. "You, my friend, are expendable. Do not forget that. Now drop that knife."

Brody turned his head and looked at Maddie, intending to tell her not to do anything stupid after he was gone because it was pretty damn clear that this wasn't going to end well for him.

"Drop it." To emphasize the request, Rick cocked the gun in his hand.

Hating this, Brody dropped the knife.

The look on Maddie's face said she knew she was now faced with a choice—save herself or save him. A few months ago, he'd have bet money on what she'd do. After all, he drove her crazy, and the feeling was mutual.

She'd have killed him herself.

Now she looked at him, the horror and regret heavy in her eyes. Her heart there, too, for the first time, visible to him, all of it.

He knew how she moved, how she thought. He'd been with her naked and not so naked, and he knew in his gut that there was nothing, nothing at all, that she could reveal about herself that would change his mind.

He was in this, heart and soul.

Knowing it, he stepped forward, closer to the barrel of Rick's gun. "You're not taking Maddie."

Ben stepped forward, too, adding his voice to Brody's. "You're not taking anyone."

Rick's gaze narrowed, wavering on each of the four of them in turn. His gun, however, did not waver, not one bit. "Are you kidding me?"

Maddie put her hand in front of Brody and shoved him back a step.

Then Leena elbowed both Maddie and Brody back. "I told you! My fight."

Brody was getting damn tired of getting shoved while trying to save his woman, but then Leena grabbed the barrel of the gun herself and put it against her chest. "It's me you want. Tiny Tim," she yelled toward the door. "This doesn't involve you. Just stay back."

Uncle Rick craned his neck to glance at the door, but there was no one in the doorway. In that split second, Leena grabbed a wickedly sharp chisel from her shelf and swung it at Rick.

Rick, no slouch in the quick mover department, sensed her motion and whipped back, aiming at Brody—except that Maddie threw herself in front of him as a shield, screaming "Nooooo."

Brody might have yelled, too. He couldn't tell over the roar of adrenaline in his body as he wrapped Maddie in his arms and tried to pivot to protect her, but the woman was strong and determined, and still screaming in his ear as she shoved with all her might.

The two of them crashed to the floor as the sharp crack of the gun went off. He actually felt the whir of the bullet as it whizzed past his ear.

Holding Maddie down, he lifted his head to see what was happening, just in time to see Leena clock Rick over the head with the chisel.

Rick's eyes, wide and surprised, locked on Leena as he staggered back a step, still in his shooter's stance. His mouth went slack as he formed one surprised word.

"Leena."

And then he hit the floor with a bone-jarring thud.

"That's bitch to you," Leena said, dusting off her hands. "Oh, and by the way? I quit."

Chapter 29

Maddie had never known panic like she knew now. Rick had gotten a shot off, but who had it hit? Beyond reason, nearly hysterical, ears still ringing, she slipped out from beneath Brody. "You okay?" she demanded, slapping her hands down his body.

"Yes." His hands grabbed hers, his gaze filled with the same panic she felt. "You?"

Heart in her throat, she nodded, her gaze going straight to Leena next, who was now standing over a very unconscious, and if she wasn't mistaken, drooling Rick.

"Hope you heard that, you SOB!" Leena sounded so cocky she might have been Maddie.

Maddie sagged in unbelievable relief as Brody surged to his feet, grabbing a roll of twine from Leena's shelf. Ben met him, and together, the two of them hauled Rick to a chair and tied him to it.

None of them had been hit. It was a miracle. And a sign. Or so Maddie hoped. A sign that this was going to go their way.

Moving close to a hog-tied Rick, she held the radio toward his mouth as his eyes slowly opened. "When I push this button," she instructed, "you're going to tell your men out there that we need the boat ready for a little ride to Nassau. You tell them that, and—"

"—And we'll let you live," Leena finished for her.

Rick snorted.

"We'll let you live," Leena repeated. "Unlike Manny."

Looking only slightly less cocky, he shut his mouth. Uncooperative.

Brody crouched in front of him. "And one other thing. Once we're out of here, you won't contact either of the sisters ever again."

Over Rick's head, Maddie met Brody's gaze and felt her heart catch. *God.* How had she gotten so lucky to have him in her life? She pushed the button on the radio and waited for Rick to talk.

"Tiny Tim," Rick said through his teeth, but said nothing else.

"Do it," Maddie said. "Tell him."

Rick nodded, but instead, he yelled, "Tiny Tim, get your ass in here—"

Before he'd even finished the sentence, there came a thud from outside in the hall, and then another, and then a single person stood in the doorway.

Rosaline.

"Where are my men?" Rick demanded from his chair, fighting his bonds.

Rosaline shrugged. "Sporting twin concussions from the brass vase I just hit them with."

Looking comically taken back by the fact that everyone had turned on him, Rick shook his head. "Rosaline—"

"Save it. I quit, too."

With a smile, Leena tossed aside the tool she still held and dusted off her hands. "Feels good, doesn't it?" She gasped in surprise when Ben yanked her into his arms. "What—"

But he just cupped her head in his big hand and shook his head. "Shut up a minute." He tightened his grip on her. "Just shut up a minute, and let a guy catch his breath."

Brody checked the knots on Rick's rope and then turned to haul Maddie into his arms, too. "Too close," he murmured, his voice thick. "Too damn close."

She gripped him tight. "It was you I was worried about."

"I'm hard to hurt."

Pulling back, she looked into his eyes, feeling her heart swell painfully. "But not impossible."

He slowly shook his head, and she opened her mouth to say something—she wasn't sure what—but Rosaline interrupted. "Come," she said. "I'll take us to the boat."

Once on Nassau, they called the authorities. Brody wasn't thrilled to find out that they were all going to be held in custody for questioning. It took a while for the police to sort everything out, but eventually, the estate on Stone Cay was siezed and held as well.

And then, after a very long day of waiting, Rosaline, Ben, and Brody were released on bail. Thanks to Noah flying in and hiring the best attorney on Nassau, a guy who turned out to be worth every penny of his outrageous fees, Maddie was released the next day as well.

The longest day of Brody's life.

Leena wasn't released until the third day when her laptop was finally accessed. In exchange for her promise to help gather further evidence against Rick, she was given her freedom. Ben had waited for her, and it was clear to everyone they wouldn't be separated again any time soon.

Rick and Tiny Tim and the others weren't released at all.

By the time Brody flew Maddie back to Los Angeles, four days had gone by. They dropped Leena and Ben in New Orleans, where Leena had decided to "stay for a while," something that had both her and Ben glowing with happiness.

Yeah, Leena was going to be just fine. But Brody didn't know if he could say the same about Maddie. She was quiet, withdrawn, saying only that she needed some time to think.

He wasn't sure what that meant.

Back at Sky High, life seemed shockingly ordinary. Except that Maddie didn't come back to work. He knew she was home, that she hadn't flown off somewhere, because he drove by her place every night to check.

She had asked for time, though, which sucked because it turned out to be the hardest thing to give.

What the hell did she need time for?

He tried to keep himself busy, tried to find the same simple joy in planes as he always had. And one morning, a week later, he stood in hangar three in front of one of their newest purchases, a sweet honey of a 1977 Grumman AA5A. The Cheetah needed some work, and he was the man to do it. Just six months ago, he'd have been all over it, filled with satisfaction and pride at his life. After all, he had a roof over his head. The books were firmly in the black. And he had a new plane to boot.

Yeah, with money finally in his pocket, he would have said life was as complete as he could have imagined it ever being.

He'd have been wrong.

He needed one thing that money couldn't buy: *Maddie*. He wanted her in his life, and he wanted her to love him. He'd never seen himself wanting such a thing, especially with a woman who'd grown up so different from himself. But he now knew that didn't matter. Money, background, none of it mattered.

The only thing that did matter was what the heart wanted. He knew what his wanted. What he didn't know was what Maddie's wanted. And though that hurt, he couldn't say he regretted the experience. If nothing else, he better understood Noah and Shayne, how they'd put their lives on the line for love.

He'd now been there.

The door to the hangar opened, and to his shock, the woman

he'd just been thinking about stood in the doorway, silhouetted by the sun behind her. His heart gave a painful lurch.

Then she walked in like she owned the place, and hell, she could have. He knew it, Shayne and Noah knew it, and she sure as hell knew it.

She looked amazing. Her hair was shorter, cut to her shoulders but her own natural fiery auburn. She wore a halter baby doll tank top over skinny jeans and mind-boggling heels. But no smile.

Ah, hell. "If you need a pilot—"

"How about a job?"

"Or that." But he sure as hell didn't want to go back to boss and employee. Or even friends.

Hell, he didn't even want to go back to only getting along in the sack, although that had its merits . . .

No, what he wanted was something far more permanent than that, and the fear nutting him up deep inside was that he was alone in that wanting.

She came to a stand next to the Cheetah, looking on top of her world and so far out of his league that if he didn't still have her nail indentations in his ass from that last time they'd been together, he might have believed he'd dreamed it all up.

In that damn workshop, she'd told him she loved him. And then she hadn't really spoken to him since. Now they were in the "real" world, whatever the fuck that meant, so—

"Nice plane," she said quietly, staring up at the Cheetah.

"Yeah."

"Do you remember what I said to you on Stone Cay?"

"You said a lot of things. You said, for instance, that I have an ego."

"I said ridiculous ego."

"Right," he said dryly. "Thank you for the clarification."

"I also said that you're big, bad, and so damn sexy that you make me melt."

He stared at her profile. "No, you never said that. I most definitely would have remembered that."

"Well, I thought it. I also thought that you make me smile. You make me laugh, too, and you make me think." She turned her head and looked at him. "You make me feel whole, Brody, when I've never felt whole before. But that's not what I was referring to." Her baby blues softened with things that made his heart pick up speed. "I meant it when I said I love you."

"You said it under extreme duress."

"It doesn't matter whether I said it while thinking we were going to die, or when you were buried deep inside me, or now, when we're just standing here . . . I mean it."

"You never said it when I was buried inside you."

"Which I plan to rectify ASAP." She let out a breath, suddenly looking touchingly nervous. "What I'm trying to say is that we *are* a unit. And that I *do* love you. So much. And . . ."

Jesus, there was an and? He didn't think he could take an and.

"And like you once said to me, I can't keep walking away from anyone and everyone who cares about me. I always thought I had to be alone to feel safe and secure, but that plan has a fatal flaw, one I never saw coming."

"Which is?"

"Alone isn't all it's cracked up to be. Which means it's time for a new plan, Brody."

"And that is?" he barely managed when she paused.

"Staying." She gnawed on her lower lip. "I thought maybe we could make this thing official. I don't really know what your plans are regarding us and this whole unit thing, if you wanted us to date or something more . . ."

He found his voice. "Something more. Way more."

"Me, too." She nodded and still looking off center, swallowed hard. "More like . . . I do more."

"Hang on." He grabbed her. "Are you *proposing?*"

"Trying." She gripped him tight. "Brody West, will you—"

"Yes." He tugged her close. "Christ, yes."

"I didn't finish even asking you yet."

"Yes to anything," he vowed. *"Everything.* As long as it's with you."

You've got to get a
HOT DATE,
the latest from Amy Garvey,
new this month from Brava . . .

This was absurd. She was just excited, a little nervous, high on possibility and the idea of a fresh start, even if she'd never imagined starting over back in quiet, boring little Wrightsville, the town she'd been dying to leave ever since she'd been old enough to understand that roads led away from it.

As she leaned against the VW, breathing in the air's cool bite, she watched Nick direct the SUV around the tangled vehicles. She'd thought a lot about what moving home would be like, about old friends and second chances and possibilities she'd never considered.

But she'd never really thought about temptation, at least not with Nick Griffin in the same sentence.

By the time Nick moved the squad car to the shoulder, and started up the chugging, shuddering VW bus to move it, too, he'd recovered from most of his surprise.

Okay, maybe not *most*, but a lot. Some, at least. And then he stepped out of the ancient bus and turned around to look at Grace, leaning against a tree trunk on the riverbank, her dark curls blowing around her face and her eyes hidden behind a pair of sunglasses, a sucker punch of shock hit him in the gut all over again.

Grace Lamb was the last person he ever expected to see in Wrightsville apart from her obligatory Christmas visit to her dad. But here she was, live and in living color, the epitome of trouble on two legs.

Two legs, he realized, that had somehow gotten a lot longer in the years since he'd seen her last. Long, slim legs in faded jeans, with ridiculous bright pink boots on her feet.

He caught himself with a cough. Grace was his best friend Tommy's little sister. She didn't have . . . *legs*. Well, yeah, of course she had legs, but not . . . *legs*. Not like that, anyway. That had definitely changed sometime in the past couple of years.

Running a stop sign and smacking into a police car, though, that was the Grace he had always known.

"Impulsive" was her middle name. Along with "reckless," "fearless," and, well, "distracted by whatever shiny new thing came along." Which wasn't a single word, but whatever. It was still the truth.

Grace had once set her backyard on fire when she tried to start the grill to make lunch for her father. Another time she'd decided to try ice fishing on the pond, only to sink into the water once she started cutting through the pond's frozen skin. She'd tried to go blond, but she'd used household bleach on her dark curls, nearly choking herself on the fumes in the process.

And that was all before she was eleven.

The girl was a walking disaster and always had been. Except she wasn't a girl anymore, and judging by the suitcases and boxes he could see through the VW's windows, she planned to be back in town for a while. Which was just frigging weird, because the one thing that Grace had always been was restless, most of all to get out of Wrightsville.

"Billy will be down any minute," he said as he walked back to her.

She tilted her head, looking up at him quizzically. "Billy?"

"Down at the precinct," Nick explained, settling his hips against the hood of the cruiser and crossing his arms over his chest. "I can't write up my own report, since I was involved."

"There's going to be a report?" She took off her sunglasses and turned horrified brown eyes on him. "It's just a little fender bender! Hardly worth mentioning, really. I can pay for the damage and no one even has to know . . ." She trailed off when he stared her down, arms still folded over his chest, immovable.

Leave it to Grace. Yeah, he'd taken care of the Great Microwave Disaster of 1988, and the time she'd lost the two Pomerians she was dog sitting, but this was a little different. It was an official police vehicle, not his own battered Jeep, and Grace, well . . . he shook his head. As far as he could tell, she had never really learned to anticipate consequences.

Like wearing jeans that looked molded to her hips, and a white blouse that didn't completely hide the outline of a lacy bra.

Not that he was looking. Definitely not. He swallowed back a growl of arousal, and turned toward the VW, gesturing vaguely. "What is all that, Grace? What are you doing here?"

He'd forgotten how blinding her smile could be, and it surprised him all over again. He was still blinking at the brilliance of it when she said, "Coming home, of course."

His eyebrows nearly shot off the top of his head. "You're . . . moving back here? To Wrightsville?"

"You don't have to say it like I just announced I'm having an alien love child and going on the talk-show circuit." She frowned, the light in her eyes turning to smoke the way it always did when she was mad at him. Boy, was that look familiar.

"Doesn't Robert work in New York?" he asked, glancing at the old bus again. And why on earth was Grace driving that thing? He didn't know Robert well, or really at all, but he did know he wasn't the vintage hippie chic type. "Commuting to Bucks County is an awful long trip."

"Robert won't be commuting." It was Grace's turn to fold her arms in front of her, but Nick was surprised to realize she didn't look upset. Instead, she was calm, almost peaceful. "Robert is moving to Chicago, to work for The Museum of Contemporary Art."

If his eyes widened any further, they'd probably roll out of his head, Nick realized with a start. "And you're . . . ?"

"Not," she said simply, and gave him another smile. The sun gleamed on her hair. "I'm starting over, Nick. I'm getting a divorce, and I'm going to figure out a career, and I'm going to do it right here in Wrightsville."

Just when he'd convinced himself Wrightsville was getting a little boring, Nick contemplated as he restrained a groan, Grace back in town, at loose ends, looking for work and maybe romance?

They were all doomed.

Some authors know that
WHEN HE WAS BAD,
he was better than ever.
Check out the new anthology from
Shelly Laurenston and Cynthia Eden,
out this month from Brava.
Here's a sneak peek at Shelly's story,
"Miss Congeniality" . . .

The doorbell rang and Irene didn't move. She wasn't expecting anyone, so she wouldn't answer the door. She dealt with enough people during the day, so she'd be damned if her nights were filled with the idiots as well.

The doorbell went off again, followed by knocking. Irene didn't even flinch. In a few more minutes she would shut out everything but the work in front of her, a skill she'd developed over the years. Sometimes Jackie would literally have to shake her or punch her in the head to get her attention.

But Irene hadn't slipped into that "zone" yet and she could easily hear someone sniffing at her door. She looked up from her paperwork as Van Holtz snarled from the other side, "I know you're in there, Conridge. I can smell you."

Eeew.

"Go away," she called back. "I'm busy."

The knocking turned to outright banging. "Open this goddamn door!"

Annoyed but resigned the man wouldn't leave, Irene put her paperwork on the couch and walked across the room. She pulled open the door and ignored the strange feeling in the pit of her stomach at seeing the man standing there in a dark gray sweater, jeans, and sneakers. She knew few men who made casual wear look anything but.

"What?"

She watched as his eyes moved over her, from the droopy sweatsocks on her feet, past the worn cotton shorts and the paint-splattered T-shirt that spoke of a horrid experience trying to paint the hallway the previous year, straight up to her hastily created ponytail. He swallowed and muttered, "Goddamnit," before pushing his way into her house.

"We need to talk," he said by way of greeting.

"Why?"

He frowned. "What?"

"I said why do we need to talk? As far as I'm concerned there's nothing that needs to be said."

"I need to kiss you."

Now Irene frowned. "Why?"

"Must you always ask why?"

"When people come to me with things that don't make sense . . . yes."

"Just let me kiss you and then I'll leave."

"Do you know how many germs are in the human mouth? I'd be better off kissing an open sewer grate."

Why did she have to make this so difficult? He hated being here. Hated having to come here at all. Yet he had something to prove and goddamnit, he'd prove it or die trying.

But how dare she look so goddamn cute! He'd never known this Irene Conridge existed. He'd only seen her in those boxy business suits or a gown that he'd bet money she never picked out for herself. On occasion he'd even seen her in jeans but, even then, she'd always looked pulled together and professional.

Now she looked goddamn adorable and he almost hated her for it.

"Twenty seconds of your time and I'm out of here for good. Twenty seconds and I won't bother you ever again."

"Why?"

Christ, again with the why.

"I need to prove to the universe that my marking you means absolutely nothing."

"Oh, well, isn't that nice," she said with obvious sarcasm. "It's nice to know you're checking to make sure kissing me is as revolting as necessary."

"I'm not . . . I didn't . . ." He growled. "Can we just do this, please?"

"Twenty seconds and you'll go away?"

"Yes."

"Forever?"

"Absolutely."

"Fine. Just get it over with quickly. I have a lot of work to do. And the fact you're breathing my air annoys me beyond reason."

Wanting this over as badly as she did, Van marched up to her, slipped his arm around her waist, and yanked her close against him. They stared at each other for a long moment and then he kissed her. Just like he had Athana earlier. Only Athana had been warm and willing in his arms. Not brittle and cold like a block of ice. Irene didn't even open her mouth.

Nope. Nothing, he thought with overwhelming relief. This had all been a horrible mistake. He could—and would—walk away from the honorable and brilliant Irene Conridge, PhD, and never look back. Van almost smiled.

Until she moved slightly in his arms and her head tilted barely a centimeter to the left. Like a raging wind, lust swept through him. Overwhelming, all-consuming. He'd never felt anything like it. Suddenly he needed to taste her more than he needed to take his next breath. He dragged his tongue against her lips, coaxing her to open to him. To his eternal surprise she did, and he plunged deep inside. Her body jerked, her hand reaching up and clutching his shoulder. Probably moments from pushing him away. But he wouldn't let her. Not if she felt even a modicum of what he was feeling. So he held her tighter, kissed her deeper, let her feel his steel-hard erection held back by his jeans against her stomach.

The hand clutching his shoulder loosened a bit and then slid into his hair. Her other hand grabbed the back of his neck. And suddenly the cold, brittle block of ice in his arms turned into a raging inferno of lust. Her tongue tangled with his and she groaned into his mouth.

Before Van realized it, he was walking her back toward her stairs. He didn't stop kissing her, he wouldn't. The last thing he wanted was for her to change her mind. He managed to get her to the upstairs hallway before she pulled her mouth away.

"What are you doing?" she panted out.

"Taking you to your bed."

"Forget it." And Van, if he were a crying man, would be sobbing. Until uptight Irene Conridge added, "The wall. Use the wall."

Keep an eye out for Karen Kelley's,
THE BAD BOYS GUIDE
TO THE GALAXY,
coming next month from Brava . . .

"Where's your dress..." He waved a finger around. "Thingy...robe whatchamacallit?" He finally pointed toward her.

She raised an eyebrow. He didn't seem to notice the clean floor. Disappointment filled her. She'd hoped for more. Silly, she knew. After all, he was an earthman and she shouldn't have cared what he thought.

"My robe was getting dirty along the hem so I removed it."

Her gaze traveled slowly over him, noting the bulge below his waist. It was quite large. Odd. She mentally shook her head.

"Your clothes are quite dirty. Once again, I've proven that I'm superior in my way of thinking," she told him.

"You're naked."

She glanced down. "You're very observant," she said, using his earlier words. "Did you know there's a slight breeze outside? It made my nipples tingle and felt quite pleasant. Not that I would be tempted to stay on earth because of a breeze."

"You...you...can't..."

She frowned, "There's something wrong with your speech. Are you ill? If you'd like, I can retrieve my diagnostic tool and examine you." He was sweating. Not good. She only hoped she didn't catch what he had.

"You can't go around without clothes," he sputtered. "And I'm not sick."

"Then what are you?"

"Horny!" He marched to the other room, returning in a few minutes with her robe. "You can't go around naked."

"Why not?" She slipped her arms into the robe and belted it.

"It causes a certain reaction in men."

"What kind of a reaction?"

What an interesting topic. She wanted to know more. Maybe they would be able to have a scientific conversation.

Kia had only talked about battles and Mala had talked about exploration of other planets, but Sam was actually speaking about something to do with the body. It was a very stimulating discussion.

He ran a hand through his hair. "I'm going to kill Nick," he grumbled. "No one said anything about having to explain the birds and bees."

"And what's so important about these birds and bees?"

He drew in a deep breath. "When a man sees a naked woman, it causes certain reactions inside him."

"Like the bulge in your pants? It wasn't there before."

"Ah, Lord."

"Did my nakedness do that?"

"You're very beautiful."

"But I'm not supposed to think so."

"No, we're not talking about that right now."

She was so confused. Sam wasn't making sense. "Then please explain what we are talking about."

"Sex," he blurted. "When a man sees a beautiful and very sexy naked woman it causes him to think about having sex with her."

He looked relieved to finally have said so much. She thought about his words for a moment. A companion unit did not have these reactions unless buttons were pushed, and even then their response would be generic. This was very un-usual. But also exciting that her nakedness would make him want to copulate. She felt quite powerful.

And she was also horny now that she knew what the word meant. She untied her robe and opened it. "Then we will join."

He strangled and coughed again and jerked her robe closed. "No, it's not done like that. Damnit, I'm not a companion unit to perform whenever you decide you need sex."

"But don't you want sex?"

"There are emotions that need to be involved. I'm not one of those guys who jump on top of a woman, gets his jollies and then goes his own way."

"You want me on top?" She'd never been on top but she thought she could manage.

He firmly tied her robe, then raised her chin until her gaze met his.

"When I make love with a woman, I want her to know damn well who she's with, and there won't be anything clini-cal about it." He lowered his mouth to hers.

He was touching her again. She should remind him that it was forbidden to touch a healer. But there was something about his lips against hers, the way he brushed his tongue over them, then delved inside that made her body ache, made her want to lean in closer, made her want to have sex other than just to relieve herself of stress.